A *Plot* for *Pridemore*

Roth has the Southern storyteller's knack for creating quirky but believable characters who will charm and alarm you and keep you glued to your chair. The action is so quickly paced, risky, and hilarious that it is easy to picture *A Plot for Pridemore* on the movie screen.

—Alarie Tennille, poet and Pushcart Prize nominee,
author of *Spiraling into Control*

In *A Plot for Pridemore* the leaders of a small town embark on a wild scheme to breathe life back into their dying community. The results are sad, comic, and ultimately terrifying. Stephen Roth keeps a steady hand on the wheel as he negotiates the twists and turns of the story and deftly introduces the reader to a diverse cast of characters, each with their own secrets, sins, and heroic qualities. The result is a supremely entertaining ride.

—Jaclyn Weldon White, author of
Whisper To The Black Candle

In his debut novel *A Plot for Pridemore*, Stephen Roth presents a funny, well-constructed misadventure about the consequences of mixing good intentions with bad strategies as the city fathers of a small Midwestern community attempt to save their town from financial ruin. The story is infused with generous portions of greed, corruption, pathos, and unintended woe as the plot to save Pridemore is executed by a group of flawed heroes who believe that the survival of their way of life hinges upon their nefarious actions. With a flair for social satire reminiscent of Joseph Heller and Sinclair Lewis, Stephen Roth reminds us once again that the ends do not always justify the means. *A Plot for Pridemore* is an all-around excellent read.

—Raymond L. Atkins, author of *Camp Redemption*,
2011 winner of the Ferrol Sams Award for Fiction

Stephen Roth's *A Plot for Pridemore* finds its harebrained, comical luck in using man-boy Digby Willers as the central game piece in an elaborate con orchestrated by Mayor Tolliver and meant to give the town "that outgrew its usefulness" a revitalizing spell of news-hour fame. As in the nineteenth-century con man tales the book evokes, deception leads to the wildest of pickles. Marry the confidence tale to our present-day mania for celebrity, and the result is a *con*-temporary story teeming with tricksters and unexpected reversals. And if you're already a fan of Mercer's own Raymond Atkins, you'll find much to love and laugh at in *A Plot for Pridemore*.

—Marly Youmans, author of
A Death at the White Camellia Orphanage,
winner of the 2010 Ferrol Sams Award for Fiction

MERCER
UNIVERSITY PRESS

Endowed by
TOM WATSON BROWN
and
THE WATSON-BROWN FOUNDATION, INC.

A *Plot* for *Pridemore*

A NOVEL

Stephen Roth

Nov 10, 2014

Ka2 –

It has been a long time! I hope you enjoy this book. Best wishes to you and the family, and let me know when you're back in the states. Best Regards,

S Roth

MERCER UNIVERSITY PRESS
MACON, GEORGIA

MUP/ P484

Published by Mercer University Press, Macon, Georgia 31207
© 2014 by Mercer University Press
1400 Coleman Avenue
Macon, Georgia 31207
All rights reserved

9 8 7 6 5 4 3 2 1

Books published by Mercer University Press are printed on acid-free paper that meets the requirements of the American National Standard for Information Sciences—Permanence of Paper for Printed Library Materials.

Library of Congress Cataloging-in-Publication Data

Roth, Stephen, 1971-
A plot for Pridemore : a novel / Stephen Roth.
pages cm
ISBN 978-0-88146-482-5 (pbk. : alk. paper) -- ISBN 0-88146-482-1 (pbk. : alk. paper)
1. Rescue work--Fiction. 2. Mayors--Fiction. 3. City and town life--Fiction. 4. Missouri--Fiction. 5. Political corruption--Fiction. 6. Political fiction. I. Title.
PS3619.T47665P58 2014
813'.6--dc23
2014000358

For Maxwell

PROLOGUE

The explosion was powerful enough to rattle the mayor's decrepit knees and leave his poor ears buzzing for some time afterward.

He and his cronies sat on a ridge a good five football fields away. The column of limestone powder that rose through the tree line had dissipated into a cloud of dust by the time it reached the three men. They wiped the dust from their eyes. In a minute, the air cleared and the birds returned to their roosts.

"Hell's bells," said the man with the sagging, hound-dog face, "that was a lot bigger than I expected."

"Yup," said the other. "I guess you could say the game is now afoot."

Hold on to your girdles, ladies, the mayor thought. He knew nothing was certain until they surveyed the damage. The blast *was* bigger than expected, leaving him a bit muddle-headed, and not just because he'd been clomping around the woods all night. He was startled by what he had wrought after more than a year of dreaming and planning. It was the right thing to do, the mayor had said to himself each night as he lay in bed, staring at the ceiling, his mind scrolling through every possible scenario.

The right thing to do. His friends might not envision it, but the mayor's plan would spring to life once the emergency crews and the excavating equipment and the cable news networks started flooding the scene. Within hours, Pridemore, Missouri, would be a national headline. Within days, it would be a household name.

Maybe, just maybe, a few well-placed sticks of dynamite could reverse two decades of decline for the mayor's little town. That was the idea, anyway.

"I sure hope we know what the hell we're doing," the hound-dog man said.

"Shut up, Chub," said the other, brushing dust from his tan windbreaker. "Everything's gonna be fine. Right, Mayor?"

The mayor said nothing, which was rare for him. He rose from his camp chair and watched the sun peek over the now-tranquil horizon. A shudder rushed up his spine. He thought he heard something above the ringing in his ears, though he might have been mistaken. It sounded like a child crying for help.

PART I

SUMMER

CHAPTER 1

The man in the charcoal suit gave a thin smile that barely registered a blip on the sincerity meter. His handshake was cool and soft. Maybe he was easing his grip because of the mayor's advanced age. Or maybe he was just a wimp. Either way, the mayor knew right off that he didn't like this guy. And he didn't feel too swell about his decision to come all the way to St. Louis to meet him.

"Trent Dodge," the man said, "VP of North American Operations."

"How are you, Trent? I'm Roe Tolliver, mayor of Pridemore, Missouri."

Dodge led the mayor into a conference room that overlooked the glass towers of a suburban office park. He invited the mayor to treat himself to some coffee in one of the tiny Styrofoam cups that lined a nearby tray, but Roe politely declined.

"So, Mayor Tolliver, how can we help you today?"

"Well, sir, as you know, my fair city was honored to be considered among the top five candidates for the new plant that Sunnyside Farms is going to build."

Dodge nodded.

"But we didn't make the next round. And I just wanted to follow up to see if there's anything I can do to make you feel more comfortable about keeping Pridemore in the running for this wonderful facility you're going to create."

He paused to allow a response from Dodge, but none was forthcoming. You pudding-headed fool, the mayor thought to himself, you should have accepted the damn cup of coffee.

"It's no secret that Pridemore has fallen on some hard times," he went on. "We were hit pretty hard by the farm crisis and have had a few big companies leave town. But I think our situation could work to your advantage. As your people know, we have a 500-acre industrial park that's just itching to be developed—prime commercial real estate where you can build and expand as you please. And you'd be Pridemore's largest employer right off the bat."

Still no response. But Dodge was kind enough to offer one of his thin-lipped smiles.

"The people of Pridemore have an incredible work ethic and a great passion for agriculture," the mayor added. "I'm sure that was plain to see when your team came to visit us."

Dodge suddenly stirred. "You mean the light show?" Actually, it was a twilight ceremony the mayor had carefully orchestrated in which Pridemore residents lined Old Highway 54 and held up candles as the Sunnyside Farms executives drove out of town. It made for a hell of a front-page photo in the next day's *Evening Headlight*. "Yes, I heard about that," Dodge said. "That was a nice touch."

"Well, thank you. And I can assure you, it came from the heart. Because the people of Pridemore—"

"Let me stop you."

The mayor let out a tiny hiss but smiled politely. He wasn't accustomed to being interrupted.

Dodge opened his leather binder and pulled out a map of central Missouri. Pridemore and four other towns of similar size were circled in red ink.

"Just bear with me a second, because I want to show you something that I think will address your concerns."

He ran a pale index finger across the map until it found Pridemore.

"You guys are here, right?"

The finger ran an inch or so to the east.

6

"And the new Highway 54 is here, eight miles away. Correct?"

Dodge peered at the mayor through designer glasses that were probably worth more than the average Pridemorean's paycheck.

"Those eight miles are why you didn't make the cut. Wherever we decide to put the new harvesting center, it is vital that it be along the Highway 54 corridor. We're going to have trucks coming in and out of the center every single day and night. We've got to be on the highway."

The mayor nodded grimly. This was nothing new. Highway 54 had been a burr in Pridemore's ass since the state decided to redirect it ten years ago.

Dodge moved his finger up the highway a couple of inches.

"Now here's Farley, which, between you and me, stands a very good chance of winning the bid. They're similar to Pridemore in size and all the other factors. Except they're on the highway, which makes all the difference."

He closed the binder and ran his hand across it like it was a dear pet. "Make sense?"

The mayor tried to collect his thoughts, seething at the arrogance of this man at least thirty years his junior trying to treat him like some junkyard dog, condensing his city (his life's work!) down to some arbitrary dot on a map. Arthritic knees or not, he felt like taking this Trent Dodge fellow by the collar and tossing him and his wingtips onto the parking lot seven stories below.

Thankfully, the nimble coolness that had served the mayor well in his many years as a trial lawyer took over.

"We've offered you a generous incentive package," he said. "One I know the other towns can't match. And we can get even more generous if need be. It won't be easy, but we'll do whatever it takes." He paused for dramatic effect. "We can make up for those eight measly miles."

Dodge frowned and looked at his binder. "Well, we have other concerns about Pridemore that kept you from being a serious candidate for Sunnyside Farms."

The mayor was losing his patience. "Like what, exactly?"

The vice president of Sunnyside held back for a moment, as if he really didn't want to throw this final punch because it was going to hurt. But he did anyway.

"Well, for instance, we feel that you have a glaring shortage of skilled labor."

That did it. Screw this garden party, the mayor thought. He slowly rose and slapped both hands on the oaken table.

"We are talking about a hog-processing plant, right, Mr. Dodge? You take hogs and you cut them up and you shrink-wrap the pieces, correct? You can call it harvesting or whatever bullshit thing you want. But it's a basically a filthy, fly-infested slaughterhouse, isn't it? So exactly what kind of *skilled labor* are we really talking about here?"

Dodge nervously eyed the door, but the mayor wasn't done.

"The people of Pridemore have harvested soybeans and corn, they have built houses, they have built roads, they have manufactured computer chips and automobile parts. I'm pretty damned sure they can hang a pig upside down and bleed him into a garbage bin."

"Okay, I think we're done." Mr. Dodge stood up and held out his hand.

"No thanks," the mayor said as he turned away. "I don't care for cold fish."

He slumped into the back of his Chrysler New Yorker and beat his fist a few times against the leather upholstery.

"Went that well, huh?" Rufus Stodemeyer asked as he started the car. The Pridemore City Council president often acted as the mayor's chauffeur when there was out-of-town business to be done.

"That godforsaken highway is going to be the end of us. Maybe it already is," the mayor said.

Stodemeyer shot him a concerned look through the rearview mirror, no small feat for a man who most days had about as much compassion as a Burmese Python.

"You want some Italian food?" he asked. "I know a good place on the Hill."

"Just drive."

The mayor said nothing for two hours, until they veered off the four-lane Highway 54 and onto the two-lane blacktop now known as Old 54, which dissected Pridemore and had served as its economic spine for generations. In its heyday, the highway was the main route for travelers headed from the cities to The Lake of the Ozarks. Back then on summer weekends, Pridemore's downtown swelled with people dressed in loud Bermuda shorts and loafers with no socks, flashing credit cards around, indulging their kids with sugary treats, and smiling easy because they were on vacation. They hailed from exotic places like Ames, Nebraska City, and Sioux Falls. They left ten-dollar tips on the restaurant tables. They made a big deal about "bargaining down" for ridiculously overpriced heirlooms and yard ornaments. The out-of-towners, for a few months at least, made Pridemore a little oasis of big-city bustle.

That was one hell of a long time ago, the mayor thought as he gazed out his car window at the empty storefronts and boarded-up buildings lining Main Street. Sad as it was to imagine, Sunnyside Farms and its filthy, sewage-belching hog plant—and its three hundred jobs—were the last chance at a better life for the town he had led for nearly fifty years.

"Hey, Rufus."

"Yeah?"

"What happened to us?"

"To us?" The councilman looked at him, eyebrow arched.

"To this town. What happened to this town?"

"Oh," said Rufus, lowering his shoulders like it was a question he got every day. "I don't know, Roe," he said after a minute. "I guess we just outgrew our usefulness."

The mayor thought about this a second, then cleared his throat with the same low, guttural grunt he used in city council meetings when he wanted people's attention. For the first time in his life, he was officially out of ideas.

CHAPTER 2

A few blocks away, Digby Willers kicked an old soda can and whooped with delight as it bounced across Main Street and clanked against a curb.

He had kicked the can through most of the downtown business strip, from Saynor Circle to the blinking stoplight at Dunbar Street. The can left scuff marks on his new pair of Dingos, but Digby didn't mind. The marks, he thought, gave the boots a real-life cowboy look.

Pang! He kicked the can into the street near the faded centerlines. It was an unseasonably hot, breezeless afternoon in late May that left the courthouse flags sagging and stray dogs sprawled and panting in the shade of a few parked cars along Pridemore's main drag. Digby kicked his can against the stucco walls of the Lizard Lounge, which had recently closed after Willie Larson shot Alan Carr in the thigh over some girl they were both seeing. Digby kept on kicking past the abandoned Westbrook Feed & Seed, and he playfully rang the big brass bell outside Truman's Malt Shop, which no one answered because the shop's owner, Ernie Tate, was in Farley getting an alternator for his Monte Carlo.

Anyone who strayed out into the ninety-degree heat at that particular moment (and most locals had more sense than to do something like that) couldn't have missed the 6-foot-3-inch, 280-pound man-child zigzagging his way up Main Street. Digby wore army fatigue cutoffs, an orange T-shirt smeared with peanut butter and jelly, and a Cub Scout cap that sat on the back of his head like a navy blue beanie. He had a round face with cheeks that turned crimson at the first sign of embarrassment, and thick lips that curled into a slow, open-mouthed smile. His hair, yellow as lemon custard, rolled over his ears in long bangs that gave him a Prince Valiant look. Digby cared very little about that. He just knew that he hated getting haircuts.

Today, the hair was matted around his brow like a helmet. His sweaty hands clutched a brand-new five-dollar bill, as well as a perfectly smooth stone that would be great for skipping if there were a lake nearby and someone to teach him how to do it.

Several other stones scraped each other in the pockets of Digby's fatigues as he hopped the curb and stepped inside Sanderson's Hardware, a jingling bell on the door announcing his arrival. He basked in the air-conditioning and wiped his face with his shirt. The clerk, a skinny kid in a bright red apron, studied him a moment, then shook his head and walked to the back of the store.

"Hiya, Digby," Red Sanderson called out from behind his old iron cash register. "Come to get your hot rod, I suppose?"

"Yessir."

"Well, let's have us a look."

Sanderson led Digby down Aisle B, where the Pinewood Derby kits were stacked on a shelf about waist high. He watched Digby pick up one kit, examine it closely, then pick up another. Aside from the clerk, he and Digby were the only ones in the store.

The Pinewood Derby for the Cub Scouts' Yellow Jacket District was more than two months away. But for Digby, who'd won the race nine of the past ten years, that was barely enough time to make a serviceable racing car from a scrawny block of pine. Each May, he bought his kit the first week Sanderson's had them in stock. He spent June and July in his mom's garage, carving the block into an aerodynamic form and sanding it to a smooth finish. He even sanded the plastic wheels because he thought it made them faster. He topped it off by painting the car blue with white numbers and red stripes. One year he painted his car green and gold, which looked pretty cool, but he lost the final heat to Timmy Thurson.

Digby returned to the blue-and-red color scheme and hadn't lost since. That was seven years ago. Competing against a field of mostly ten- and eleven-year-olds, he was the Dale Earnhardt of Pinewood Derby racing in Pridemore.

Naturally, parents complained. The scouting committee hemmed and hawed for years on the issue, briefly making Digby an "honorary" racer, meaning whoever finished behind him could get a trophy, too. This pleased absolutely no one, and the grumbling intensified. When it came to racing little blocks of pine down a thirty-foot ramp, Digby Willers was as polarizing as Rush Limbaugh or the Dixie Chicks. You loved him or hated him. There was no middle ground.

Sanderson watched for several minutes as Digby sat cross-legged on the floor, staring at seven or eight kits spread out before him. Sanderson was exceedingly patient, something he honed after taking on a grenade in North Korea and spending a year in a VA hospital as they put him back together again. He could spend hours playing with his grandkids or creating a landscape of his lake house in needlepoint. Or he could sit behind his register, read an old paperback, and wait to hear that bell on the double doors. Sometimes hours would pass between the rings.

"You gonna pick one out? They're all the same, you know," he said with a wink as Digby arranged more kits on the floor.

Digby stared at Sanderson as if the old man couldn't possibly be serious, then returned to studying the kits. After a few minutes of pondering, he chose a favorite, helped Sanderson return the other kits to the shelf, and followed the old man to the cash register.

"You give 'em hell this year, Digby," Sanderson said, ringing up the kit and putting it in a paper sack. "You hold on to that trophy."

Digby nodded and grinned. He waved to Sanderson and the skinny clerk as he skipped out the door. The soda can was right where he left it, so he gave it a nice, swift kick.

"That's a good boy right there," Sanderson said. "Wish there were more like him."

"That boy is twenty-two years old going on two," the clerk said with a snicker. "What do they call it—water on the brain?"

The old man glared at the clerk before tossing him a plunger from Aisle C.

"Clean the toilet, smart guy," Sanderson said.

CHAPTER 3

The mayor was in a thoroughly foul mood by the time he got home. He sat for half an hour in the darkness of his living room, staring at the blank television screen and mumbling to himself.

"What's with you tonight?" his wife asked him, her plump figure silhouetted by the light from the kitchen. "You want a beer?"

"No, I don't want a beer," he huffed, brushing a *TV Guide* off his lap and onto the carpet.

"How was St. Louis?"

"Wonderful. Just wonderful."

He tried adjusting his lounger to a reclined position. There was some whiz-bang button under the arm you had to push that he could never find.

"'Wonderful,' my ass." She stepped into the den, her round face crinkled with concern. "You haven't said two words all night."

"It's nothing," he said, feeling a little bad now for being a grump. Margaret was mostly a good wife, but she hadn't learned in nearly sixty years of marriage that the best thing to do when he was in one of his moods was to leave him the hell alone. He was entitled to a crappy mood every now and then and shouldn't be made to feel guilty about it. His fingers found the button on the side of the chair, but he couldn't push it in for some damned reason.

"Well, I'm off to Bridge Club," she said, sighing as she lifted her purse from the back of a chair.

"Uh-huh," he mumbled, still fiddling with the button.

"There's leftover lasagna you can heat up if you get hungry."

"Great."

"Anything else before I go?"

"You can fix this rotten, stinking chair!" he yelled, burying his fist in the leather upholstery. He'd spent six hundred dollars for the piece of crap, waited two months for delivery, and the damned thing wouldn't even recline. Didn't anything work like it was supposed to?

Margaret bent over the armchair and pressed the button, easing the mayor back into a more comfortable position. She clicked on the television and handed him the remote.

"Better?"

"That makes you feel so good, doesn't it?" he growled.

"It does, actually." She touched his cheek affectionately. "My little Grumpy Monkey."

"Stop it," he said, almost smiling but fighting it off. He didn't want anything to spoil his mood.

The mayor usually wasn't one to sulk. Well into his eighties, he led a vigorous life. He'd retired from his law firm because law had bored him for years. But he still ruled the City of Pridemore with heavy-handed gusto. He put in forty-five hours a week at City Hall in addition to public meetings, ribbon cuttings, trips to the state capitol, and other appearances that came with the job. He signed off on every piece of city business before it reached even the committee level. No summer intern was hired, no sidewalk repaved, without Mayor Roe Tolliver's approval.

Aside from that, he had a few hobbies. Fishing, coin collecting, an electric train set he was building for a great-nephew. And, of course, there were his memoirs, the definitive chronicles of the Tolliver family's first college graduate and high-level public servant. He'd been stuck at 1991 for several months. The years that followed were too depressing to contemplate, much less articulate. It had been, he thought, a long, slow crawl to oblivion.

The mayor farted softy as he turned on the TV and clicked through the channels. Happy talk on the six o'clock news (stupid shit). A game show involving blind dates (stupid shit). A congressional hearing on C-SPAN (stupid, stupid shit).

Maybe he'd watch a video? He glanced at his wife's movie collection, alphabetized from *Annie* to *Dr. Zhivago* along the living room bookcase. One tape wrapped in clear plastic caught his eye—it had probably been on the shelf for years and never even been opened. He shook his head, his theory proven: Margaret bought more damned movies than she had time to watch.

With a grunt, the mayor pushed himself from the armchair and reached for the tape. *The Baby Alison Story*. He didn't know this one. He ripped off the plastic wrapping, popped the tape into the VCR (he was too prudent to buy into the DVD fad), and settled into his chair.

A little girl with a bandage around her head appeared on the screen. Something familiar about that image, the mayor thought. A few frames later, a square-jawed man in his sixties appeared, a grain elevator and a church steeple peeking over his shoulder. He looked to be one of those where-are-they-now TV actors who probably hadn't worked steadily since the 1970s.

"Prairie View, Ohio," the actor said. "A small town halfway between Cleveland and Dayton. Few people beyond this rolling farmland had heard of Prairie View before September 23, 1989.

"That's the day two-year-old Alison Funderburk slipped down a long-forgotten well in the woods behind her home. And everything changed for this tiny town of less than five thousand God-fearing people.

"Soon, the world was at Prairie View's doorstep."

The screen cut to shots of television trucks lined up in front of what appeared to be the Prairie View courthouse. Dan Rather, Tom Brokaw, and Peter Jennings were doing live shots from the Funderburks' modest ranch home.

Tolliver remembered the story now. It had taken teams of emergency workers something like six days to rescue the little tyke, and the country—the world—had been caught up in the calamity. He remembered attending a Pridemore High football game and the PA announcer interrupting the action to say, "Folks, the little girl in Ohio has been rescued from the well." There were cheers and high fives on both sides of the stadium. Some people got teary-eyed. All for a little girl they'd probably never meet.

The mayor watched as the rescue workers gingerly pulled Alison, blue eyes peering through layers and layers of blankets, from the well and into the arms of her parents. It was powerful stuff, and the mayor blinked out a tear or two. The TV actor went on to describe the avalanche of cards, gifts, and letters that descended on Baby Alison's family for months, even years, after the crisis. The Funderburks attended a state dinner at the White House. A millionaire formed a trust fund for the kid's education. Prairie View became a destination for thousands of people inspired by Baby Alison's story. Some drove their recreational vehicles hundreds of miles off the beaten path just to take snapshots of the family's home.

He paused the video. Rewound the last five minutes and played the part about Prairie View over again. A tourist mecca. A little town in the middle of nowhere Ohio. The story was preposterous, but there it was. The events surrounding the life of a two-year-old girl had changed the course of that town and its people forever.

The mayor rose from his chair, ignored the pain in his joints, and shuffled into the kitchen for a beer. He would have danced into the kitchen if his poor body allowed it.

The mayor knew from experience that, in almost every courtroom trial or public hearing, there comes a point when you get the break you need: a prosecutor gets sloppy during cross-examination or a councilman bumbles the facts on a zoning ordinance. Through sixty years of defense law and politics, the mayor always seemed to find those little creases in the enemy's armor that he could split wide open before they knew what hit 'em. When those moments came, a giddiness invaded his body so suddenly that he often wrapped his arms tightly around his waist to keep from having a full-fledged giggle fit. The regulars who watched trials from the balcony at the county courthouse would tell you that to see Roe Tolliver stooped over the defense table with his arms folded like a straitjacket and a hand over his mouth was to know the old codger had the prosecution right where he wanted them.

Alone in his den, with one hand clutching a Budweiser longneck and the other holding a cheap cigar he kept hidden in his fishing tackle box, the mayor let the titters roll up and down like someone was running a goose feather over his body. He sensed an opening, and he was going to ram through it like a full-throttled locomotive.

The mayor looked again at the frozen TV image of poor Baby Alison, blue eyes pleading from beyond that dirty bandage around her head.

For the first time in God knew how long, he felt a true tinge of hope for his little town.

The five men ate lunch every Monday at Carl's Machine Shed, just a couple doors down from City Hall. They used to meet at Lucy's Garden Cafe, but Lucy's closed and moved to Hendersonville after the state redrew Highway 54. Carl's was the last decent restaurant in what remained of Pridemore's business district. It had excellent patty melts and open-faced beef sandwiches, and the waitress knew better than to linger while the men talked business at their table in the back room.

With the exception of Mayor Tolliver, the men at the table were all in their fifties. Though none had done hard labor for many years, their hands were rough, and their necks and faces were wrinkled like brown paper sacks from years of working in the sun. Their shoulders were big and wide, and they walked around town with the sinewy grace of central Missouri boys who knew their way around a plow.

Though they varied in intelligence, none of the men lacked ambition. They had achieved success in a town where the average income was $20,000 and college degrees were rare as April snow. Chub Hughes ran M&M Construction Co., the biggest cement and commercial contractor in three counties. Larry Truesdale was publisher of the *Evening Headlight*. Thomas Treadwell was the county prosecutor, and Rufus Stodemeyer doubled as owner of Stodemeyer Ford-Lincoln-Mercury and city council president.

They were what you might call the town power brokers, and their weekly back room lunches were Pridemore's worst-kept secret. The mayor liked to meet on Mondays to give the boys a preview of what would happen at that evening's council meeting and open the floor to suggestions. The mayor and his men were in line on most issues—raised voices and rambling debates were rare at Carl's Machine Shed. But no sewer project, committee appointment, or zoning ordinance was approved in the city without Chub Hughes, Larry Truesdale, Tom Treadwell, and Rufus Stodemeyer knowing about it first.

Today was different. The mayor knew he would have to do a little selling. He had the waitress roll in a television and VCR so he could show *The Baby Alison Story* while his friends ate their sandwiches.

"Now, what's the point of all this again?" Stodemeyer asked when the video concluded.

"The point," the mayor said, rising from his ice tea and half-eaten patty melt, "is how something as simple as a two-year-old girl falling down a well can change the course of history."

The four men stared at him as if he'd announced that *Horton Hears a Who* held the key to the cosmos. The mayor would be eighty-eight in August, and, like many his age, he sometimes rambled on about things that had little to do with the here and now. The publisher, Truesdale, had watched him while away hours at the *Headlight*'s microfilm machine, often grumbling about a story the newspaper got wrong, say, thirty years ago.

The mayor smiled to himself as he stood over the men. Giddiness shivered through his nervous system, temporarily relieving the chronic pain in his knees, as well as the constipation that had kept him plugged up for three days. He'd worn his "victory suit," a gray, pinstriped number he reserved for key council votes or visits to the statehouse. He had on silver cufflinks with engraved dollar symbols and a silk tie that depicted Old Glory, the blue field of stars fading into vertical red and white stripes. Not his favorite, but he felt it set a patriotic tone appropriate for the occasion.

"First of all, what I'm about to tell you absolutely, positively cannot leave this room," he began. "Whether or not we buy into this, we must agree to that."

The men nodded. They knew how to keep a secret.

The mayor went into his spiel about how Baby Alison had transformed the tiny town of Prairie View. How her ordeal became the topic of media coverage around the globe even years after the event. He told the story of a town in Iowa called Valmont that was so decimated by the 1993 Mississippi River flood that it had to be moved a mile away. Television crews from as far away as Japan were on hand as semitrucks carried the town's buildings to safety atop a river bluff. On a darker note, Simpson, South Dekota, became a cult novelty when the townspeople conspired to kill a local drug dealer who was untouchable by the law.

"People get shot every day in the city, and nobody gives a damn. It's buried in the six o'clock news and that's about it," the mayor said. "But a spot of trouble comes to a small town, and the media just about wets itself in excitement.

"You see, small towns hold a sacred place in the hearts of Americans, particularly those who've never lived in one. It's all supposed to be River City, Iowa, with a dash of Mayberry R.F.D. thrown in for good measure. Bad things don't happen here. Bad people don't live here. And when they do, the townspeople pull together and make things right again. That's just the way it is, according to the mythology."

Blank stares around the table. Treadwell coughed into his napkin. Stodemeyer glanced at his watch. They think I'm nuts, the mayor thought as silence swallowed the room, but what I'm about to say will make their short hairs stand on end.

"My friends, Pridemore is dying. I've banged my head against the wall for ten years trying to figure a way to save it. And, let me tell you, salvation ain't coming with a new curb and gutter project or a Burger Bomb franchise on Main Street. This town needs something powerful."

He leaned in close, looking each one of them in the eye before whispering in a southern Missouri twang he'd been turning off and on like a light switch for as long as he could remember. "I want to create an event that will stir peoples' hearts and minds. I want something so simple and dramatic to happen here that every news broadcast and every newspaper in America will lead in with a dateline from Pridemore, *Missourah*.

"I've got a germ of an idea that might do the trick. But I need a little help from my friends."

Chub Hughes was the first to speak. He was a heavyset man with graying sideburns and a doleful face that reminded some of a basset hound. His manner was slow and methodical, and he rarely spoke up before hearing what everybody else had to say. Nobody considered him the sharpest tool in the box, but, being the only general contractor in Pridemore County, Chub didn't need to dazzle folks with his intellect.

"You mean to tell me, Roe," he said, "that the only way to resurrect the town is by dropping a little bitty girl down a twenty-foot well?"

Stodemeyer slammed his fist on the table, rattling glasses and rousing Treadwell from the nodding refrains of a nap.

"I'm not gonna stand for using some two-year-old girl as bait for a newspaper story. You try a damned stunt like that and I'll see you all in jail. I don't care who the hell you are."

"Hold on, Rufus, hold on," the mayor said, clamping a weathered hand on his friend's shoulder. "That's not what I'm saying. That's not what I'm saying at all. You fellas ain't listening to me."

He straightened his American flag tie and wondered how Reagan might speak to a room of business leaders. The Great Communicator would probably take a quick breath, smile disarmingly, and tell a little story. Parables were good at a time like this, the mayor thought. But judging from the stolid looks on their faces, his colleagues were in no mood for smoke and mirrors. So he cut to the chase.

"The idea is to create some sort of calamity, some sort of crisis, but we control it from beginning to end, see?"

He looked at Treadwell and saw a hint of a smile on the prosecutor's big, bovine face. It was the face of Middle America, staring up at the Great Communicator and asking for a helping hand.

"Here's a for-instance," the mayor began, and he went on to describe the scenario he'd hashed out over six beers and two cigars the night before. The plan had kept him up until two in the morning, plotting and scheming. There had to be some kernel of genius to it for him to stay up that late. He was usually out like a baby by nine o'clock.

The plan was immense and convoluted, with several layers of deception built in. Somehow the mayor hit the highlights in fifteen minutes. When he finished, he found himself standing over his friends with both hands raised, as if bearing witness at a tent revival. He folded his arms tightly around his chest and swayed back and forth as the power brokers churned his idea over in their heads.

"That," Stodemeyer finally said, "is the dumbest thing I ever heard."

Larry Truesdale sucked thoughtfully on his well-chewed straw. Carl's Machine Shed didn't allow smoking, and the newspaper publisher had to do something to ease his oral habit.

"It might work," he said, "if you get the right people."

"It *will* work," the mayor said, "and the people we need are in this room."

"I don't like the idea of a kid being involved," Treadwell said.

"It's not gonna involve kids!" the mayor cried. "Have I said anything about kids?"

"Baby Alison is a kid," Chub noted.

"Baby Alison is old enough today to drive a car, and she's got nothing to do with this," the mayor said. "I promise—no kids!"

Chub learned back in his seat and put his Popeye-sized forearms behind his head.

"So what do you need from us, Roe? I got to be in Farley for a bid proposal at two o'clock."

"Well, I'm certainly going to need your expertise, Chub. You're the only contractor we've got."

"I've never done anything quite like this," Chub said. "It'll take time to work out a plan."

"Time's all we got," Truesdale said with a chuckle. "Time we got plenty of."

"Larry's right," the mayor agreed. "This isn't the kind of thing you do overnight. In fact, I wouldn't want to try it until next summer, once the rainy season's past us. So that gives us more than a year to plan this thing, plan it down to the last detail."

He placed his hands on the table and leaned toward his friends with an expectant smile.

"What do you think, boys?" he asked. "Wanna give it a go?"

The men shifted in their seats. One of them burped softly. This was pretty far-out stuff for a Monday at Carl's, where discussions usually centered on things like picking a new chairman for the United Way campaign.

And who could blame them for doubting? The idea was bizarre, morally indefensible, and illegal. It meant possibly spending the rest of their lives in prison if they were caught. Yet there was something thrilling about it, a last-ditch gambit to bring the town some meaning on its way to total irrelevance.

It was, as they say, a hell of a way to go.

The four men sat there, blinking.

"It's a lot to absorb," the mayor finally said. "Y'all wanna to go home and mull it over? That's fine. That's fine.

"I would just ask that you not mull it over with your wives or your children, or even your dog or cat," he added, peering into four pairs of eyes. "It is vital that you keep this information confidential. Including you, Larry."

Truesdale stared at the remains of his beef sandwich. The mayor hadn't forgotten 1997, when the publisher used a bit of inside information for an editorial. He was kicked out of the lunch group for two years after that.

The mayor sat down, crossed his legs, and placed a napkin over his knee. The waitress cleared the table and brought out ice cream and peach cobbler. Conversation turned to kids, the planting season, and the latest episode of *Dancing with the Stars*.

The men filed out after dessert, leaving the mayor and Chub Hughes alone. It was Chub's turn to pick up the check.

"How'd I do?" the mayor asked, watching his friend finish his cobbler.

Chub dabbed his napkin in a glass of water and wiped his big, somber mouth.

"Well, this town needs something."

The mayor leaned in and placed a hand on the man's big arm. "I need you with me on this. I need you to bring the others along, too."

The contractor rose, brushed the crumbs off his khakis, and checked his watch.

"I'll try, Mr. Mayor," he said. "I'll sure try."

CHAPTER 4

Expelling a long, low groan, Pete Schaefer slapped the facsimile from Edwards Funeral Home on the computer clipboard and started typing: *Naomi D. Elbert of Marshall City, formerly of Brush Hill, died Sunday, May 25, at Truman Retirement Center. She was 81.*

Before anything else Monday morning, Pete's job required him to type the obituaries of everyone who had died over the weekend—often a lengthy assignment given the number of blue-hairs in the region. Right now he was on obit number 8, his mind so far removed from what he was doing that he'd unwittingly invented two new ways to spell Naomi.

Pete found it hard to concentrate on the obits, or "oh-bitches," as his coworkers sometimes called them. After a year at the *Pridemore Evening Headlight*, the formula was so ingrained that he would merely slap the funeral notice on the clipboard and let his fingers clack away at their fifty-words-a-minute pace. This freed him to contemplate the newsroom's avocado-green decor, the florescent light that flickered annoyingly over his head, and a faded poster that advertised the Affair on the Square arts and crafts show from 1986. *Funeral services will be held 2 p.m. Tuesday at the Edwards Funeral Chapel with the Rev. Edwin Hodge officiating. Visitation will take place prior to services.*

Edna Bright fastened one of her Jimmy Carter grins on Pete as she waddled past his desk. It was a rare morning when he beat her to work. Plump and cheery as a Christmas ham, she was the *Headlight's* society editor and probably the most contented person Pete had ever met. Watching her swing an oversized purse around the back of her chair while singing an off-key version of "Escape (The Piña Colada Song)," he wondered if Edna Bright wasn't the source of the old notion that all fat people are jolly.

Pete kept his head down, pretending to focus on his work. *Survivors include one sister, Maureen Dowell of LaGrange; two sons, John Elbert of St. Louis and Duane Elbert of Wellsville; and a daughter, Yula Mae Lowry of Forest Park.*

Edna nibbled a doughnut and slurped her coffee while reading the *St. Louis Intelligencer*, occasionally clucking an "Oh, my," or a disapproving "Ew!"

Then silence. No slurping. No ews. Peter sensed her beady eyes, dark as night, watching him.

"Hiya, Pete," she said when he finally looked up. "How's your morning?"

Slowly turning from his computer, Pete decided to shock her with a smile of his own. Not one of those put-on numbers he gave the cut-and-paste girls in production that even they could see through, but a real, genuine smile.

"How are you, Edna?" he asked so naturally you would think he said it every morning.

Edna wasn't surprised. If anything, she seemed encouraged.

"Say Pete, did you catch *The McClusky Files* last night?"

"*The McClusky Files*," he said, vaguely recalling the show in which an aging actor plays an aging detective. "Is that the one that's set in Miami?"

"No, you're thinking of *Randy Slaughter, Medical Examiner*," she said. "*McClusky Files* is in L.A."

"Of course."

"I just really love that McClusky, don't you? I mean, he's nice and polite like a gentleman should be, but he's tough, too. He always gets his man and he's not afraid to call a spade a spade, if you know what I mean." Edna smiled. "I can tell that's probably the way he is in real life, too."

Pete gave one of those half laughs that most people would read as a sign of disinterest. Not Edna.

"Last night was one of the better ones," she said. "McClusky and these other people are guests on this millionaire's yacht, you see. And, almost as soon as they all get on board, the millionaire disappears."

"Really?" Pete said.

"So all of a sudden, people just start disappearing: the millionaire's wife, the movie star—"

"The Professor and Mary Ann?" he offered.

Edna giggled to show she caught the reference, and went on.

"Usually I'm pretty good at picking out the murderer before everyone else. But I didn't have a clue on this one. Jerry thought it was the millionaire, but what does he know? I mean, he's the only guy in Rotary who thought O.J. was innocent, you know?"

"Right."

"Just when we're at the part where McClusky's gonna nail the bad guy, I get this phone call from my daughter, Alicea. She's about your age, you know."

Edna was shaking now, her banshee cackle filling the mostly empty newsroom.

"So I get off the phone and I rush back to ask Jerry whodunit. Well, he's already switched the channel to SportsCenter. Took me six phone calls to find out it was the Portuguese deck hand who strangled 'em all with a piano wire and threw their bodies overboard.

"*Ewww,*" she said. "I almost strangled someone myself last night!"

"That's funny," Pete offered in a tone that suggested he didn't think it was funny at all. He gave her a tight smile and returned to his computer.

Edna let out a huff and left her desk for another cup of coffee. Pete felt pretty evil for leading her on like that. He could be mean when he was depressed, and he was depressed nearly all the time lately.

He thought about starting another conversation when Edna returned. But the other staffers were ambling in, and he needed to call the area cops to see if there'd been any overnight car wrecks. Obits and road fatalities—it was some sweet gig he'd scored for himself more than a year removed from journalism school. Woodward and Bernstein had better watch their jocks.

From the corner of his eye, he watched Edna settle into her seat. He'd come up with something thoughtful to say to her first thing tomorrow, even if he had to watch network television to do it.

The afternoon sun sprayed rivulets of light through the dusty blinds that hung over Pete's futon. Angela sat up, crossed her skinny legs under the sheet, and watched Pete sift through the dirty clothes, old magazines, and sports gear that cluttered his bedroom closet.

"What are you looking for?"

He smiled as his fingers grazed the beat-up leather briefcase.

"My soul," he said, pulling the briefcase out of the closet and opening it.

"Wow," she said as he pulled out a fistful of typed pages. "You wrote all that?"

"It's nothing. Maybe two hundred pages in all, double-spaced."

"That's nothing?"

"Not for a book," he said. "You heard of Schubert's unfinished symphony? This is Schaefer's unfinished novel."

"Wow," she repeated, plopping next to him on the floor. Save for the three-legged recliner that tilted like a sinking ship in Pete's living room, there were no chairs in his one-bedroom apartment, so the two spent most of their time on the futon or the floor.

"You never told me you were a writer," Angela said.

"I'm a newspaper reporter. You know that."

"Yeah, but I didn't know you were a *writer*," she said, laughing and folding her arms across her chest. "What's it about?"

"Oh, your typical coming-of-age, loss-of-innocence love story."

"Sort of like *Great Expectations*?" Angela suggested.

"Yeah," Pete said, and he gave her a soft kiss. "Except with zombies."

"Can I read it?"

He flicked through the pages before finding a chapter he liked, the one in which Sully and Bart take Bettger down to Creepy Woods for one last bong hit.

He ran his hand through Angela's long dark hair and studied her crinkled brow as she read, making note of whether she smiled at the funny parts. She giggled once or twice, always a good sign.

That giggle reminded him of Angela's current status on the high school varsity cheerleading squad. Most of the time, Pete thought her comparable to the somber, artistically inclined women he'd dated in college. The crinkle in Angela's brow gave her a thoughtful look that seemed older than her years, and she could quote whole passages of Dickinson or Thoreau. He would almost start to take her seriously until, in a beautifully unguarded moment, she'd relate a fart joke she learned in study hall or clumsily pick the chords to "Smoke on

31

the Water" on his guitar. That's when the giggle came out, and it was suddenly *Saved by the Bell* time at Pete's place.

He loved and detested that giggle. Loved its affirmation that he could make someone laugh at a time in his life when he didn't laugh much at all. Hated how it reminded him that what he was doing with Angela went beyond the bounds of acceptable adult behavior. He'd tried many times to tell her this. Well, once or twice. But Angela would just giggle and kiss him and tell him to shut up, and Pete would mind his manners as they crawled back onto the futon.

They had met in October at a downtown festival called Olde Pridemore Days. He'd seen her around town a couple of times, hanging at Truman's Malt Shop with her high school buddies or passing through the newspaper office to drop off her "Teen Beat" column. But Olde Pridemore Days was the first time they really talked.

He remembered almost every detail of that day: she wore a spaghetti-string halter top and a pair of ripped-up blue jeans, edgy stuff for a Sunday in Pridemore. They spent the day walking around, eating sno-cones and funnel cakes, making fun of the lame country/western act on the main stage. They talked about books and music, and how cool it would be to move to Paris, just living and writing like Hemingway and Fitzgerald and those other Lost Generation guys.

They made out that night on the courthouse steps, an encounter that soon led to Angela's afternoon visits to Pete's apartment when she could slip out of her independent studies class. In the first four visits, Pete was able to pull back, throw on his jeans, and mumble something about getting Angela back to school before the start of seventh period. The fifth time they reached the precipice, an unseasonably warm February day when Pete was supposed to be covering a livestock show in Hodgeville, Angela straddled his waist, grabbed his shirt with her fists, and said in a husky voice, "I'm not taking no for an answer."

Pete gave in. He hated himself for it, but not enough to stop meeting Angela at his place most Wednesday afternoons. He was weak. He was stupid. But mostly he was bored. She was the only girl he'd met since moving to Pridemore, and he was tired of pretending he didn't like having her around.

"How long ago did you write this?" Angela asked when she finished the chapter.

"It's been a while. I haven't really touched it since college."

"You ought to finish it," she said, pulling him close. "I mean, think how much you've improved as a writer since then."

"Really?" he asked. "You think it needs work?"

"I dunno. I mean, this part about the guys drinking and partying, making all the pop culture references—it's funny, but it's kind of played out, you know?"

She wiped a strand of hair from her mouth and gave a half-smile.

"It kinda reads like a beer commercial."

He was still reeling from the blow as they drove to the high school in his beat-up Ford Explorer. *Kinda reads likes a beer commercial.* This from someone who ate Oreo cookies icing first, who'd only recently shifted her musical allegiance from Beyoncé to Taylor Swift. It was a mistake letting her read his book, he thought. Did he expect an educated response from someone who was struggling to maintain a B average in junior English?

Come to think of it, this whole thing was a mistake. And driving Angela to school was beyond dangerous. They were getting very careless, Pete knew.

He watched her light a Marlboro while grooving to a pop song on the radio. It was amusing to watch her smoke because she hadn't mastered how to tap the ash off a cigarette.

"What did I tell you about smoking in my truck?" he asked.

"That I'm allowed to do it except when you're pissed over something I said about a book you wrote."

"I'm not mad."

She leaned across the gearshift and kissed his cheek.

"I'm such a meanie," she said with a pout that was both cute and condescending. "I guess when you've been reading *Crime and Punishment* for two weeks, everything else reads like a beer commercial."

"Oh, so now I'm not even as good as Dostoevsky?" he said, breaking into a grin as they approached their drop-off point near the gym.

She gave him a kiss that surprised him with its deepness. It was the kind she had planted on him that night at the courthouse steps.

"I love you," she said in a throaty whisper. "I know you hate that, but I do."

"Okay," Pete said, handing Angela her books as she stepped out of the truck. "Just don't tell your daddy."

Pete was explaining his premature baldness to a waitress when his buddy, *Headlight* sportswriter Dave Felton, walked into One-Eyed Willie's, the only Pridemore establishment left with a liquor license since the Lizard Lounge closed.

"Yeah, my brother's losing a little on top himself," the waitress said. "He's pretty freaked out about it."

"It's genetic, you know," Pete told her after a sip from his longneck. "It's passed down from your mother's side of the family."

The waitress pondered this for a minute.

"But my mom's not bald," she said.

Felton and Pete exchanged the same weary look they shared in the newsroom whenever Edna referred to the president's anti-terrorism policy as The War on Towel Heads.

Like two strangers in a strange land, Felton and Pete clung to each other almost out of necessity. They were both about the same age and both St. Louis natives. They both enrolled in journalism school with grand thoughts of someday working for *The Washington Post* or *The New York Times*, and they both graduated into a crappy job market with $18,000 salaries at a newspaper they'd never heard of. ("This," Felton said after a couple of whiskey shots one night at Willie's, "is what is known as paying your dues.")

Meeting once or twice a week at Willie's had become something of a social highlight for Pete. He cringed to think what Pridemore would be like if he didn't have a friend around.

He nodded toward the baseball highlights on the overhead TV. "Cards took a pounding today."

"No pitching, yet again," Felton replied.

Pete ordered another Bud Light and surveyed Willie's decor of birds, bayonets, and batting helmets. It beat looking at the clientele, which this night consisted of two utility workers and a woman with mall bangs dancing alone. The jukebox was playing its usual mix of Three Dog Night, BTO, and, in a token nod to the '80s, Night Ranger.

"Larry asked about you today," Felton said. "He's starting to wonder where you're spending your Wednesday after-noons."

"I'm spending them at home," Pete said with a shrug. "Comp time."

Felton shook his head and laughed. "You're an idiot."

"What?"

"He's gonna find out."

"I guess I'll be out of a job, then.

"It's kind of like detonating a highly sensitive explosive," Pete added after some thought. "You never know when it's going to just blow up in your hands."

"Don't romanticize it, Schaefer. You're screwing your boss's daughter. Your boss's *seventeen-year-old* daughter." He laughed as he fished in his shirt pocket for a lighter. "You're just an idiot, that's all."

"You said that already."

The door creaked open, and Felton and Pete glanced back as if they expected Angelina Jolie and Scarlett Johansson to drop by for drinks on their way through town. But it was just some grubby guy in a shirt with his name on it. The dancing woman left her spot at the jukebox to give him a lingering hug.

"Done any work on your book lately?" Felton asked.

"Looked at it today, that's all," Pete said with a sigh. "How's yours coming?"

"I can't summon the muse," the sportswriter said. "Every night, I sit there, blinking at a blank screen. I end up watching reruns of *Seinfeld* and falling asleep on the couch."

Pete laughed. "It's this town, you know? It's sapping our brains."

"Yeah," Felton agreed, mashing his cigarette into an ashtray. "I need to get out of this fucking town."

Pete looked at the TV, which was flashing highlights from the previous night's Marlins-Phillies game.

"Florida would be nice," Felton said, reading Pete's mind.

"I've got an uncle in Jacksonville," Pete said. "We could crash at his place until we found jobs. Maybe we could open a hot dog stand on the beach, or whatever."

"Felton's Franks, we'd call it," Felton said.

"That could give us some cash until our novels got published. We'd open for lunch at eleven and close around two so we could get some beach time—"

"—and watch the sun go down each evening with our beautiful, bikini-clad girlfriends," Felton added. "When do we leave?"

"Tomorrow," Pete said instinctively. "How much money you got saved up?"

"About two hundred—give or take a hundred."

"I've got about five hundred," Pete said, really thinking now. "So we've got enough for the drive and maybe a week after that."

"Should we give two weeks' notice?"

"In two weeks we'll lose our nerve," Pete said. "It's gotta be now."

Felton took a thoughtful drag from his Camel and grinned. Meatloaf was on the jukebox now, wailing about how two outta three ain't bad.

"You don't even have an uncle in Florida, do you?"

The door opened. Felton and Pete glanced back, in case a starlet appeared.

CHAPTER 5

"Well, the ol' boy's finally gone wacky, hasn't he?"

Rufus Stodemeyer let out a little snicker as he said this. The owner of Pridemore's only car dealership was a short, barrel-chested man with small black eyes and a crew cut he'd worn since his time in the Missouri National Guard more than thirty years ago. He was a mean, petty man whose boorish behavior would have made him an outcast in town were he not also its wealthiest citizen.

"Yep," Stodemeyer said, staring down the length of his pool cue like it was a gun barrel. "The ol' boy's gone wacky-do."

He was taking a few shots at the mayor while Larry Truesdale lined up one of his own: a difficult bank shot that would sink the seven ball and keep alive his hopes of beating the car dealer on his own billiard table.

"Ha!" Stodemeyer said as Truesdale hit the cue ball so hard it bounced off the table and rolled beneath a rubber tree plant.

"I don't think he's crazy at all," said Chub Hughes. The general contractor sat in a leather armchair, chewing thoughtfully on an unlit cigar.

"Me neither," Truesdale said. "Eccentric? Yes. Crazy? No."

"Well, I've served on the council with that crackpot for fifteen years and, believe me, the man's 100 percent toys in the attic," Stodemeyer said as he retrieved the cue ball. "Must I remind you gentlemen of the Torch Fiasco of '96?"

He was, of course, referring to the summer many years ago when the Olympic torch was scheduled to proceed through

Farley on its way to Atlanta. Just days before the torch came through central Missouri, Mayor Tolliver told the Olympic Committee they'd better redraw the route through Pridemore if the torch bearer wanted to avoid a blockade of county sheriff's deputies on Highway 54. After some heated phone calls, the Olympics people decided it would be better to cooperate with a crazy old mayor than explain to the international press why the torch was a day late to the Opening Ceremonies.

"That was a fine moment for this town," Tom Treadwell, the county prosecutor, said between sips from his margarita.

"You'd think so, wouldn't you, Tom?" Stodemeyer said "Since you're the one who signed off on the roadblock."

"Come off it, Rufus," Truesdale said. "We know why you want Tolliver out."

Stodemeyer just grinned as he lined up another shot. For years, he'd waited in the wings as the mayor's handpicked successor. He'd backed the mayor on every council vote, defended him in the newspaper, gone with him to Jeff City every January to grease political palms. For years, he'd been the good soldier only to watch the mayor put off retirement time and again by running for "one last term."

He thrust the cue stick, sending the eight ball flying into the corner pocket. Truesdale groaned; Rufus Stodemeyer had won again.

"Can you fault me for wishing the old man would just go away?" he asked.

Chub sat in his chair, chewing his cigar and watching the other three men rack up a game of Cutthroat. A quiet, morose man who had worked his way up from plow hand to owning a construction business worth ten million dollars, he hated conflict and acrimony. Stodemeyer's comments about the mayor were all the more annoying because, come Monday's council meeting, his lips would return to their familiar place on the mayor's fanny. Chub saw through Stodemeyer's big talk, his hot pink Mustang with dealer's plates, and his two-piece, custom-made pool cue. He'd like nothing more than to break that stick across Stodemeyer's National Guard buzz cut. He'd do it, too, if the son of a bitch didn't happen to be his biggest client.

As owners of three Ford dealerships in the five-county region, the Stodemeyers had more money than anyone else in Pridemore and didn't seem to care who knew it. Their three-story Colonial Williamsburg-style house towered over the respectable split-levels and ranch homes that lined Waverly Lane.

The home was filled with furniture and artwork the couple had collected from Europe and Asia. Upon walking into the living room, the first thing you saw was a massive painting of human and animal parts strewn across a dark landscape. It was hideous, Chub thought, until Stodemeyer's wife explained it was a print of *Guernica*, Picasso's portrayal of the Spanish Civil War. Now he kind of appreciated it. Karen Stodemeyer might be a humorless, uppity bitch, Chub thought, but at least she had interesting taste.

Her husband's basement was a different world. Filled with lava lamps, sports memorabilia, beer signs, and pinup girls, it looked like a ninth grade boy's tribute to the good life. In the middle of all this were the pool table, a fifty-inch flat screen TV, and a couple of beat-up leather armchairs with stuffing peeking out the corners. The wife clearly had no hand in decorating this part of the house.

"See that one, boys?" Stodemeyer said, pointing his cue stick at a forlorn-looking buck's head with antlers as wide as a Lincoln Continental. "Got that one in Alberta last spring. A twelve-pointer!"

Feeling he'd heard enough, Chub rose from his chair, picked up a cue stick, and tossed it on the pool table.

"Damn, Chub!" Stodemeyer said. "That's a forty-dollar cue you almost smashed."

"I just wanted to get you boys' attention and remind you why we're here."

"What?" Treadwell asked. "To discuss the mayor's cockamamie plan?"

Chub settled into the armchair with a legal pad on his knee. He stared his colleagues down until they put away their sticks and found somewhere to sit.

"Now fellas, you know I'm not prone to galloping off on some damn fool idea. I've lived in this town my whole life. And I'd like to think folks see me as a steady, solid, God-fearing guy."

"Amen to that," Truesdale said.

"What the mayor proposed last week made me nervous," Chub continued. "Actually, it made me sick to my stomach."

He looked across the room to find Stodemeyer stifling a yawn. The little shit.

"I couldn't believe how a man I've admired my whole life could come up with a plan that was so dishonest, so manipulative of other people.

"But coming home from work that night, I drove past the boarded-up storefronts on Main Street, past the baseball park covered with weeds, past that pothole at Marley and Houston that's bigger than a cast-iron tub."

The men nodded knowingly.

"And I thought about what the mayor said, about how this town needs something bold, something powerful. And he's right, of course."

Chub chewed off a piece of his cigar and spit it into a plastic cup he'd been holding.

"I don't know what to think of the plan," he said. "I know it's not perfect, but does anyone have a better idea?"

"I can sure as shit think up something that won't land us all in jail," Stodemeyer said. "And I don't see how this is gonna get Pridemore out of the fix it's in."

Chub nodded slowly. "It is a delicate situation, to be sure."

He turned to Truesdale, the *Headlight* publisher, who was nursing his rum and Coke. He was a tall, broad-shouldered man with neatly coiffed hair, a hint of baby fat that favored his jaw and cheekbones, and perfectly aligned teeth that, despite a perpetual nicotine habit, remained alarmingly white. In a town where most folks wore boots and open-collared shirts, Truesdale was a suit and tie guy. Tonight was as casual as he got: tan loafers, navy slacks with a tight crease, and a white shirt with his monogram on the breast pocket. The guy looks like he's in a brandy commercial, Chub thought.

"The plan has got potential," Truesdale said. "It's the kind of story the press could really go for, if the timing's right."

"Which means what?" Treadwell asked.

"You want to stage this thing when the chances of being overshadowed by a bigger story are low," the publisher said. "For instance, you wouldn't do it in August or September, because that's hurricane season. You'd want to avoid October, because that's the World Series, or January, because that's the Super Bowl."

"Which leaves us with what?" Stodemeyer asked.

Truesdale picked an invisible piece of lint from the crease in his slacks and released it into the air.

"May isn't bad," he said. "In fact, that's Sweeps Month, when the local TV stations are looking for blockbuster stories to boost their ratings. The mayor's plan could be just what the doctor ordered."

"Sweeps Month," Treadwell said, shaking his head as if he couldn't believe the cynicism of it all.

Chub looked at his watch. If they wrapped this thing up in twenty minutes, he could get home in time for *Survivor*.

"So, Larry, you like the plan?" he asked.

"It's got potential. But it's in the baby stage."

"Agreed," Chub said. "We don't have to lay this all out tonight, but I'd like to get back to the mayor with some sort of consensus. I, for one, think we should move forward with the plan because I can't for the life of me think of anything better."

He eyed each of his colleagues.

"So, Larry, you're open to the idea?"

"Sure."

"Rufus?"

"I think it's the stupidest damned thing I've ever heard of."

"All right. Tom? How 'bout you?"

The county prosecutor rubbed his hands together, obviously pleased to be the swing vote. For someone like Treadwell, graceless and dull, any scrap of attention was like finding a four-leaf clover in a field of green. He sat for what seemed like a minute with a clenched look on his face before responding.

"I don't like it."

It was a deadlock. There was only one fair way to break the tie, the four power brokers agreed. And that was, of course, in the realm of sport. And, because this was Stodemeyer's house, it would be decided on the pool table. Whoever shot a ball the closest to the bumper without hitting it would be declared the winner. Treadwell and Truesdale demurred. It would be Stodemeyer and Chub, the two best players.

As he placed the cue ball on the table, Chub wondered if he even cared to win. But he was kidding himself. Right or wrong, any chance to wipe the smirk off that flat-topped goon's face was satisfaction enough. Remembering it was a fast table, he tapped the ball with just enough force to make it bounce off the other end and come to a stop about six inches from the bumper. A good shot, but probably not good enough.

Stodemeyer approached the table with the bow-legged swagger of a cowpoke who'd done it all. He placed a little chalk on his stick (as if that was even necessary), set up the six ball, and leaned over the table. He pumped the stick through his index and middle fingers like a well-oiled piston as he lined up his shot.

"Watch," he said. "And learn."

And Stodemeyer hit what was possibly the worst shot of his life. Off the side of the tip, with that horrible wood-meets-ivory cracking sound, the ball careening into the corner pocket. The car dealer unleashed a scream and hurled the stick into a hanging fern.

Chub shook Stodemeyer's hand and hung his cue stick on the rack near the cigar humidor.

"Well," he said. "I guess I'll give the mayor the good news."

Once outside the oak doors that graced the Stodemeyers' front stoop, Chub stopped, glanced around to see if anyone was looking, and let out a war whoop that would make an Apache brave proud.

He climbed into his SUV and backed down the winding driveway, careful not to drive over Karen Stodemeyer's begonias.

CHAPTER 6

Digby Willers smiled as he ran his finger along the smooth piece of pine that would be his entry in the Yellow Jacket District's Pinewood Derby. What just a few days ago had been a simple block of wood now bore the unmistakable contours of a 1970 Corvette, Digby's favorite sports car and the inspiration for all nine of his champion racers.

He held the block up to the desk lamp that was the only light in the one-car garage. There were still some rough spots, so he pulled the folded piece of sandpaper from his shorts for the umpteenth time that day and ran it over the wood with the slow, circular motion of someone polishing a rare coin. The scratching of sandpaper against wood kept time to the music in his head, the latest hit from boy-band idol Dakota Marx:

> *Girl, you know what's in my heart.*
> *But I don't want to know,*
> *Just where you get off tellin' me,*
> *which way my love should flow.*
> *Girl, you know you are my sun,*
> *And you know you shoot the moon.*
> *And I've got a funny feelin',*
> *Things'll be all right soon.*
> *All right soon. All right sooooooon…*

Digby didn't know all the words. But he liked singing the tune, especially when he was doing something that didn't require much thought. He had been a huge Dakota Marx fan for more than a year, and he badgered his mother for weeks to buy him the new CD, which came with a full-sized poster of Dakota and his band that Digby immediately hung in his bedroom. "All Right Soon" was his favorite song on the album, and he practically jumped out of his skin whenever it came on the radio, which was often that summer.

It was near midnight, but still hot and stuffy in the garage. He stepped away from his work now and again to wipe his face or breathe in the evening air. Digby wouldn't sleep tonight until the piece of pine was smooth as glass. Tomorrow, he would paint it crimson and blue, apply the Penzoil and Beechnut Chew decals, and, finally, attach the well-sanded plastic wheels.

A wood shelf over the carpenter's table displayed his Pinewood Derby winners, all of them red and blue cars of varying shapes and refinement. If you lined them in chronological order, you could track his progress from the chunky editions of the first few races to last year's rocket-sleek model.

Those cars were the pride of the Willers family, which consisted of Digby, his mother, and a couple of cats named Peanut and Romeow. They lived in a white, split-level house that, frankly, had seen better days. Paint peeled from the vinyl siding, the storm windows hadn't been washed in years, and the front yard, which Digby rarely got around to mowing, was a blanket of dandelions.

Susan Willers had little time to worry about that. She worked most nights as an RN at the county hospital, a position she attained after years of waiting tables, cleaning houses, working the Burger Bomb drive-thru, and, finally, getting her nurse's certification. She was a broad, unsmiling woman with large hands that felt firm as C-clamps as one gripped your shoulder and the other rooted deep between your cheeks for a prostate check that seemed anything but routine (nurses weren't supposed to do such tests, but Dr. McNamara was only in town three days a week). She looked ten years older than she was, used nothing in the way of beauty products, and could often be found near the emergency room entrance sucking on a Winston Light. Her coworkers called her Big Tobacco, though never to her face.

The icy exterior Susan showed the outside world seemed to melt around Digby. She coddled him as if he were still that tiny kid beaming in the Olan Mills portraits that hung over the mantle. When Digby wanted to be a pilot a few years back, she bought him a $200 remote-controlled airplane that he assembled and promptly crashed into the Harpers' garage. When he decided he wanted to be a magician, she bought him an elaborate magic kit and took him to watch the world-famous what's-his-name (the one who married a supermodel) attempt to make the St. Louis Arch disappear.

Now he was into Dakota Marx, and Susan was dead set on taking him to see the superstar perform on his "Nothing Matters" tour, though she didn't know how she would scrape together three hundred bucks for two tickets to the Kansas City show. She would hold off fixing the air-conditioner in the Pontiac if need be. She could bear the summer heat a helluva lot easier than the thought of letting Digby down. He was such a good boy and asked for so little as it was.

Pop stars and magicians came and went, of course, but the Pinewood Derby was a lifelong commitment, something Digby relished every summer since joining Troop 66 (at a time when he was two years older than the other scouts and several inches taller). Scouting, it turned out, wasn't his bag—he dropped out after severely bruising another kid's rump in dodge ball. But Digby was hooked on the derby from the first time he entered it; he loved the anticipation of blue-clad scouts huddled around the big ramp, waiting for the scoutmaster to lift the gate that would send the cars flying, six wooden racers of various shapes and colors rattling down the thirty-foot ramp and spilling onto the gymnasium floor. Digby won six heats and the championship trophy that day, the first thing he ever won in his life.

He had competed every year since, despite rumblings from parents. "Look, he's a nice kid and, of course, he is *different*," they would suggest, "but how long is this going to go on? The *real* scouts don't even have a chance."

Sometimes, he felt bad about winning. He knew how upset people got. And why wouldn't they? The cars were all made out of the same wood, all weighed about the same, all rolled down the same ramp. How on earth could he keep winning the thing year after year?

He sometimes thought the derby was a curse, like his pea-sized brain. Both made him different. Both made kids keep their distance on the street and grownups whisper about him in the grocery store. He prayed about it sometimes. He asked God to end the winning streak, which he felt would make him seem a little more normal. It helped to be normal in Pridemore, where everybody knew you, or at least talked about you like they knew you. But Digby realized his prayers were half-hearted. If he really wanted to end the streak, he just wouldn't enter the damn race at all.

He looked at the derby winners up on the shelf and thought about how quickly they would burn with just a match and a little kerosene. Of course he would never do that to the most prized things in his life. Still, he imagined how they would look, decals peeling away, plastic wheels melting, crimson and blue bodies turning black. It was crushing to think about, but also a little exciting.

Digby had been experimenting with a cigarette lighter he swiped from his mother's purse. He tried smoking one of her Winstons, which only made him cough. But he liked what the lighter could do to his collection of plastic model planes and his GI Joe action figures. Sitting in the gully behind the house where no one could see, he watched the flame turn one toy after another into gooey gunk, like those melting faces in *Raiders of the Lost Ark*. He would do this until the fumes made him dizzy or he heard his mom calling him. Digby liked what the lighter could do. It had the power to change things.

He looked up as a pair of headlights flickered past the garage door windows. He heard the car pull up the gravel drive next door and listened carefully as the driver killed the motor, opened the door, and muttered a curse word as she dropped her keys. It was Miss Hurshey, the Willerses' next-door neighbor and one of the few women in town who wasn't married or divorced. She was Digby's babysitter back when he needed one, before he was a big boy.

As he had many times before, Digby turned off the desk lamp, slipped through the side door, and crawled under the honeysuckle bush where he could see into Miss Hurshey's bedroom. He liked her long hair, her clingy skirts, and the pretty underwear she sometimes wore on the nights she came home late. Some nights she brought a friend, and the shade was drawn. But most nights she came home alone, the shade would be up just a tad, and Digby could watch Miss Hurshey peel off her skirt and stockings, letting her black hair flow over her bare shoulders. Those nights in the summer when the fireflies were flashing and the air was sweet with honeysuckle, she was the most beautiful thing he'd ever seen that wasn't on television.

Digby watched until Miss Hurshey turned off her light. Then he crawled back to the garage, turned the lamp on, and returned to sanding and singing his favorite Dakota Marx tune.

Things'll be all right soon, all right soon, all right sooooooon…

CHAPTER 7

Pete Schaefer idly sketched a buxom mermaid on his notepad as he waited for the members of the Pridemore City Council to detach themselves from the Mister Coffee machine and start their six o'clock meeting. The council met at City Hall every other Monday, and it was Pete's job to attend on the off chance that something newsworthy might happen.

The meetings were usually as scripted as a pro wrestling match, minus the camp value. Everyone knew that Mayor Roe Tolliver had eight of the ten members in his back pocket. About an hour before every meeting, the eight toadies gathered in the mayor's office, where they were briefed on the council's agenda and how they were supposed to vote. Pete sometimes arrived at City Hall just in time to see a few of them scurry out and gather around the coffee pot, where conversation turned to somebody's honor roll kid or the sad state of University of Missouri athletics. The council had worked this way for as long as anyone could remember.

Pete didn't know much about government protocol, this being his first year covering the city beat. But he knew that a meeting of more than three council members was a quorum, which meant it should be open to the public. He'd talked to his editor, Beatrice Reilly, about doing a story on the pre-meeting meetings, but Larry Truesdale pooh-poohed the idea in his usual backslapping way.

"The mayor would never let me hear the end of it," the publisher said with a chuckle when Pete pitched him the story. "Roe doesn't even like reporters attending the *real* meetings, truth be told."

"I don't know why. Nothing ever happens in them," Pete said.

"Now listen here," Truesdale said, pointing a half-smoked cigarette in Pete's direction. "People in Pridemore were doing things a certain way long before you came here, and they'll keep doing them long after you've gone. Mayor Tolliver didn't get elected to ten straight terms for nothing, understand?"

"Yessir."

Truesdale smiled big, revealing two rows of shiny teeth. He held the expression until it seemed less like a grin and more like a predatory baring of enamel.

"Great!" he said. "Now here's a story you might be interested in..."

He rattled on about some twenty-two-year-old guy who kept winning the Cub Scouts' wooden car derby (whoop-de-do!) and sent Pete slinking out of the office with a phone number and an order to check out the story.

So city business went on as usual, and Pete covered all the meetings, sometimes drifting into a fog while staring up at those eleven faces behind their comically ornate dais. He wondered about their lives: how many of them had enjoyed a hearty, nutritious breakfast that morning, how many of them would go home that night to a loving spouse, and how many of them would fall asleep in the white glare of late-night talk shows.

Mostly, he sat and doodled in his notepad, as he was doing when Bryan London marched up and placed a hand on his shoulder.

"Peter," he said with an impish wink.

"Hi, Mr. London."

"What have they got for us today?"

Pete glanced at his agenda. "Looks like curbs and gutters, and a liquor license for the Lizard Lounge."

"Mind if I borrow that?"

"No problem." Pete handed over the sheet and returned to his doodling.

London thanked him and climbed behind the dais to his seat just left of the mayor. Bryan London was one of only two councilmen who weren't part of the mayor's rubber stamp committee (the other, Sid Walsh, lived most of the year in Florida). London opposed the mayor on almost everything, from where to put new sidewalks to whom would serve as grand marshal of the Pridemore High School homecoming parade.

The way Pete understood it, the two men had been political allies and best friends until ten years ago, when London decided Roe Tolliver had been mayor long enough and ran against him in the city election. Of course, London lost by a huge margin and had been the council pariah ever since, so much so that the city clerk was forbidden to provide him agenda items for the weekly meetings.

Just another tidbit the *Headlight*'s readers would never know, Pete thought as the meeting began with a solemn thud from the mayor's gavel. Pete looked around the room. There were about twenty people gathered in metal folding chairs to watch the meeting. Half of them were Boy Scouts trying to earn their merit badges.

The council chambers, as they called it, could have been any room in any aging government building in the country. The ceiling was all tubular florescent lights flickering among yards of textured ceiling panels yellowed from decades of cigarette smoke. The floor was black-and-white linoleum tiles, and the windows were guarded by wide, metallic blinds that probably hadn't been dusted since the Carter administration.

The only unusual thing was the council's oaken dais, carved in an ionic style and coated with enough lacquer to fuel a three-alarm fire. The edifice was huge and out of place, reminding Pete of the monolithic slab in the opening of *2001: A*

Space Odyssey. The mayor and his ten council members sat a good two feet above everyone else, allowing them to peer down imperiously at whoever stood before them.

The meeting began with standard city stuff. The council activated $700,000 in bonds to finish a drainage project along Coleman Street. The public works director notified council members that the swing set at Tillman Park was rusty and needed to be replaced. The council voted nine to one to grant a new liquor license to the Lizard Lounge, which had temporarily closed after one ol' boy shot another ol' boy over some waitress who couldn't care less about either one of them.

"The Lizard Lounge doesn't have a wheelchair ramp," Bryan London protested. "You can't give a liquor license to a bar that doesn't meet the Americans with Disabilities Act."

"Handicapped people shouldn't be out drinking anyway," the mayor muttered after tallying the vote. "Next item!"

This one caught Pete by surprise: "A proposal to annex the Dragon's Ice House into the City of Pridemore." It wasn't on the agenda.

"What the hell is this?" London said.

"Just a little something I came up with," the mayor responded, lowering his eyelids in serene innocence. "Dragon's Ice House is one of Pridemore County's few natural wonders, and I thought it would useful to have it in our city after all these years."

"Nobody shared this with me," London said, his face reddening. He was a heavy, excitable man whose face turned beet red, arteries bulging like mountain ranges on a relief map, when he didn't get his way. This happened at least once every meeting.

The mayor turned his chair, which was just a little taller and grander than those of the other council members, and gave London the pitying look of someone who was dealing with an extremely slow child.

"Then I guess," he said, "I will go over it again."

He explained how it was his dream to take over Dragon's Ice House, a deep chasm on the outskirts of town that led to a large network of caves, some of which had never been explored. The mayor always thought the Ice House would be a nifty tourist attraction, sort of a Pridemore version of Fantastic Caverns down in the Ozarks. Folks would come from miles around to crawl into the Ice House, so named for the chilly temperature within its limestone walls, and learn a little about the caves that tunneled for miles beneath the Missouri farmland.

Annexing Dragon's Ice House made sense, the mayor said, because the state had earmarked $140 million in its budget for tourism. If it acted fast, Pridemore could get a hefty chunk of that money to develop the site.

"I talked to our state representative Chester Maddox the other day, and Chester thinks he can get us ten million in matching state money for the project," the mayor said.

"But we haven't got ten million to begin with!" London cried, his face as red as a fire engine. "We can't even get the damned streets fixed, and you wanna spend ten million dollars on an amusement park?"

The mayor shot him a concerned look. "I know there aren't a lot of sacred things in this world, but I would ask you to refrain from using profanity when we are discussing city business in this chamber."

The mayor stood and opened his veined hands, palms facing the audience. He was a tall, bony man who only looked more grotesque the closer you got. His skin was gray and almost transparent under florescent light, revealing every blood vessel and liver spot in detail. Atop his head sat the most hilarious rug Pete had ever seen, a dark brown number that didn't even attempt to blend with his white temples. Tonight, the mayor was wearing a seersucker suit and a tie that featured a bald eagle flying with a formation of B-2 bombers. It was the kind of getup you might expect from a car dealer announcing his Fourth of July sale.

"I'm just an old man," the mayor said. "Just an old man with a lot of old dreams. One of those dreams is to get this city going again."

He turned to London.

"You can have the best streets in the whole dad-blamed world, but that isn't going to bring us back to where we were, among the elite communities in this state."

The mayor pressed his hands together and crouched slightly like he was trying hard to squeeze a diamond from a lump of coal.

"This Dragon's Ice House idea, it's kind of risky. Maybe it's stupid, I don't know," he said, shaking his head with apparent self-doubt. "But I keep thinking, if we can do something to bring people back here, to show them we're still here, alive…"

He looked out at the audience. "You ever feel like we're stranded on this remote island, and the rescue planes are flying over our heads every day? And we make fires and jump around and yell at them to come save us, but they just keep flying by, like they don't hear or see us? Or maybe they don't care."

Mayor Tolliver stood there, motionless save for two pale blue eyes that darted from one council member to the next. He finally sat down and threw his hands up.

"I'm a dreamer, always have been," he said with a sigh. "Guess that's my weakness."

London rolled his eyes.

"I think the mayor has a fine idea," said Gloria Bush, the council's lone female and one who spoke so seldom that she rarely bothered to turn on her microphone. "Dragon's Ice

House, I think, would make an excellent attraction for Pridemore."

"Great idea!" said Bernie Alsop, glancing sideways as if seeking the mayor's approval. "I move we schedule a public hearing on the annexation for Monday."

"What are we voting on?" asked Sutter Mardock. He was a former mayor himself, and, at ninety-five years old, the senior member of the council.

Gloria Bush leaned toward the withered man and said in a loud, enunciated voice, "We're voting on whether or not to take over Dragon's Ice House so that we can turn it into a fun park."

"Oh," Mardock said.

"You can't be serious," London said. "This hasn't even been through the planning committee."

"Bryan," the mayor said, "we must move swiftly."

"I second Bernie's motion on the ballot issue," Council President Rufus Stodemeyer said. "All for putting Dragon's Ice House on the July 7 ballot, say 'Aye.'"

There was a chorus of ayes. London voted nay and suggested he might bring up the matter with the American Association of City Councils.

"To hell with this," Pete heard him mutter as he stomped down the aisle and out of the room.

Some of the council members grinned. As reliable as the seasons, London stormed out of a council meeting at least once a quarter.

With three gavel snaps, the council adjourned, and everybody gathered around the coffee pot to talk about the Cardinals' lack of a bullpen.

Pete drifted through the group, mumbling a few questions and jotting down answers in his notebook. His hands got sweaty and sloppy with the note-taking, and he sensed that the government gray walls were closing in on him. His throat clenched up and his eyes got watery and he dropped his pen on the floor. He sometimes got this way in social situations where he knew he didn't fit in.

Pete picked up his pen and strode out of the building to his Ford. He revved the engine a couple of times, threw it into drive, and peeled out of the parking lot and onto Old Highway 54. He hung his arm out the window and felt the hot summer breeze.

The truck's speedometer inched above seventy as Pete passed the city limits. Out in front was darkness, with just a few farmhouse lights in the distance. It reminded him of trips his family used to take every summer to the beach, where the ocean at night was an endless canvas of black, save for the lights of a few shrimp boats in the distance. Pete drove toward the lights, past rows and rows of corn and soybeans and tobacco and more corn that he couldn't see, all the while repeating his alone-in-the-car mantra, *"Hate this place, hate this place, hate this place."*

He reached the faraway lights to find that (surprise!) they were farmhouses. The distance held more lights. He drove toward them until he reached the county limits and, with a sigh expelling all the air from his 160-pound body, he turned back toward town.

CHAPTER 8

Mayor Tolliver picked up the next day's paper and scanned the banner headline, "Cave Project to Mine Tourist Treasure." The story was even worse, quoting liberally from Bryan London about how the city was broke and the project hadn't gone through the proper channels. There was only one quote from the mayor, but it was a gem: *Mr. Tolliver said he wasn't fazed by his colleague's early departure from the meeting. "Bryan and I have been at this a long time," he said. "You tie two tomcats by their tails and throw them over a clothesline, one of 'em's bound to get scratched."*

He picked up the phone and dialed the reporter's number.

"*Evening Headlight.* Pete Schaefer speaking," a monotone voice answered.

"I do not speak in idioms."

"What?"

"You had me comparing last night's meeting to a cat fight. I don't talk like that."

"Mayor Tolliver?"

"I suggest you check your notes."

"Well, I—"

"I realize you're new to this job, but I have a reputation in this town. And your story makes me sound like some cornpone stooge out of *Hee-Haw.*"

The mayor paused. He heard a manic shuffling of paper on the other end of the line.

"Mr. Mayor, I've got the quote right here in my notepad."

"I don't care what you've got. I know what I said. Something to the effect that Mr. London and I have had our disagreements over the years but have nothing but the utmost respect for each another as public servants. I might have even said his conduct was a bit out of line, but there was nothing whatsoever about cats and clotheslines."

"But why would I—"

"Peter, I've got to go. Please be more careful with your reporting from now on. This is important business that we do here."

The mayor paused before taking his final jab.

"Have you tried using a tape recorder?"

Before the reporter could answer, Tolliver dropped the phone receiver onto its cradle and giggled in spite of himself. It really was indefensible, picking on some kid young enough to be his grandson. But dammit, no one made Roe Tolliver look like a monkey's uncle in his hometown newspaper, even if he did say the exact words the reporter had written. He missed Beat O'Reilly, who covered City Hall for years and would always clean up his quotes, sometimes throwing in a sparkling metaphor for good measure. She understood what the mayor *meant* to say. The two of them had a relationship.

He leaned forward in his swivel chair to reposition a pillow at just the right spot above his pelvis. His back had been killing him nonstop for the past six years, leaving him stooped over with his neck craning forward like some kind of damned turtle. He used to be six-foot-three when standing straight in that erect, military posture they drilled into him at Fort Leonard Wood. Strong as a horse and pretty good-looking to boot.

"Mayor?" a woman's voice called over the little intercom that was perched on the corner of his desk.

"Yes, Briana?"

"Digby Willers is here."

"Let 'em in."

The big oak door slowly opened, and the retarded boy who had been delivering his mail for the past year marched in with a big smile on his face. Probably thinks I'm gonna give him one of those candy bars like I did the other day, the mayor thought as Digby handed him a bundle of letters held together with a rubber band.

"Well, well, my boy!" he said in as buoyant a tone as he could muster. "How goes the mail room today?"

Digby pulled off his Cub Scout hat and wiped a bead of sweat from his forehead. He worked in the basement, the only floor without central air.

"Hot down there."

"Hot, eh?"

"Hot as a house fire," Digby said, leaning over the mayor's desk to watch him go through the mail.

"That right, huh? That must be pretty darn hot."

The mayor leafed through the letters, which consisted of junk mail, a couple of bills, and an angry note from Stanley Redler, who wrote or called every day about utility workers tearing up his yard. Another senior citizen with too much damned time on his hands.

"Almost Pinewood Derby time, isn't it, Digby?" the mayor asked, not looking up from his mail. He couldn't recall if it was or it wasn't, but, like everyone else in Pridemore, he was well aware of Digby's winning streak.

"Yeah. 'Bout four more weeks."

"You gonna win this year?"

"Hope to," Digby said, tugging the brim of his Cub Scout cap over his eyes.

"Hope to?" The mayor stared at the boy looming over his desk. God, he's a big son of a bitch. About 6-foot-3—tall as the mayor used to be—and 280 pounds, if he were to guess. Would have been a heckuva lineman for the high school football team.

"Don't give me any of this 'hope to' crap. You think I got to be mayor because I *hoped* it would happen?"

The boy shrugged his shoulders. "Guess not."

"Look, these Cub Scouts are a tough lot. I know for a fact that one of them loads his little car up with BBs so it'll go faster and whip your ass. They're gonna be gunning for you, Digby. They always will. So you need a little more than just hope. You've gotta *know* you're gonna win. And you know how you do that?"

"How?"

"You work your tail off, that's how. And always with one eye over your shoulder to see if anyone's gaining. That's how you win—by always striving to be the best.

"Never do anything half-assed, son," the mayor advised. "Go all the way, or don't go at all."

Digby looked him right in the eye, nodding slowly as if he had learned something profound. It gave the mayor the willies, this huge kid looking at him so seriously all of a sudden. So he changed the subject.

"Now, Digby, I counted at least three bills in this stack, and you know our arrangement. I can't maintain my supply of Kit-Kat bars if I have all these bills to pay."

"Okay," Digby said, a smile slowly forming on his round, doughy face. The mayor suspected he wasn't the only candy supplier on Digby's route, as evidenced by the chocolate smears on the boy's hands and, sometimes, the envelopes he delivered.

"I'm going to let it slide this time," the mayor said, opening a desk drawer and pulling out a Kit-Kat bar. "But no more bills! We have an arrangement."

"Yessir."

The mayor laughed. The kid was a good egg, which was more than one could say for the scruffy-headed punks who rolled their skateboards up and down the steps of City Hall and wouldn't look you in the eye when you lectured them about respecting public property.

"Well, scram!" he said. "I got work to do."

The big boy clomped out the door in his tan-colored Dingos, and the mayor glanced at his watch. Three o'clock. The state legislature would be breaking out of session about now. That meant Representative Chucklehead might actually be in his office for a change. The mayor leaned across his desk and shuffled his crooked fingers through a Rolodex of yellowed business cards. He found the number he wanted and punched it into the dial pad.

"Representative Maddox's office," a young woman answered.

The mayor inhaled deeply before he replied.

"*Don't throw bouquets at me,*" he sang. "*Don't please my folks too much…*"

"Mayor Tolliver?"

"*Don't laugh at my jokes too much…*"

"I know it's you."

"*People will say we're in looove,*" he finished, holding "love" as long as he could without erupting into a hacking cough.

"Mr. Mayor," the girl said, giggling, "you are so bad."

"Not bad, my dear," he said. "A baritone."

The girl—Linda was her name—tittered some more. Whenever he visited Chester Maddox's office in the state house, he always brought roses or a box of chocolates for Linda. She was a leggy gal in her early twenties with blond hair that went halfway down to her plum-shaped ass. She would gush and giggle and make a big deal out of whatever the mayor brought her, which made visiting Chester at least somewhat bearable. He was certain Chester was banging Linda, though he wondered what a sweet young gal could see in a career state representative from Pridemore County.

"You've got a nice singing voice, Mayor Tolliver," she said in a southern Missouri twang that made nice sound like *nahhce.* "When you gonna come down and see us?"

"In good time, my dear. Is your boss in?"

"He just got back from the floor. I'll put you through. You take care of that baritone, now."

"People will say we're in looove," he sang, but the phone clicked over before he finished.

"Good morning, Mayor Tolliver!" a cheery male voice boomed.

"It's the afternoon."

"It is, isn't it?" Chester said after a pause. "We were on the floor debating this transportation bill, and the time just slips by. Well, good afternoon, then!"

"Chester, I don't have time to dick around," the mayor began. "We just approved an ordinance annexing the Dragon's Ice House into the city, and I'm gonna need you to get me some of that tourism pie you and your buddies are carving up."

"How much you need?"

"At least five million."

The representative let out a long, low whistle. "I dunno, Roe. There won't be much left after the cities take their share. Most folks down here never heard of Dragon's Ice House."

"But you can educate them, can't you, Chester?" the mayor said softly. "You know, this would go a long way in repaying your debt to Pridemore."

Chester Maddox had been Pridemore County's representative for six straight terms and was perhaps the man most responsible for its economic demise. As a first-term member of the House Transportation Committee a decade ago, he somehow missed the crucial vote on whether to draw the new Highway 54 through Farley instead of Pridemore. The committee voted five to four in favor, mostly because Chairman Enos "Suds" Hewitt was a Farley man. Chester's whereabouts that day were never confirmed, but one story had him shuttling some gal to Planned Parenthood in Columbia.

Whatever the reason, Chester Maddox screwed up big time. The fact that he was still in office had less to do with his political acumen than with Pridemore County's maddening tendency to always vote Republican, no matter what scoundrel the party put up.

Still, the man could be useful. Chester was a ranking member of the Economic Development Committee that doled out the money for city museums and state parks. He had power. He had influence. He had a chance to make up for his mistake.

"I dunno, Mr. Mayor," the representative said. "I dunno."

"I'm not asking you to put a man on the moon, Chester. Just get me on the agenda for the hearing, introduce me to the people I need to meet, and I'll do the rest."

"I'm just saying it's gonna be a battle," Chester said. "The St. Louis Zoo needs a bunch of money, and they want to build an aquarium in Kansas City. I'm just not sure how people are gonna—"

"Chester!"

"Yessir?"

"If you screw this up, if you so much as get in my way down there, I'm going to…" He paused. Do what? After the Highway 54 mess, he went seven years without speaking to the representative. If Chester botched this, the mayor would have to get really unpleasant. He wasn't above digging up an old mistress or a drinking buddy to prove his point. And Chester had some of both.

"Let's just say I've still got some political capital in these parts," he finally said.

"Yessir."

"Now, get to it," he growled.

"You have a nice day, Mr. May—" was all he heard before slamming down the phone.

CHAPTER 9

Twenty miles south of Pridemore on Old 54 was some of the best bass fishing in all of Missouri. Quantrill Lake, named for the Confederate sympathizer who raped and pillaged much of eastern Kansas, during the Civil War was a rambling body of water with fingers stretching into three counties. A domain of the US Army Corps of Engineers, Quantrill had only one Marina where mostly local anglers stored their boats.

Fishing was what brought Chub Hughes and Mayor Tolliver to the lake in the pre-dawn hours. Fishing and the need for a quiet place to talk business. They slipped Chub's twenty-one-foot Pro Sport Bumblebee into the water just as the sun was peeking over the trees. There was a crispness in the air despite the fact that it was early July and the thermometer would be pushing ninety degrees in a couple of hours.

Chub drove the boat to a distant cove, and the two men cast their lines near a clump of reeds where the fish might be biting. At seven o'clock that Saturday morning on Quantrill Lake, Chub popped his first can of Miller High Life. For the life of him, he couldn't think of a place he'd rather be.

He lazily reeled in his line as the mayor jabbered on about this and that. A quiet man, Chub enjoyed the mayor's company because Chub knew he wouldn't have to say much to keep a conversation going. It was an unspoken agreement between the two men that whatever time Chub didn't utilize to express his thoughts, the mayor would gladly use to pontificate about everything from American foreign policy to the decline of the Broadway musical.

Chub enjoyed that high-pitched, stump-speech voice that, when it got going, had the clickety-clack cadence of train cars speeding down a track. He liked how the mayor talked, even when he wasn't listening to what the mayor said. Like now, for instance.

"Goldwater was right," said the mayor, casting his line into the water. "'Bomb 'em! Bomb 'em where they live.' It sure would have beaten the hell out of ten to fifteen years of protracted war."

"Yup," Chub said softly.

"I don't think people understand that when they elect a president, he only has so much control over the machine. The military, government bureaucrats, private industry...they'll all be around long after a president's time is up."

"Yessir," Chub said. He felt a tug on his line, but he jerked his rod too soon and the fish got away. Probably nothing but a bluegill anyway. He reeled in and checked his hook.

"That's what I like about City Hall," the mayor continued. "No term limits in Pridemore. A man can invoke real change and stick around to see it through."

You'd sure know about that, Chub thought as he reached in his cooler and pulled out another beer. He popped the tab and took a sip, letting the taste rest on his tongue before swallowing it down. He understood why they called it the High Life—drinking a beer on your own Bumblebee 2100 Pro Sport with midnight-blue racing stripes and a 250-horsepower engine, not really caring if the fish are biting or not, just savoring the moment. To borrow a phrase from another beer commercial, it didn't get any better than this.

The boat had been Chub's favorite toy since he bought it the spring before last in Columbia, talking the salesman down a couple thousand from the $32,000 sticker price. He'd taken it on the lake almost every weekend that first summer. One quiet morning like this one, he'd pushed the Bumblebee up to around eighty miles per hour, roaring through the straits like an F-16 and blowing the hat off his balding head in the process. If you were to give Chub a choice between a hot night with Jennifer Aniston and taking the Bumblebee for a spin on Quantrill Lake…after some consideration he would probably take Jennifer, provided he didn't have to talk to her. But it would be a close call.

Sadly, this was Chub's first time on the lake this summer. Despite being the only general contractor in Pridemore County, M&M Construction Co. had fallen on hard times and needed his attention. Commercial and public projects had slowed to a trickle, and Chub, who'd hoped to retire in a year or two, instead had to sign a new line of credit to pay off the new headquarters his partners talked him into building a few years back.

"Have you finished the study?" the mayor asked.

"The what?"

"The feasibility study. How's it going?"

"Oh." Chub set his beer down and turned toward the mayor. It was time to talk shop. "I had Lewis go down there and look at the site. Kind of rough country out there. It's gonna take some heavy firepower to blast through those rocks. Gonna be noisy too."

"If we get the money for this tourism project, you can make all the damned noise you want," the mayor said, casting his line with a jerky motion. The lure dropped three feet from the boat, and he cursed softly. "The question is, how long and how much?"

"Like I said, we're still in preliminaries, but I'm going to say at least six months. We've done demolition before but nothing like this. It's going to take some time, and it's going to be expensive."

Chub made a forty-foot cast into the reeds that hugged the shoreline. "The other day after our lunch meeting, you told me to talk to the guys to see if I could get their buy-in on this little adventure."

"And?"

"Well, they think you're crazy, but that's nothing new," he said with a grin.

"Crazy like a fox," the mayor corrected him.

Chub told how the four men voted on the idea and how he broke the split decision by embarrassing Rufus Stodemeyer on his own pool table.

"No kidding?" the mayor said, hugging his sides to keep from giggling. "I'd love to have seen Rufus's face when that happened."

"Priceless," Chub said.

He looked the mayor in the eye, not an easy task with the old man wearing a floppy hat that had the words "Here, Fishy, Fishy!" embroidered on the brim.

"It's a tough call," he said after a few moments. "There's a lot that can go wrong with your plan."

"I beg your pardon," the mayor said as he put a rubber worm on his hook. "I never promised you a rose garden."

"I can only hold the guys at bay for so long. They'll want more information."

"Like what?"

"Well, for one thing, who are we going to use in this scheme of yours? Who's going to be, you know, the—"

"The patsy?"

"Well, yeah."

"I've been thinking about that."

The mayor shifted in his seat to face Chub, almost knocking him in the head with his fishing pole. He looked at Chub with wide, dancing eyes that seemed to say, *"Prepare to be impressed!"* The general contractor felt a tinge of excitement as the mayor started to explain.

"I've got an idea of someone I'd like to use, though nothing's set in stone."

The mayor laid out the final piece of his plan, the human-interest angle that would make Pridemore a front-page story from coast to coast. It would have to be handled delicately, he warned, with no small amount of deception directed toward the person in question. He hadn't worked out all the details yet, but the broad strokes were already crystallized in his mind.

"And the rest will come together in time," he finished. "You know what a detail person I am."

Chub stared at the mayor for several seconds before reaching into his cooler and pulling out yet another High Life. He'd done a lot of talking today, and Chub Hughes would rather wade naked through a nest of water moccasins than go yammering his fool head off all morning.

"So that's it, huh?" he finally said. "Well, I'll be buggered," he added for good measure.

"Work with me on this," the mayor said, holding a gnarled hand to his heart. "Please."

"Dang." Chub reached into the cooler and tossed out a beer, which the mayor caught with surprising ease. He took a sip and smacked his lips loudly as Chub cast his line one last time. Soon it would be time to rev up the Bumblebee and cruise back to the marina. There was a foot-high stack of invoices waiting back at the office.

He felt a little tug on his line, pulled the pole up, and started reeling. But he jerked too sharply and, again, the fish got away.

Chub sighed and reeled in the line.

"Okay," he told the mayor. "Let's give your plan a try."

CHAPTER 10

The Monroe P. Tolliver Athletic Center roared with the unrelenting clatter of nearly a hundred boys' sneakers squeaking against the rubberized basketball court that would host the 21st Annual Pinewood Derby for the Yellow Jacket District. Each of the blue-clad Cub Scouts held a seven-inch scrap of wood carved to resemble a race car. The first heat wouldn't start for thirty minutes, but the scouts were already testing their cars, hurling them across the floor, crashing them into the wall or a bystander's leg, and then picking up the cars and hurling them again.

"Ain't this a trip?" Larry Truesdale said with a chuckle. "Ain't they the cutest things you ever did see?"

Pete Schaefer wondered if his publisher meant the cars or the scouts. It must have been the latter because the cars, for the most part, sucked. Some were scarcely refined from their original rectangular form. The handful of Pinewood racers that looked like actual cars were probably the work of the little urchins' parents, Pete figured.

He was certain that the last place he wanted to be at nine o'clock on a Saturday morning was standing next to Larry Truesdale in a gym full of screaming kids. The headache from the night before was like a thousand little pins piercing his skull. Each squeak of a sneaker, each smack of a car against the wall, drove the pins a little deeper. He should have stayed in Columbia. He was three-quarters into a twelve-pack at two in the morning and contemplating what friend would lend him a sofa to sleep on when he remembered this little assignment. So he made the hour-long drive back to Pridemore and crashed on his own couch, a recent purchase from the clearance aisle at Furniture World. He woke up roughly ten minutes ago, allowing time to down a Pop-Tart, brush his teeth, and slip a reporter's notebook in the back pocket of the wrinkled khakis he was still wearing from the night before.

That was the beauty of living in Pridemore, Pete thought with a little smile. You could get anywhere in town in about as much time as it took to take a leak.

"How ya doin', buddy?" Truesdale asked some kid with a bowl cut. "Did ya bring your good-luck charm?"

The boy, whom Pete took to be Truesdale's son, pulled a small brown object from his pocket. Upon further inspection, Pete saw it was a buckeye.

"He's been rubbing that buckeye all week," the publisher said. "Earned him third place last year, didn't it, buddy?"

The kid nodded slowly, avoiding eye contact with both Truesdale and Pete, then scampered away, buckeye in one hand and wooden car in the other.

Pete stood there, grinning stupidly. He watched a young woman saunter up to Truesdale and give him a hug. She was wearing ripped blue jeans that clung to her hips and an undersized T-shirt showing just enough midriff to give Pete the first tinge of arousal.

"Angela, I'd like you to meet Pete Schaefer," Truesdale said, turning toward the reporter. "Pete, this is my daughter, Angela."

Pete stood there, blinking.

"I know him, Dad." Angela took Pete's hand but fastened her eyes on a spot just to the right of his head. "We met last year at Olde Pridemore Days."

"That's right!" the publisher said with a boisterous laugh, though Pete couldn't figure out what was so funny. "Peter's one of our top young reporters."

Angela rolled her eyes, like she so often did around Pete. It was the kind of *who are you kidding?* glance that could stop you in mid-sentence, even if you were winning an argument, even if you were her dad and one of the most powerful men in town.

"Isn't he your *only* young reporter?" she asked.

Truesdale paused a moment, perhaps searching for the proper, adult response.

"Oh, hush!" he finally said. He pulled the girl toward him and kissed her forehead. She giggled her daddy's-little-girl giggle, flashed Pete a lightning-quick roll of the eyes, and ran off to hurl cars across the floor with her kid brother.

The reporter maintained his idiot grin.

"Ain't she a peach?" Truesdale said.

She certainly is, Pete thought. Here he was, practically having a coronary while Angela chatted amiably and got the hell out of there before he said something incriminating. One glance Pete's way and Truesdale surely would have noticed a twitch or a stammer, something to give away the fact that, two days ago, the top young reporter had Angela bent over his brand-new sofa, both of them drinking freely from the chalice of delicious, guilt-ridden sex.

Bless her heart for running away! Pete was beginning to realize that his cheerleader girlfriend was pretty good at this cloak-and-dagger shit. Almost too good. He sometimes got a strange vibe from Angela. Her smile, soft and warm and winning, was all his. But those dark eyes seemed to focus on something just beyond him, like she was working out an elaborate calculation in her head.

"There he is!" Truesdale suddenly boomed. "The man of the hour!"

Trudging across the gym was a large young man wearing a Cub Scout hat, cowboy boots, and a Mountain Dew T-shirt that spilled like a gown over his muddy jeans. The Cub Scouts and their parents stopped what they were doing to watch him approach the registration table, a brown paper sack under his arm. His shoulders hunched and his head bowed as if there were a hundred pounds set squarely on his back, and Pete felt a pang of guilt for gawking at this seemingly burdened kid. After what felt like an eternity, Digby Willers reached the registration table, where an elderly gentleman waited to sign him in.

"Hiya, Digby," the man said.

"Hi."

"You gonna give 'em hell today?"

Digby glanced at the man with a trace of a smile before looking back down at his sign-in sheet.

"Yeah," he said. "Ain't no shot for what I got."

The old man broke into a laugh that was really more of a cough, but it eased the tension. The parents returned to chatting and the scouts went back to crashing cars.

"That's your boy," Truesdale whispered, as though Pete hadn't figured that out yet. Digby Willers was Pete's reason for being here, to report on whether this man-child could win his tenth Derby title in eleven years.

This was about as big as it got in Pridemore, so big that Pete's editor, Beat Reilly, agreed to hold the press-run back an hour so the Saturday afternoon *Headlight* could print an exclusive on the race. The only reason Pete was deemed worthy of covering such a story was because the paper's senior reporter was on a rafting trip in Colorado.

Pete watched Digby walk to a corner of the gym and plop Indian-style on the rubber floor. He opened his paper sack and pulled out his Pinewood racer with the care of someone holding a precious bird. The Number 3 car was painted in metallic crimson and blue, like all his winners sported over the years. Pete wasn't a classic car expert, but he recognized the contours of an early model Corvette in Digby's creation.

Pete pulled out his notebook and walked to the spot where Digby sat Zen-like, idly rolling the racer between his thick hands and singing to himself. As he approached, Pete recognized the words from one of those teenybopper ballads the radio had played about a million times that summer.

"Dakota Marx, right?" Pete said. "You like his music?"

Digby eyed him warily. "Yeah. He rocks."

Pete feigned a laugh and introduced himself as a newspaper reporter. He asked if Digby could answer a few questions before the race.

"Sure," Digby said, gingerly putting the Corvette back in its sack. "You guys do a story on me every year 'bout this time."

Pete nodded vigorously. It was nice to know that he'd again be sailing uncharted journalistic waters with the *Headlight*. He set about asking the usual hard-hitting questions, which ranged from "How did you get into Pinewood Derby racing?" to "How much longer do you plan to compete in the Pinewood Derby?" Digby responded to each with several seconds of pained silence before providing the shortest answer possible. Looking at his notes later, Pete would gather this information: *started racing age 10 or 12; Mother bought first P-wood Derby kit; likes to work on the cars "a lot" b/4 derby; favorite race car driver is Dale Ernhart (sp?), thus all cars must have No. 3; doesn't appear bothered by drastic age difference—will continue racing as long as "fun"; likes "plain" M&Ms as opposed to "peanut"; paints cars red/blue b/c favorite team is KS Jayhawks.*

"Do you think it's fair that you're so much older than the other boys in the race?" Pete finally asked.

Digby crinkled his brow.

"I love to race. Racing is fun for me."

"I know it's fun for you, but I mean you're, what, twenty-two?" Pete said. "Most of the kids here are ten, eleven years old at the most. Doesn't that give you an advantage?"

Digby gave him a kind smile that suggested he'd love to help Pete if he could, but he had no idea what the reporter was talking about. Pete was about to try the question from a different angle when a whistle blared from the registration table.

"Gotta go," Digby said.

He scooped up the paper sack and leapt to his feet, almost dropping into a sprinter's four-point stance before running as fast as he could to the great wooden ramp that spilled out from one corner of the gym. Pete watched Digby go, shirttail flapping over his butt like a tattered flag. Glancing at his scrawled notes, he hoped he'd collected enough information to file his story.

Roe Tolliver filled his toy gun with fresh caps and beamed like a kid on the last day of school as six Cub Scouts took turns placing their cars in the slots atop the Pinewood Derby racing ramp. All eyes were on Digby Willers's Number 3 car, which had breezed through the first three rounds, winning each race by more than three lengths. No matter where Digby slotted his car, it was as if that particular lane somehow tilted slightly steeper than the others on the ramp. Nobody seemed surprised, numb as they were to so many victories by Number 3 over the years. This car, it seemed, would soon take its spot next to the other winners in Digby's garage, never to be seen by the public again.

Or maybe not, the mayor thought as he readied his cap gun to fire off the final heat. This field of six had a couple of hot contenders in the Number 7 car, which Bobby Matthews had carved into a likeness of a Porsche 911 convertible, and Andy Bold's Number 12 car, which looked pretty snazzy in Oakland Raiders' silver and black. Both looked to have the aerodynamic chops to blow past Digby, though the mayor wouldn't necessarily bet his lunch on it.

He chuckled to himself as the crowd of kids and adults huddled around the well-oiled ramp for the final race. He used to hate this ceremonial shit. Always fancied himself more of a policymaker than a politician—he only cut ribbons and kissed babies because that was what you had to do to stay in office. The mayor didn't like touching people, nor did he like being touched, and you usually had a lot of both at these sorts of things. He also didn't much care for folks whose working knowledge of the Bill of Rights was limited to the Second Amendment. This crowd had some of that: one guy wore a muscle shirt with a cartoon assault rifle and the familiar inscription, "My cold, dead hands." A real classy getup for a scout jamboree.

But the mayor had mellowed enough over the years that being among the masses didn't bother him as much—it was nothing a vigorous scrubbing with Ivory soap couldn't cure once he got back to the house. Besides, he'd just gotten an exceptionally good piece of news from none other than Chester Maddox. The slow-witted state representative, no doubt attending the Pinewood Derby to grease a few palms himself, had told the mayor that he'd collected enough committee votes to direct eight million dollars to the Dragon's Ice House project.

"You're kidding me, right?" the mayor had said.

"No, sir. I wouldn't kid about something like this."

The mayor nodded curtly, but inside he was doing a touchdown dance.

"Chester, you pull this one off, and I'll damn well put a statue of you next to City Hall."

The mayor still felt giddy a few moments later, standing before more than two hundred current and future voters who awaited his signal to send the racers streaking down the ramp. You could almost hear a pin drop. It was a moment of crowd control few people got to experience, and the mayor, for one, found it thrilling. Staring at the masses who stared back at him, he had a tiny appreciation for how Hitler must have felt standing inside that stadium in Nuremberg, tens of thousands under his spell. He knew the comparison was twisted, and he certainly didn't advocate fascism, but that's how he felt right now. The great ones understood his exhilaration.

He pointed the gun toward the ceiling and beamed at the crowd with a mouthful of yellowed dentures.

"Gentlemen, start your engines."

He fired the toy gun. The gate lifted and the cars rumbled down the track with the scraping clatter of plastic wheels on wood.

The race was over in seconds, but what transpired during that span would be the subject of porch-swing chatter for weeks to come. Two cars in the far right lanes took the early lead: Andy Bold's Oakland Raiders car and Bobby Matthews's Porsche. Digby Willers's Number 3 trailed by a full length, and the other three cars brought up the rear.

In horse racing, an experienced jockey will hold his mount back for the first half-mile, letting his rivals tire out so he can pass them in one late but perfectly timed surge of speed. In oval-track car racing, a driver will practice the art of drafting, riding in the wind-resistant vacuum of the car just in front of him, allowing him to use less throttle and fuel while keeping the same speed.

After year upon mind-numbing year of watching the event, the mayor had learned that there are no such strategies in the Pinewood Derby. Ninety-nine times out of a hundred, the car that grabbed the lead out of the gate was the winner. The ramp simply wasn't long enough for the others to catch up.

Halfway down the ramp, Bobby Matthews's Porsche pulled almost a full length ahead of the silver and black car, with Digby's Number 3 lingering in third. In any other race, that would have been the finishing order. But less than fifteen

feet from the finish line, something got under Bobby's car—
some theorized it was a hair-thin bump where two planks of
wood dovetailed together, though, after a careful, post-race
inspection, the scoutmaster reported that the ramp was smooth
as glass. Whatever the reason, something caused the car to flip
out of its lane as if propelled by a steel spring, make a 360-
degree corkscrew in the air, and land on its side in the adjacent
lane, directly in front of Andy Bold's Oakland Raiders car.

The cars collided with a terrific pop and slowed to a halt
no less than a foot from the finish. Digby's car sailed past them
to collect his tenth Pinewood Derby trophy.

There was a beat or two of silence as the big crowd
processed what just happened, and then an eruption of noise,
most of it the negative kind.

"Bastard!" one man standing near the mayor yelled. He
was a big man with rugged brown skin—probably came
straight from a soybean field to watch the race. The man pulled
the bill of his mesh cap over his eyes and swore again.
"Bastard!"

The mayor felt an adrenaline surge as children and adults
swept past him to mob Digby Willers, who was trying to reach
the scorer's table to accept his award. Some clapped him on the
back, but others, most of them far enough away to avoid
retribution, shook their fists and yelled profanities.

"Fuckin' retard!" one scout spat. In all his years, the mayor
had never heard the F-word used in a public setting in
Pridemore. He fought the urge to slap the little punk upside
the head.

At the scorer's table, Andy Bold's mother had to be
physically restrained from grabbing the trophy and running
out the door. With the crowd surging around him, Scoutmaster
Tompkins announced Digby the undisputed winner of the 21st
Pinewood Derby and handed him a foot-high edifice of chrome

plastic and aluminum that probably cost ten dollars at the Army Surplus store in Farber.

You'd think it was the Stanley Cup the way people thronged the winner as he tried to make his exit. Someone's tennis shoe flew through the air, a white blur that just missed the back of Digby's head.

Before he realized what he was doing, the mayor shoved his way toward Digby, holding his cap gun high so he could bring it down on some miscreant's head if need be. A pretty stupid thing for a eighty-seven-year-old to do, jostling his way through what amounted to—what did they call it?—a mosh pit of boys with a few teenaged delinquents thrown in for good measure. He probably wouldn't have done it, had he stopped to think about it. But something called him to act. He couldn't just sit back and watch the whole town beat up on this kid.

"Follow me," the mayor said, grabbing a fistful of Digby's shirt and tugging him toward the back exit.

After a good bit of jostling through the crowd, the two of them stumbled out the door and into the piercing sunlight. The mayor placed his hands on his knees and inhaled the thick, humid air with a wheeze that came out like a C note. It wasn't even eleven o'clock in the morning and he already needed a nap.

"You okay?" Digby asked.

"Yes, yes, my boy," the mayor said, still catching his breath. He walked over to a nearby bench and sat down with an emphatic grunt.

Digby looked down at him with a confused smile. He didn't seem to recognize the mayor from his daily mail deliveries at City Hall. He was just a boy, the mayor thought, with his Cub Scout hat and cowboy boots and his shirttail hanging out. He carried the Number 3 car and the gleaming aluminum trophy underneath a forearm as thick as a four-by-four plank.

"Thanks for getting me outta there," Digby said after a long pause. He dug in his pocket with his free hand. "Want some gum?"

"You're welcome, and no thank you," the mayor said. He gripped the edge of the bench and prepared for the agony of standing on his tired old knees.

"Well, I guess I owe you."

"I guess you do." The mayor stood and gave a wink that belied the pain shooting up his leg and lower back. Like nails being hammered into a piece of driftwood, he thought to himself as he shuffled to his Chrysler New Yorker, which had leather seats that were probably 140 degrees about now. Before lowering himself into the steamy car, the mayor looked back and watched his young friend, who would soon play such a crucial role in Pridemore's future, make his way home while idly kicking an empty soda can.

PART II

SPRING

CHAPTER 11

Driving down Main Street in his Ford Explorer, Pete Schaefer slowly realized that, for the first time in months, he could roll down his window for some purpose other than hastily grabbing a burger from the drive-thru. Though it was the middle of March and technically still winter in Missouri, the Good Lord granted a reprieve of upper-fifties sunshine before the thermometer plunged south for another round of teeth-rattling misery. Pete made the most of it, rolling up his shirtsleeve and propping a milky forearm out the window. It was a Sunday afternoon and he was in no particular hurry.

The chill from the open window reminded Pete of early spring campouts by the lake with high school friends. He missed those excursions—charcoal and kerosene, Milwaukee's Best in a silvery can, fearful excitement that the next pair of headlights coming around the bend might belong to a sheriff's deputy. And the soapy cleanness of Karen Wilhelm invading Pete's senses as she pressed against him in his sleeping bag. That happened on the first camping trip of senior year, after Pete built up enough liquid nerve to sit next to her in front of the bonfire. It was a seminal moment for him: the first girl he really kissed. And while whatever he and Karen Wilhelm had was gone by the time the sun peeked over Tarwater Lake, he distinctly remembered how she smelled (Ivory Soap blended with Inhibition, a popular teen fragrance at the time), and Pete had sought it ever since among the handful of women he had the good fortune to know in an intimate way. So far, his search had been unsuccessful.

Pete took his hands off the steering wheel and closed his eyes as his truck cruised down Main Street at twenty-five miles an hour. He envisioned the night with Karen by the lake. He cursed himself for never getting up the courage to call her afterward. They could have had something, even if it only amounted to a summer fling before college. But as with so many things in Pete's life (his book, his career, frayed relations with both of his parents), he never followed up.

If Pete had opened his eyes at that moment, he'd have seen ample signs of downtown Pridemore's continued decline. The Reading Lamp bookstore and Ernie's 66 Filling Station were recently boarded up, and the city took a jolt when Sanderson's Hardware Store, after more than fifty years in business, closed in February. Red Sanderson finally decided to retire. Pete wrote a piece about Red's last early-morning cup of joe with cronies on the store's final day, and the old guy liked the story so much that he gave Pete the "D" from the red block letters that spelled "SANDERSON'S" over the store's awning. Pete kept the memento propped in his bedroom window.

He opened one eye as he approached the intersection of Main and Purcel, where he would turn right and proceed three blocks to the *Evening Headlight*'s offices. Though he hadn't lived in Pridemore long enough to wax any real sentiment over the loss of Sanderson's, Pete took the hardware store's closing as another sign that he needed to get the hell out of Dodge. That's why he visited the newsroom on off days. It was a great time to work on his news clippings and cover letters without anyone nosing around.

A Beatles tune played on the radio as Pete turned onto Purcel, and he pondered the relevance of "Here Comes the Sun" to his current situation. It had indeed been a long, cold, lonely winter, little darlin'. He had broken up with Angela just before Christmas, and, while he knew it was the right thing to do, it sure didn't make life any more fun. Added to the bleak winter landscape was the fact his sportswriter colleague and drinking buddy Dave Felton had landed a job with the *Wichita Express* in January. Pete helped load the U-Haul and bought Dave a beer at One-Eyed Willie's before watching his friend drive into the worst winter storm of the year. He assumed Felton made it to Wichita, though he never got a phone call. Depressed, he spent weekends huddled under his down comforter, munching Cheetos and watching college basketball. He worked on his novel a little but couldn't seem to finish the chapter where the hero, Bill Sullinger, kills his roommate in a horrible waterskiing accident.

When he wasn't feeling too down, Pete scanned the want ads and trade publications for jobs. He spent one afternoon hunched over his computer and came up with a gem of a cover letter for Pat Hutchins, human resources coordinator at the *St. Louis Intelligencer*. Of course, he was running a 101-degree temperature at the time.

> *Dear Ms. Hutchins,*
>
> *I am writing in response to your advertisement for a copy editing position on the metro desk. God, how I hope you haven't filled it.*
>
> *I am a 23-year-old graduate of the University of Missouri School of Journalism who has labored for the past 19 months as a staff writer at* The Pridemore Evening Headlight. *My responsibilities include writing obituaries and commodity market reports, covering area cops and city government, some photography, and, when I have time, penning the spare high school football story. While I have not yet been assigned an afternoon paper route, I am expecting that to occur any day now as it is one of the few assignments at* The Headlight *I haven't been asked to take on, at no addition to my lucrative base salary of $18,500.*
>
> *Not that I'm complaining. The diversity of my work at* The Headlight *has given me a rich appreciation of how a publication operates on every level, and, now that I have that experience under my belt, I feel ready to work at a <u>real</u> newspaper. Though I have little*

copy editing experience since college, you can rest assured that, in hiring me, it would be the equivalent of rescuing a drowning man from the precipice of Niagara Falls. In other words, I would be your loyal dog for life.

Please help me. When I took the job at The Headlight, *my plan was to hang out for six months or so until something decent came along. Nearly two years and a lingering recession later, I fear that* The St. Louis Intelligencer *may be my last hope for journalistic happiness. I dearly wish to remain part of The Fourth Estate, but Pridemore and its inherent lack of even one tolerable bar to hang out in have me wondering if that telemarketing job I passed up during a recent visit to Kansas City wasn't, in fact, a viable career move.*

Please respond if you'd like to give a poor boy a break. You might be interested to know that I am 10 percent Cherokee Indian, just in case you have any quotas to fill.

Your Friend,
Peter Schaefer

Someone at the *Intelligencer* responded to Pete's missive with a handwritten note stating that the copy editing position had been filled and that he shouldn't bother applying to the newspaper ever again. Pete was impressed the venerable newspaper took time out of its busy day to basically tell him to fuck off. He Scotch-taped the reply to the side of his computer terminal where everyone at the *Headlight* could see it.

It was shortly after Valentine's Day when Pete took Angela back. Throughout the winter, she periodically showed up and rapped at his door like a lost puppy. He'd fix her a cup of Swiss Miss, let her cry all over his sweater, and send her back out into the night. One evening, she refused to leave until he read her a story from one of the books that lined the shelf he'd rigged from cinderblocks and particleboard. He selected *The Killers* from a book of Ernest Hemingway short stories. Aside from being one of Pete's favorites, *The Killers* was dark, foreboding, and completely devoid of romance. He could read it in about ten minutes and get Angela out the door in time to catch *The Daily Show*.

Angela had huddled close to Pete as he read. He reached the part where Nick was warning the washed-up prizefighter, Ole Andreson, that two guys had been sent to kill him and he'd better get out of town when Angela rested her head in his lap and let out a sigh. She smelled like lilacs, not Pete's favorite scent (*Karen Wilhelm!*) but pleasing enough to set his heart thumping. It had been two months since he and Angela had been together, and he'd almost forgotten how it felt to wrap his arms around her, pull her close, and inhale that sweet scent. Tomorrow, he would have to start again at the business of getting rid of her.

He was weak when it came to girls. Weak and inexperienced and stupid. Besides, it was lonely in Pete's one-bedroom apartment. So he took Angela back, and the two returned to their cycle of afternoon delights. That, more than anything, was why he had to get out, Pete thought as he pulled into the newspaper parking lot. He was to the point where he almost felt sorry for Larry Truesdale, so much that he had walked into the boss's office the other day intending to clear the air, job be damned. The man deserved to know. Maybe Pete could put it in the kind of glad-handing, Rotary Club terms to which Truesdale was accustomed.

"Hey, guy! How they hangin'? Just popped in to tell you that my roundup on the state legislature session will be done by Friday and, by the way, I've been banging your daughter and just thought you should know."

"Well, well, my boy! This calls for a celebration. Look through my desktop humidor and fire up a cigar that suits you!"

"Yes?" Truesdale looked up from his desk through a haze of cigarette smoke.

"I, uh, just wanted to know if I could take off early this afternoon."

"Doing some fishing?"

Pete slowly nodded. He was actually planning to take Angela to Quantrill Lake after cheerleading practice, though fishing wasn't on the agenda.

"Well, catch one for me!" the publisher had said, looking back down at whatever he was reading.

Pete shuffled out of the office that day, feeling havoc in his digestive region. He couldn't level with Truesdale, especially since he'd been on a bit of a roll lately. Pete's stories about the pending project to transform Dragon's Ice House into a tourist attraction won a Missouri press award. Amazingly, the state lawmakers had earmarked eight million dollars to go toward blasting a giant hole in the ground that would allow sightseers to walk into the very depths of the cave and view stalactites, cave coral, and other geological treasures that you currently had to worm through foot-wide crevasses to see. The big question was how Pridemore would come up with the matching funds from its depleted reserves. The mayor wanted to do it without raising the local sales tax, which would be fiscally ruinous, as far as Pete could tell. He subtly argued this point in his stories, and, though nobody in Pridemore seemed to give a damn, Truesdale circulated a memo commending Pete for "great shoe-leather reporting" (whatever that meant) when the award announcement came.

So he couldn't just tear Truesdale's heart out and stick it on a pike. Small-town huckster though he was, Larry had been an okay boss, even going to bat for Pete in a couple of disputes with Mayor Tolliver. Pete had some semblance of compassion for the guy, which is why he finally decided it was best to get another job and book it out of town.

He unlocked the service entrance to the *Headlight*'s office and walked into the dark newsroom. It was mercifully quiet. Waiting for his computer to boot, Pete picked up the phone to check his voicemail. He quietly prayed that the *Ft. Lauderdale*

Post-Accord had called about the health care reporting job. Instead, he heard the low voice of one of his deep background sources, really his only deep background source: "The usual place, Schaefer. And bring your notepad."

The usual place was Saul's Good Time Barbecue and Fillin' Station, a sort of down-home restaurant/convenience store ("Liquor Guns and Ammo Sold Here," a big sign declared out front) about a mile past the county line. The deep background source was Bubba Bell, director of public works for the city of Pridemore. He was late, as usual.

Pete sat in a booth near the back of the restaurant, staring idly at the Coca-Cola signs, John Deere hats, and ancient farming tools strewn around the place as though a tornado had blown them in from the countryside. A series of yellowed poster boards lined the walls with pieces of verse that documented what Pete assumed to be every year Saul's had been in business. The one hanging in front of him read,

> *In the year nineteen hundred seventy-two*
> *we elected Nixon and Agnew, too*
> *Mark Spitz won medals, all of them gold*
> *and 5,628 was the number of pork sandwiches Saul and Barb sold!*

Not the best rhyme and meter, Pete thought, but the sandwiches were very good. He was about to order the beef-on-bun when he saw Bubba roar onto Saul's gravel drive in his Ford F-250 with "City of Pridemore" emblazoned on the door. A few moments later, he burst through the double doors with such exuberance that Pete half expected him to break into song.

To call Bubba Bell a big man would be like calling the *USS Enterprise* a big boat. Bubba filled a room with his girth, accentuated on this day by a red hunter's cap and a bright orange parka he wore over several layers of clothing. His neck was thick as a medicine ball, supporting a broad, doughy face flush from the wintry cold that had returned to Pridemore overnight. His goatee was a tiny dirt-brown ring besieged by fat, rosy cheeks from above and that impressive neck from below. Bubba liked the beard, he once told Pete, because it made his face look thinner.

"Howdy, Saul!" he roared at the restaurant's proprietor, who was immersed in a morning crossword puzzle at the front counter.

"What say ya, Bubba?" Saul said. "Kinda chilly out there?"

"Shit, yeah! Fixed a busted main over on Seventh and Camelot, and it took us more than an hour just to dig down to it." Bubba laughed hugely. "Ever been knee-deep in frozen turds, Saul?"

"Can't say that I have."

"Really not so bad," he said. "The cold keeps it from smelling so God-awful."

He unzipped his parka and draped it over a chair at Pete's table. "You should thank the sweet Lord you've got one of them sit-down desk jobs."

Pete nodded and pulled a notebook from his coat pocket. He had met Bubba six months ago at One-Eyed Willie's, and the two quickly bonded over margaritas and a shared disdain for the lack of a decent bar scene in Pridemore. Since that time, Bubba periodically filled him in on what was happening at City Hall. He sometimes called Pete's apartment late at night with drunken complaints about the city's crumbling infrastructure and how that somehow impaired to his ability to find a woman.

Pete never asked Bubba why he agreed to talk off-the-record about city business. He initially thought the public works director had some sort of axe to grind. But the more Pete got to know him, the more he realized Bubba was one of those rare sources who just got a kick from seeing his inside information show up in the daily paper. A strange fetish, but God love him, Pete thought. As a reporter covering small-town government, you couldn't ask to have a secret source much deeper inside the city machinery.

Today's topic was the Dragon's Ice House project and how the hell Pridemore planned to pay for it.

"They've got to pass a bond issue," Pete suggested as a waitress refilled his ice tea.

"Nope," Bubba said, his face slightly smeared in barbecue sauce. "The project kicks off April 1, so there's no time to do a referendum even if they wanted to, which they don't."

"What choice do they have? They've got to match half of the state's eight million, and the city's broke."

"So's everybody else in Pridemore," Bubba said. "The mayor knows proposing a tax hike in this town is suicide, even for him. Folks around here don't take much to raising taxes."

"How else are they going to do it?"

The big man looked at Pete with a raised eyebrow, then dipped a mammoth pork sandwich that the menu dubbed "The Marshall City Mayor" into a little dish of barbecue sauce. Bubba took a bite, then held the sandwich between two fat fingers and chewed thoughtfully.

"An interesting question, young Skywalker," he finally said. "How *will* they raise that money? You know about the city's reserve fund, right?"

"Sure." Pete knew that Pridemore kept a few hundred thousand on hand for disasters like a tornado or a flash flood.

"Well there's *another* fund." Bubba looked left and right before leaning across the table. "Okay, this is off-, off-, off-the-record, all right? You can't write about this, and you certainly didn't hear it from me, dig?"

"Sure." Pete put his notebook down.

Bubba leaned in closer. His breath smelled of onions and beer.

"There's another fund that the mayor's been quietly putting money into for, like, a million years, okay? A nickel here, a dime there sort of thing—it goes back to the days when the city had this huge surplus, and the mayor was siphoning off dollars into a secret account because the state had rules that a city could only be so much in the black, follow?"

"Yeah."

"Well, nobody knows how much money is in this fund. Not the city council, not the city manager. Only the mayor knows. And word is that he's going to dip into this fund to help pay the city's part of Dragon's Ice House."

"Just a minute," Pete said, rubbing a hand along his receding hairline. "You're telling me the mayor's got millions of dollars in a secret slush fund?"

"Could be," Bubba said in a raspy voice that was his version of a whisper.

"That's illegal."

"You write anything about that and I'm toast. They're already going through every computer file and desk drawer to try and find out who your snitch is."

"I'll just need a paper trail," Pete said, unsheathing his pen and starting to jot in his notebook. "An internal memo, canceled checks, something like that."

Bubba chuckled and took a bite from his Marshall City Mayor. He looked at Pete and laughed some more, his man breasts bouncing beneath a flannel shirt.

"What's so funny?"

"Son, you got a lot to learn about Pridemore politics," he said. "There ain't no checks and there ain't no paper trail. Hell, the state auditor's been trying to nail ol' Roe for twenty years. You really think he's gonna let some kid reporter take down his kingdom? I mean, you're a smart guy, Pete, but whoa!"

Pete felt a burning sensation rise from his chest and through his neck and ears. It wasn't the healthy dose of Saul's

"Your Butt in Space" hot sauce so much as the sense that Bubba had lured him to this hillbilly joint on a freezing day just to tell Pete what he couldn't print. The public works director must have noticed Pete was getting hot, because he stopped laughing and took a gulp from his 46-ounce Gut-Buster.

"All right, here's something else," Bubba said. "My office sees every plan for every project that gets done or doesn't get done in the city, right? We're the ones who say, 'You can hook your building right here to the water supply,' or 'You can't dig there because you'll hit a gas line,' you know?"

"Yeah."

"Dragon's Ice House is three weeks from breaking ground, and I ain't seen one single blueprint for the thing. Neither has the city planner. We went in to talk to Tolliver about it and he basically said, 'It don't concern you.'"

He ran a napkin across his face before continuing. "Now, don't you find that a tad strange?"

"I do."

"I do, too. Hey, Saul!"

The restaurant owner ambled over from his spot near the cash register.

"Saul, I'd like you to meet Pete Schaefer, one of the best damn reporters the *Headlight* ever produced."

Saul shook Pete's hand.

"Pleased to meet you, Mr. Schaefer. I read your stories every day."

"Thanks," Pete said. "You make a pretty mean brisket."

"Best damn brisket in central Missour-ah," Bubba said, slapping Saul square on the back. "I got the check, Pete. Don't you worry 'bout that."

A few minutes later, standing in the lot outside Saul's Good Time Barbecue and Fillin' Station, Pete asked Bubba why he had called the old man over. "Aren't you nervous about people knowing our, uh, relationship?"

Bubba laughed as he sat in his truck with the door half open. "Ol' Saul's known me since I was a knee-high little pecker. He ain't telling nobody nothing."

"What about the other people in the place?"

"What about 'em?"

"It's just that what you're telling me is kind of, well, sensitive."

"Shit, Pete! You worry too much."

His truck roared off in a hail of dust and gravel as Pete hustled back to his Explorer. Huddled over its air vents, waiting for the engine to warm, he flipped through his notes and wondered how he might confirm Bubba's tale of secret funds and under-the-table chicanery. If Pete could substantiate even part of it, he'd have one hell of a story to write.

CHAPTER 12

Something smelled good downstairs, the mayor thought as he buttoned his khaki shirt. Margaret had a chicken in the Crock-Pot and Dave Brubeck on the hi-fi. The smell of simmering meat and the snappy opening to "Blue Rondo a la Turk" gave the dimly lit Tolliver home a cozy charm that it normally lacked.

He pulled an olive green army jacket over his slight shoulders and stood in front of the full-length mirror. His woolen pants were a little tight in the midsection, but otherwise the standard-issue uniform fit about as well as it did on March 29, 1944, when he first tried it on. That was the day they shipped him out to Fort Leonard Wood for three months of basic training. He was eighteen and fully prepared to run his bayonet through every Jap from the Marshall Islands to Tokyo. His older brother, Mickey, was a Marine corporal already bound for the South Pacific. Another brother, Billy, had fought in North Africa and would soon be part of D-Day. Runty little Roe Tolliver, too small to start on the high school football team like Mickey did, too slow to play guard on the basketball team like Billy, was ready for this war. It was to be his deliverance.

So he thought. Both brothers died in combat before the year was out—Mickey in Peleliu and Billy on Omaha Beach. Roe, for his part, helped lead the liberation of Fais Island, a phosphate atoll in the Caroline Islands. Most people had never heard of it. No reason why they would. There was a small radio station and six Japanese soldiers on the whole damn island, and four of them committed hara-kiri before Sergeant Tolliver and his men got to them. The mayor still had a ceremonial loincloth that the natives bequeathed him for freeing the island and leaving the tribe a portion of the company's K and C rations. He kept it with his medals and a Jap rifle (from one of the suicides) in a footlocker in his attic.

He stared into the mirror, snapped his arm in a tight salute, then snapped it back down and stood at attention, shoulders squared and gut sucked in. Nothing made him sicker than to watch the current president make a rubber-wristed attempt at military protocol as he got on and off his helicopter. Is it asking too much, the mayor said to his cronies on more than one occasion, for one of the Joint Chiefs to show that pissant how to make a decent, proper salute?

After the war, it was off to Mizzou on the GI Bill. Then law school. Then clerking for a Jeff City firm, where he met a pretty secretary named Margaret Bloom. They watched *The Treasure of the Sierra Madre* on their first date.

Then the usual stuff. Got married. Went to work. Started a law practice in Pridemore and, like many of what they were now calling the Greatest Generation, felt a calling to get into public service. He served six years on the city council before running for mayor, and was surprised as anyone when he won. In his initial term, he opened Pridemore's first city pool.

He and Margaret put off having a kid for a few years while his career grew. By the time they really started trying, they were in their thirties and wondering if they hadn't waited too long. After two years of intermittently hopeful and frustrating sex, they were delighted when Margaret's doctor confirmed the happy news. Jack Nathan Tolliver entered the world on May 31, 1955, at a whopping eight-and-a-half pounds and twenty inches.

Jack was a tough little bug—elbows and knees all scarred up by the time he was three from climbing trees and falling off his tricycle. He would need every bit of that toughness. A few weeks before his seventh birthday, Jack was diagnosed with leukemia. The next year was spent shuttling back and fourth to a clinic in Boston, where Jack had a series of aggressive chemo treatments.

Sometime during that awful year, when things were especially bleak, the mayor sat alone at O'Hare International Airport, watching planes take off and land while awaiting his connection to Boston.

"Amazing, isn't it," someone next to him said, "how they get those big hunks of metal up in the air?"

"Yeah," said the mayor. "Makes you wonder why they can't fix something like cancer."

Jack died on September 19, 1963, eight weeks before Kennedy was shot. In those days, you didn't talk about something as horrible as a kid dying. There were no support groups or charity walks. There would be no second child— Margaret's hysterectomy a few years after Jack was born took care of that. All you could do was throw away the toys and the car bed and the clothes and the Dr. Seuss books and try to get on with your life.

The mayor did that, pouring himself like never before into his practice and local politics. He never spoke of Jack to anyone, not even to Margaret. Never visited the gravesite. For many years, he had kept a small photo on his office desk. That was it.

Looking back on it now, he had probably been something of a basket case when he'd met Beatrice Reilly. The editor of the *Evening Headlight* wasn't much to look at today, with her lumpy sweaters and grey hair pulled back in a bun. But five decades ago, when she came to Pridemore fresh out of college…. Well, let's just say if you didn't look twice at those big, green eyes and that golden hair spilling down her shoulders, you weren't a man in Roe Tolliver's book.

He was playing doubles tennis with a few pals at the country club when he saw her walking onto the court with some good-looking guy who was probably her boyfriend. This was back in the days of the tennis skirt, and Beat was wearing a white, pleated number that stopped a few inches short of her well-tanned knees. Her long hair was pushed back in a braid that playfully swayed back and forth when she returned a shot. Now and then, one of her volleys had bounced to the mayor's court, and the girl smiled demurely as he and his buddies scrambled to retrieve the ball.

There was a patio outside the courts where the men drank beers between matches. The mayor sat there, nursing his drink for an hour while waiting for the blond and her boyfriend to finish their set.

"You must be the new reporter," he said after she'd taken a sip from the nearby water fountain.

"I am," she replied, dabbing her forehead with a towel. Her boyfriend was talking baseball with a couple of the guys.

"I," he said, offering his hand, "am Monroe Tolliver."

"Well," she said, "good for you."

He smiled broadly. He was in his late thirties then, and people would sometimes note what a bright, charming smile he had. The kind, they said, that could light up a room.

"You don't know who I am, do you?" he said.

"Should I?"

"Maybe."

She put a hand over her eyes to shield them from the sun. She had a round face with big eyes that seemed intent on taking everything in. Her smile, in addition to flashing a set of perfect white teeth, bore a peculiar cockiness that probably shattered a lot of male egos back in school.

"So who are you?"

"I'm the mayor."

Her lips parted slightly, not enough to express complete surprise.

"Gosh," she said. "I should have known that."

He unleashed an easygoing laugh, or at least that was the intent. Coming out, it sounded a bit overdone. He reached out and patted her arm.

"Not a big deal," he said. "Drop by City Hall next week and I'll show you the ropes."

"I'd like that," she said.

He'd reached into the cooler next to his chair and pulled out a Budweiser. Late afternoons in the summer, when the sun stayed up past nine, he was always at the tennis courts mixing it up with the boys and getting a buzz on. It beat the hell out of the quiet and emptiness at home.

"You drink beer?" he asked.

"Sure," she said, taking the bottle from his hand.

It was the beginning of a wonderful friendship, at least in his mind. He taught her everything he knew about city politics. Well, almost everything. Beat was smart, though a bit too much of a know-it-all for Roe's taste. The cocky little smile wasn't a front—she really believed she was hot shit. He didn't care for some of the stories she wrote, but they were usually balanced and fair. At the very least, she made a point of cleaning up his grammar for print, something today's reporters weren't much interested in doing.

The boyfriend eventually took a sales job in St. Louis, but Beat stayed, churning out two or three stories a day from her Underwood typewriter and usually going through a pack of Lucky Strikes in the process. Roe wondered why she stayed. She didn't have family here. She had enough talent to latch onto to one of the bigger newspapers but didn't seem interested. Nor did she care for the burly farm boys who could twirl her around the dance floor with their vise-grip hands but weren't much for talking about the Warren Commission findings or the growing discontent with Vietnam.

He wondered a lot of things about Beat Reilly until one June afternoon when he took her for a ride in his brand new, cherry red Mustang convertible. Just a ten-mile jaunt from City Hall to the old gas station at the stoplight where 54 and Route MM intersected and then back into town again, enough time to get some wind in your hair, gaze at the endless sea of waist-high cornstalks, and take a few sips from the Budweisers poking out of the ice-filled cooler in the back seat. He got the little car up to around eighty miles an hour on a long stretch of Missouri blacktop that split the landscape as far as could be seen. Beat fiddled with the radio dial before settling on a rock-and-roll tune with which Roe was entirely unfamiliar. Some guy singing about a girl named Peggy Sue. She leaned back in the seat, sipped her beer, and let the breeze lift a few strands of golden hair.

"This," she said in that southern Missouri twang he'd come to love, "is heaven."

Roe Tolliver, hero of Fais Island and winner of a Purple Heart for spraining his ankle while jumping from his bunk during an air raid, had never done anything daring or stupid his entire life. He wasn't one for spontaneity or grand gestures, especially not in the courtroom. He was a plodder, plain and simple. Someone who planned and worked for everything he'd gotten in life.

Without really thinking about all that, he downshifted the Mustang and skidded onto a dirt road that cut through the cornfields. They sped down the road, kicking up pebbles and dust until he swerved against the stalks, killed the ignition, and planted one of history's all-time sloppiest kisses on her lips. It took a moment for Beat to push him away, straighten her sunglasses, and manage a look of smoldering fury. He kissed her again, this one a little longer and more precise, before she gave him the brush-off. Her lips were full and soft and had the faint taste of cigarettes and beer. Her shoulders and neck smelled like jasmine. Something called Chanel No. 5, she told him later.

They sat in that car, necking like a couple of teenagers while the radio played rock and roll. He would hear a lot of Chuck Berry, Little Richard, and some English band called the Beatles that summer. He would learn which dirt roads offered the most privacy as the days got hotter and the cornstalks grew taller.

That was almost fifty years ago, and not a day passed when he didn't think about it. All told, the fling lasted three months. Roe called it off in September, knowing it was a matter of time before word got back to Margaret through bridge club or altar guild or one of her other activities. Beat took the news well. Didn't even tear up as her head rested on his lap and he stammered through his rehearsed excuses and apologies. When it was time to go back into town, she sat up, fished some bright red lipstick from her purse, and slowly ran it across those soft lips as she looked in the side-view mirror. He tried to keep his eyes on the road, but he saw that cocky little grin mocking him from the passenger seat. It would take him years to realize that Beat was doing more than just keeping a brave face. It was a smile of, if anything, relief.

The mayor stared hard into the full-length mirror in his darkened bedroom, an eighty-eight-year-old man who still fit into his army uniform. Big flipping deal. It occurred to him that this might be the last time he ever wore it. That didn't depress him so much. He was tired of trying on the uniform. He was tired of council meetings on Monday nights and empty storefronts on Main Street. He was tired of having to sit down every morning to take a piss because, when you're an octogenarian with ruined knees, you sit down every chance you get.

It probably wouldn't have been much better had he said to hell with it all in 1964 and kept driving Beat down Highway 54 toward St. Louis, but he'd like to think so. They would get a place in the heart of the city. He'd start a new practice. They'd take in an art film or the ballet on Saturday and top it off with some fine Italian food on the Hill. Then they'd come home to their maintenance-free, pet-free condominium, he and his wife with the soft twang and the golden hair, who hadn't aged a minute from the time he saw her stride onto that tennis court like a Hollywood queen.

Without really thinking about it, he pulled the 9mm pistol from his holster and pressed it to his temple. He cocked the gun and pulled the trigger with a lifeless click, knowing there were no bullets in the chamber. Life was never that convenient, and, besides, he couldn't stand the thought of Margaret finding his brains splattered all over their king-sized bed. That was not how he wanted to go.

He slipped the pistol back into its holster and began the slow, draining process of taking off his uniform. First the jacket, then the belt and the trousers, then fumbling to unbutton the shirt. Was it worth all this trouble just to try it on?

"My liege!" his wife called from downstairs. "Your dinner awaits!"

He looked in the mirror at his sagging, naked body before slipping on a bathrobe.

"Okay," he said with a grunt. "Be down in a minute."

CHAPTER 13

Until the state allotted millions of dollars to turn them into tourist attractions, the Lewis and Clark Land Bridge and Dragon's Ice House were two of the best-kept natural secrets in all of Missouri.

Visitors savvy enough to spot the bullet-ridden sign off Old Highway 54 ("Girl Scout Camp, 2 miles") would turn onto the gravel road that wound through a forest and ended at a gurgling freshwater stream called Moss Creek. They could park their cars in a small glade and take an unmarked path along the creek until they reached Lewis and Clark Land Bridge, a mossy rock formation that the two great explorers were rumored to have crossed sometime in 1804, even though they made no record of it in their journals and Pridemore was a good twenty miles from the famed Lewis and Clark trail.

Following the stream beneath the land bridge was not for the squeamish. It was a long, dark, misty passage where the temperature plunged about twenty degrees and the natural bridge's slimy ceiling was low enough to touch. Those who finished the trek found themselves at the edge of a jagged twenty-foot gash in the ground that led into blackness. This was Dragon's Ice House, so named because the limestone rocks at its entrance looked like enormous teeth and its cool cave walls could refrigerate a twelve-pack of beer in the middle of July.

The Ice House led to a network of caves that stretched as far as seven miles under the Missouri bedrock. There were winding passages, underwater streams, cathedral-sized caverns, and crawl spaces barely wide enough for an average-sized person to wiggle through. It was a spelunker's playground, and many who explored the Ice House rated it among the best in the Midwest for experienced cavers.

It also was a popular make-out spot for Pridemore teens. At twilight on summer evenings, kids would sit at the cave's mouth and watch tens of thousands of bats pour out, their flapping wings blotting the sky. Taking a girl to the Ice House to see the bats swoop so close that you could reach out and touch them was a rite of passage for Pridemore boys of a certain age, just as young males in Pamplona might be expected to run with the bulls. The crushed beer cans, Mardi Gras beads, and women's underwear scattered around the cave entrance were testaments that the generations-old ritual was still in practice.

This spring brought a different set of visitors to Pridemore's natural wonders. Since early April, the machine-gun thumping of jackhammers had echoed through the woods at a constant pace. Chainsaws screamed and tree trunks groaned as they crashed to the ground. Cement trucks rumbled up and down the gravel road while work crews cleared brush to make way for a two-lane drive.

Chub Hughes stood over a blueprint inside what he called the War Room, a white, doublewide trailer marked on all sides with the M&M Construction Co. logo. The trailer stood a few hundred feet from the Lewis and Clark Land Bridge, right where the blacktop road would soon feed into a parking lot with sixty-five car spaces and a tourist information center. Chub's crew was four weeks into the project and already behind schedule, which pissed him off even though he knew it probably didn't matter. The parking lot, the information center, the moving walkway underneath the land bridge, and the boats that were to follow an underwater track along Moss Creek had as much chance of being built as a Dollywood in Damascus. There wasn't enough money to finish the work, even with the eight million in state funds. Finishing, of course, wasn't the point anyway.

It was the damnedest project Chub had ever worked on, and, the more he thought about it, a wasteful thing to do to a scenic piece of undeveloped land. The Ice House had a dear place in his heart, as it was where he first summoned the courage to kiss a girl. He'd had his first beer near the mouth of that cave, too, come to think of it. To be party now to its exploitation gave him pause...until he remembered the $700,000 profit his company stood to make on the project.

Chub glanced out the window to see a couple of his orange-vested road crew smoking cigarettes and laughing. Fuming, he opened the window and poked his head out.

"Hey, ladies!" he bellowed. "It ain't lunchtime yet!"

The two men shrugged their shoulders and shuffled back to the job site. As general contractor overseeing public projects, Chub had long ago resigned himself to being surrounded by some of the stupidest people in the tri-county region. But this generation of construction workers, with their tattoos and their earrings and their insistence on playing "tunes" at work, really pissed him off. Give him five minutes alone with these punks, and he'd beat all their sorry, PlayStation-playing asses, herniated disc and all. Chub wasn't so far removed from the crew to forget the brawls in the roadhouse after work, when it felt almost liberating to plant your fist in another guy's face. And if the guy hit back, you were usually too drunk to feel it until the next morning.

"Go on, you faggots!" he yelled out the window, and immediately felt like an idiot. The two kids were too far down the road to hear him, and they were probably plugged into their iPhones anyway.

He returned to his table and rolled up the blueprint of the parking lot and the elevated walkway to reveal a much smaller map with dark blue lines that ran hither and yond with no discernible purpose. They outlined, roughly, the Ice House's meandering path under the Missouri farmland—no one knew for sure where the cave actually ended. It would be his job in the coming weeks to figure all that out, to learn every square inch and stress point of the damn thing while most of his employees were busy laying blacktop a few hundred yards away.

He sighed as he looked at the map. All in all, it was a pretty solid plan, one that took six months to conceive and that Chub felt he could execute for less than $170,000. He only needed four men to carry it out—subcontractors he trusted and who were desperate enough to work late nights and sign airtight confidentiality agreements.

None of the workers knew the full scope of the plan. Still, Chub worried. Some nights he'd lie awake in bed, images of bright orange jumpsuits, gang showers, and basketball courts with chain nets filling his head. Chub had seen every episode of *Oz*, the HBO series about prison life, and deciding whose bitch he would become or learning how to make a shiv from a government-issued spoon wasn't how he wanted to live out his golden years.

It shouldn't come to that, he thought as he stared at the map. It couldn't. Otherwise, he'd never have hopped onto this pony ride. Despite running a company that was nearly a million dollars in debt and in danger of losing its line of credit, he was not a man given to ventures whose outcomes he didn't have a strong hand in deciding.

"This is a damn solid plan," he said, as if willing it to be so.

CHAPTER 14

"Yo, Willers!"

Digby looked up from his lunch to see a tall man with stringy blond hair smiling down at him. He wore a tattered "Yo Quiero Taco Bell!" tank top that revealed an upper body tanned and toned from years of hard labor. The guy's name was Travis. Everybody called him Drag-Ass because that was the kind of nickname they stuck you with in the construction business. Especially, Digby supposed, if you had long, blond hair, you smiled a lot, and you spent a lot of time in your car smoking tiny, rolled-up cigarettes.

"Mind if I sit down?"

Digby scooted to the edge of the tailgate to make room for his new friend, who sat with the kind of prolonged grunt you'd expect from a much older person. Travis set a thermos next to him and opened a beat-up lunch box painted with Scooby-Doo characters. He pulled a sandwich out of a zip-lock bag and groaned dramatically.

"Corn beef again, can you believe it?" he said. "My old lady, that's all she knows how to make. Corn-fuckin'-beef sandwich."

Digby snickered in spite of himself at this funny way of mixing a dirty word with everyday words. He didn't really trust Travis, mostly because Travis made fun of him around the other guys in the crew, then acted like they were best buddies when it was just the two of them. It was hard to tell who was real—his pal Travis, or Drag-Ass, the guy who cracked everybody up with his jokes, most of them about all the different things he wanted to do to women. Digby put up with Drag-Ass's antics because Travis was fun and easygoing, and he was the closest thing to a friend Digby'd made since joining the road construction crew more than three weeks ago.

"What you got there, sport?" Travis asked.

Digby held out his Dakota Marx lunch box and recited its contents: "Red Delicious apple, ham-and-cheese-with-mustard-on-rye, and two Hostess Twinkies with banana crème filling."

"Banana crème filling? Ain't heard of no Twinkies with banana filling."

"It's a special deal," Digby said before biting into one. "My mom got them at the store and said they're doing them with banana filling for, like, a year."

"That a fact?" Travis pulled one of those homemade cigarettes out of his shirt pocket and lit it. He sucked on the thing until his eyes got so narrow he looked Chinese. Digby couldn't help noticing that Travis hadn't touched his corn beef sandwich.

"Hey, brother," Travis said after another puff. "Why don't you let me try one of them Twinkies."

Digby eyed his friend suspiciously, then looked at his Twinkie. He didn't particularly like the banana crème filling, but the Twinkies were rare, a special edition, and he didn't know if he would ever have the chance to eat another one.

"C'mon man," he said. "Just one bite."

Digby considered for a moment whether his friendship with Travis was worth one extremely rare Twinkie.

"You can have my apple," he offered.

"Now, Digby, when we were having lunch the other day, and that coon starting getting on you about your little trips over to Dragon's Ice House, who was the only person to stand up and tell him you could do whatever you wanted on your lunch break?"

Digby didn't remember anybody standing up to the black man named Charles, whom everyone called "foreman" and whom some people, like Travis, called other names whenever Charles wasn't around.

Travis gave him a big smile that was more frightening than friendly. He wore a diamond in his right ear that glared sunlight into Digby's eyes.

"Puh-lease, Willers," he said. "Please-give-me-one-of-them-fancy-new-banana-crème-filled-Twinkies, sir!"

Digby smiled weakly and handed over a Twinkie. Travis tore through the plastic bag and inhaled the treat in two bites.

"Mmm," he said, wiping bits of frosting from his beard with a dirty hand. "You're a prince of a man, Digby Willers. Don't let no one tell you different."

Digby nodded and put a half-eaten sandwich back in his lunch box. He didn't feel hungry all of a sudden and knew there wasn't much time left on his break.

"Where you going?"

"Up there," Digby said, nodding toward Moss Creek.

"The Ice House, huh?" Travis said with a grin. "Well, I'll cover for you, but don't be long."

Digby put his lunch box back on the yellow school bus that some of the workers rode to and from the site, and he started his daily walk up the little trail that ran along the creek and under the land bridge.

Sometimes he walked all the way to the jagged hole in the ground that was big enough to drive a truck through. A couple of times, he dared to creep a few feet into its mouth, but the sight of something—once, it was a swallow's nest nestled in the rocks, another time it was a zipper spider's web—sent him scrambling back to daylight.

Some days, when he was far enough along the trail that no one could see him, Digby pulled off his work boots and socks and waded into Moss Creek, the rushing water so cold it turned his toes blue. He searched the creek bottom for skipping stones until his legs couldn't stand the cold, and then he hopped onto the wide, flat rock where he'd left his shoes and examined the treasures he'd collected. One day he was sure he'd found an Indian arrowhead, only to be told by his crewmates it was probably just a jagged piece of limestone. Still, he put the rock on his nightstand when he got home, next to the seashells his aunt had brought back from the Gulf of Mexico.

He had just rolled up the cuffs of his jeans for a wade in the creek when the thumping bass of rap singer Shockley P. Morris started pounding away from a distant boom box:

Cold-cocked, I'm your favorite villain,
Shell-shocked, she's ready an' willin'.
Jedi fame, like old Ben Kenobi,
Play my game, get mo' bitches than Kobe.

This was Digby's signal that lunch break was over and it was time to get back to work, so he pulled on his socks and work boots and trudged back down the trail. Soon the gurgling creek water was drowned out by the noise of jackhammers and chainsaws and the big trucks rumbling down the road. The noise drove Digby a little crazy. It was a lot different from his job at City Hall, where he pretty much sat all morning in the break room, playing his Gameboy, until the mailman came by at noon.

Digby had that job longer than any other, which meant he'd worked in the City Hall mail room a little more than a year. Until one day the mayor called Digby into his office and told him that the city couldn't afford a courier anymore and would have to let him go. Digby wasn't exactly sure what that meant, so he kept showing up at 9:00 a.m. until the mayor called him into his office again.

This time the old man had a big smile on his face like he was about to share a very interesting secret. The mayor didn't smile often, but when he did, Digby was amazed at how much his teeth looked like canned corn.

"I might have a solution to your employment problem," he said.

"Really?" Digby wasn't aware that he had a problem, but he was willing to give the mayor a chance to explain himself.

The solution, it turned out, was a construction project at a place called Dragon's Ice House. It was going to become one of the most important attractions in all of Missouri, the mayor said, and the project team needed creative young minds like Digby's to bring it to life.

The idea of helping to build a tourist spot thrilled Digby; he pictured a Magic Kingdom-style experience with sky buckets, water flume rides, and a fairy-tale castle. While he'd never been to Walt Disney World, he had a well-thumbed book with photos and illustrations on how the park was built. He spent the weeks prior to his new job flipping through the book's pages, humming "When You Wish Upon a Star" and dreaming up ideas for Dragon's Ice House. He decided the project could definitely use a monorail.

Chub Hughes's hound-dog scowl on Digby's first day at work was a clue that the contractor didn't expect creativity from his road crew. Mr. Hughes was a mean-looking man, and the few words that came out of his mouth were usually unpleasant. Digby was glad that the boss spent most of his time in the big, air-conditioned trailer that was off limits to regular workers.

The foreman, Charles, gave him a blue hard hat and some steel-toed boots but forbade Digby from operating any of the heavy machinery, which was disappointing. His work was limited to tasks like holding the mixing truck's arm so it poured a steady flow of concrete that formed the curbs and gutters. When he tired of that, they had him walk up and down the road, making sure the new layer of asphalt was nice and smooth.

The work was dull, so it wasn't uncommon for Digby's mind to wander. Today it ambled down a gravel road much like the one he was working on. But this particular road was on the other side of town, covered in weeds that were waist high in some places. He'd discovered it a few weeks ago when he had nothing better to do but wander the country lanes that shot off the highway like so many streams from a river. This road, which had no name as far as Digby knew, led to an old barn that looked like it was abandoned a hundred years ago. An oak tree had grown through its collapsed roof, and sunlight shone through the wood planks in its walls. The barn was big and brittle and at least a half mile from the nearest living soul. It was just right for what Digby had in mind.

He'd experimented with fire for more than a year, first melting GI Joes and Star Wars figures with his mom's cigarette lighter, then sneaking into the woods behind the house to burn little piles of brush. He sat for hours watching the flames skip and dance, easily turning the twigs and branches to ash, and imagined what they could do to something much larger. The old barn was the perfect place to find out, a two-story structure that would surely go up like a pack of matches. Of course, he would need something stronger than Mom's lighter if he wanted to have a real show. Over the past two weeks, Digby had quietly filled a cardboard box with a variety of household items—hairsprays, rubbing alcohol, furniture stripper, paint remover—and planned to carry it off to the barn while his mom worked the overnight shift at the hospital.

It would surely be a sight to see, when he had enough firepower to make it happen. Digby closed his eyes and imagined the rickety structure fully consumed, columns of red flame filling the black sky…

"Willers!"

He looked up to see Charles's big face about an inch away from his nose. Charles was a black man, but his face took on a reddish tint when he was mad about something. It was red now.

"The hell is this?"

He pointed to a spot where the concrete, still pouring from the mixing truck, had piled over the tops of Digby's work boots.

The foreman ran to the truck's gearbox and shut the mixer down. He helped Digby pull one leg, then the other, from the hardening gray substance.

"I'm sorry," Digby said softly.

"This is one of the easiest jobs on the crew, and you're fucking it up. I'm not going to tell you again to get your head in the game, understand?"

"Yessir. I will."

"You better," Charles said, but with a little less edge in his voice. "Clean this up and get back to work."

Digby picked up a leveler and smoothed out the concrete as best he could. He kept his eyes fixed on the ground as his crewmates hooted at him.

"Nice job, Willers!"

"Looks like a Clydesdale shit over there!"

The sound of one familiar voice, slurred and dumb, made the muscles in the back of his neck tighten.

"My name is Digby, and I'm *retard-ed*."

He looked up to find his friend Travis (or was it Drag-Ass?) baring his teeth and making a donkey laugh for the enjoyment of three coworkers.

"C'mon, man, say it," Travis said. "My name is Digby. And I'm *re-tard-ed*."

The others laughed, but with less gusto. Travis walked toward him, still wearing that grin. Digby looked around. The foreman had moved on down the road.

"Say it just once, boy," he said. "Say it for your buddy Travis."

A burning fury rose through Digby, and his eyes welled up with tears. It was that scary feeling from recess, when the boys used to pelt him with rocks or push him into a sticker bush. That shameful, burning feeling never told Digby whether to run and hide or make his hand into a fist. So he just stood there.

"F-fuck you, Travis," he said softly.

"What'd you say?"

"Fuck you!"

"Fuck me?" Travis said, drawing closer. "Gee, Digby, that's a flattering thing to say. I'm going to have to think about that one here for a second. Let me see. Oh, yeah…I don't fuck RETARDS!"

The other guys stopped laughing.

"That's enough, Drag-Ass," one said. "Leave 'em alone."

By now, Travis was so close to Digby that their noses almost touched. Travis's breath smelled like rotten food, but Digby forced himself to stare into the man's dark eyes. He noticed dried-up clumps of banana crème in Travis's beard from the Twinkie he'd eaten less than an hour ago, when it was just the two of them. When they were friends.

The thought of sharing a Twinkie with this man made him feel sick. Travis must have noticed something, because he smiled in an almost friendly way and his voice turned soft.

"You wanna hit me?" he said. "C'mon. Hit me."

Without thinking, Digby grabbed two fistfuls of blond hair, pulled Travis toward him, and bit into his ear. His teeth lingered around the earlobe even as Travis squirmed, the salty taste of sweat and blood faintly reminding Digby of those vegetable juices his mother used to make him drink. He hadn't had one of those in years.

"Oh, my God!" Travis screamed. "Get him off!"

Digby felt heavy hands on him, trying to pull him away. He resisted a few more seconds—hearing the screams and knowing their source was oddly satisfying—before relaxing his jaw and watching Travis collapse in the pile of soft concrete.

Travis held both hands against his head in a weak attempt to stop the blood from flowing.

"Jesus Christ!"

Digby sat down, or maybe it was those heavy hands that actually *set* him down. They stayed on him for a long time, but Digby didn't notice, didn't hear Travis calling him a cunt and a retard and a motherfucker. He sat on the ground Indian-style, his tongue working something around his mouth that was sharp and pointy like a thumbtack. What on earth was it? He spit it into his palm: a diamond-studded earring covered in blood and saliva.

He studied the piece of jewelry, working his little finger around its tiny diamond and prongs, before gently tossing it to its owner, who was lying, arms and legs akimbo, in a reddish-brown concrete puddle while the workers treated his wound with duct tape.

Digby leaned back, closed his eyes, and everything went black.

CHAPTER 15

Susan Willers was taking a smoke break near the entrance of the Pridemore County Hospital when an intern rushed out to tell her she had an urgent phone call. A feeling of dread washed over Susan's size-28 body. She knew it could be only one thing.

"Well, who the hell is it?" she asked anyway.

"They won't say," the intern said. "They just said it was important and I should get you right away."

"Shit, Karen," she said, tossing her cigarette to the ground and mashing it under a white clog shoe. "If it's a sheriff's deputy or coroner calling, your ass is grass."

Susan walked calmly through the double doors to the nurse's station, but she felt her chest thumping like a bass drum as she picked up the phone.

"Susan Willers," she said evenly.

"Miss Willers, we need you down here," a gruff voice said. "It's your boy, Digby."

Five minutes later, she was roaring down Old 54 in her 1986 Fiero, thinking about how they better not have touched a hair on that boy's head or there would be one pissed-off fat lady at the M&M Construction site. The guy on the phone, Chub-somebody, assured her everything was under control. So then why the hell did they need her to break from her afternoon shift? The ER was unusually busy today—they'd just hauled in some poor devil with half his ear chewed off—and she hated to leave the staff unsupervised for no good reason.

She pulled a Marlboro Red from the breast pocket of her nurse's scrubs and flicked her Bic with the other hand. She'd run out of Winston Lights earlier in the day and had to bum a couple of smokes from Brenda. The Marlboro Reds were a little on the harsh side for her, but they would do in a pinch.

Susan Willers was a senior RN at the hospital. She'd earned her nurse's license and a dependable salary ten years ago. But those eight-hour shifts of back-wrenching toil had taken something out of her. She was a large, loud-mouthed woman who took pleasure in berating the staff nurses and even, on occasion, the doctors. The cigarettes, a habit she'd picked up at age fourteen and had long since given up trying to shake, seemed to wash the worry lines from her broad, ruddy face as she took a long, satisfying drag.

Digby was the product of her marriage to a shoe salesman named Stan Willers who disappeared shortly after it became apparent that his son was, as they gently put it nowadays, "developmentally challenged." "Retarded" was the word they used back in the 1980s, and Stan apparently was such a shining example of human intellect and accomplishment that he couldn't bear the idea of raising a kid who would never read above the first-grade level. The son of a bitch just took off one day, leaving behind a vague note about "getting his head together" and moving in with his sister in Des Moines. Susan and Digby hadn't received so much as a Christmas card since.

Susan never touched another man, so great was her rage at the entire species. All of them except for Digby, who wasn't so much a man as he was a 280-pound boy with peanut butter and jelly on his T-shirt. She smiled, recalling how her baby once declared, after watching *Peter Pan* on video for about the six hundredth time, that he would someday travel to Never-Never Land and become one of the Lost Boys.

That was ten years ago, but not much about Digby had changed besides his shirt size and appetite. He would never, ever grow up to be a man, and that was a good thing.

"Because then I'd have to castrate him," she muttered to herself as she swerved the Fiero onto the gravel road and past the sign that read "Girl Scout Camp, 2 Miles."

An orange-vested worker stopped her about a mile down the road, where a large, balding man waited in a golf cart. He helped Susan emerge from her tiny car and introduced himself as Chub Hughes, the project's general contractor.

"I don't care if you're the goddamned Earl of Sandwich," she said. "Where's my baby?"

The contractor opened his mouth as if to say something, but instead he expelled a soft moan. He motioned for Susan to climb into the golf cart.

"He's down the road a piece."

They rode another half mile, past the work crews and rumbling machinery, to the white doublewide trailer. Susan and the contractor walked inside to find Digby sitting at a conference table, starting blankly ahead, an unopened can of Coke in front of him.

"My God," the nurse said.

"He's been this way for two hours," Chub said.

Susan pulled a chair next to her son and cradled his head in her arms. She brushed his yellow hair gently with her fingers and, after a few minutes, got him to take a sip from his Coke.

"That's my baby," she cooed. "That's my good boy."

Chub pulled a Diet Dr. Pepper from a mini-fridge.

"Can I get you a drink, Miss Willers?"

The nurse shot him the dark glare she liked to use when a person—usually a man—said something stupid.

Chub shrugged his shoulders and popped open his soda. He leaned against the conference table and sipped the drink as Susan whispered little words of encouragement to her son.

"He was saying something earlier, real softly," Chub said. "He kept saying it over and over like one of those phrases the Indians use. What do they call it?"

"A mantra?" she asked.

"That's it—a mantra. He kept saying, 'All right soon, all right soon, all right soon,'" he said. "This went on for about an hour, and we couldn't get him to snap out of it. So we called you."

Susan smiled at her son and rubbed the back of his neck with one hand while her other hand tipped the Coke can against his lips.

"That's a line from his favorite Dakota Marx song," she said. "He's a big fan."

Digby was starting to get some color back in his face. He burped softly as his mother pulled the Coke away and wiped his chin with a shirtsleeve.

"He gonna be all right?" Chub asked.

"Well, it's a little hard to tell, since he's obviously traumatized," she said as evenly as she could manage. "The question I have for you is, what did you do to my boy to put him in this state?"

The contractor pulled a swivel chair from behind his desk and sat with a soft grunt. He crossed one leg over the other so that one tasseled loafer was pointing in her direction. Looks wise, he was nothing special: short and stumpy with a fringe of gray hair around a bald dome and a sad, jowly face. But the guy had that blasé, chief executive manner about him, as if the world was his personal crapper and it was everyone else's job to wipe his ass. He was the most fraudulent form of male, all brassy and bossy and cock-of-the-walk, but wheel him into the clinic with a busted knee or a slipped disc, or, better yet, have him bend over for her rubber-glove-and-KY treatment, and she'd bet two-week's salary he'd be sobbing like Tammy Faye Baker in a Barbara Walters interview.

"It's not what we did to Digby," he said calmly, almost smugly. "It's what Digby did to one of our workers."

The contractor went on to explain how Digby wound up with a piece of Drag-Ass's earlobe in his mouth, which led to a brief tangent on corporate liability and workers disability.

"Bullshit," she finally said. "My boy wouldn't bite a man's ear off."

"I got at least ten workers who *saw* him bite a man's ear off," the contractor said. "Jiminy Christmas, look at the blood stains on him."

She looked at her son's T-shirt and noticed for the first time that half of Yosemite Sam was covered in crusty burgundy. She remembered the clinic staff wheeling in that long-haired freak clutching the side of his head and screaming bloody murder just a few minutes before she got the call from Chub Hughes.

"Well, somebody must have done something," she said. "He wouldn't do this unprovoked."

The contractor nodded and brushed a microscopic piece of lint from his khaki slacks.

"Look, I'm not going to read you the riot act," he said. "Fact is, we like Digby. We think he's doing a great job. The workers—most of them—think he's a great guy.

"It's just that, well, the road crew can be tough sledding. Some of the guys may not take into consideration that a kid like Digby is different. Hell, some of 'em are probably borderline retarded themselves."

He quickly restrained a chuckle upon seeing the nurse's scowl.

"Anyway, I'd like to propose a new arrangement. Since I'm personally fond of Digby and the crew can be a little rough, I'd like to assign him to special duty as executive assistant to the general contractor, who is, of course, me."

She said nothing. If this guy was expecting Susan Willers to hurl herself to the floor in gratitude, he had another thing coming. In fact, she was thinking about hurling something else as she took in his self-satisfied smirk. He was lucky there were no table lamps in easy reach.

"Hey, he'll work the rest of the summer in air-conditioned comfort!" Chub said.

She let the contractor sit there for a few beats with that dumb grin on his face. This pious bastard thought he was doing her some kind of a favor.

"If you think," she said, "that I would have my son work another minute with these fucking animals, then you don't know me or my son very well, Mr. Hughes. I've seen enough of your crew, parading around with their shirts off and listening to their jungle music. I was against Digby working here from the start, and coming down here seals the deal. It's no place for a child to be."

"Well, I—"

"Well, you've said enough!" Her massive chest was heaving now as if it might burst any moment from its monarch-blue top. "Be thankful, Mr. Hughes, that we are not the litigious type. Although I might reserve judgment on that until we get Digby's CT scans back from the lab."

She held out her hand, which was the signal for Digby to grab it and follow her. Dazed though he was, he took the hand and meekly trailed her out the door.

"What is it?"

Caller ID was the mayor's favorite invention of the past two decades. It not only told him who was calling, thus allowing him to escape frivolous conversations with one of Margaret's mahjong buddies or an angry voter, but also helped him to skip inane greetings and get right to the damn point.

This evening's caller, Chub Hughes, would understand. He wasn't much for small talk himself.

"We got a problem," the contractor said.

The mayor muted his TV, which beamed a History Channel documentary on Luftwaffe bombers.

"I'm listening."

Hughes sighed heavily, indicating that this was particularly painful news.

"The Willers kid."

"Yes?"

"There was an incident on the road crew. His mother took him off the site today and he's not coming back."

"Not coming back?" The mayor shifted his lounger to an upright position.

"I don't think so. No sir."

The mayor glanced at the cuckoo clock that hung over the television. Nearly eleven. Hughes wouldn't call this late unless it was something dire, like al Qaeda bombing City Hall.

"Now hold on, Chub," he said. "What kind of an incident happened today?"

Chub explained Digby's unprovoked attack and how his mom came and raised all sorts of hell.

"I've been trying to get her on the phone ever since, but she won't pick up."

"Well, try her again."

"Pardon?"

"I said, 'Try her again,'" the mayor said. "I don't care if you have to bump the kid up to general contractor. Just get him back to work."

"Look, Roe. The kid bit a guy's ear off today. Bit the earlobe clean off. Took three men to get Digby off him, and blood was everywhere." Chub sighed again. "And the mother's just impossible to deal with. A crazy woman. They're just not very good people, Roe."

The mayor felt a throbbing that started in his chest and ran down his left arm. He didn't like being questioned. It was bad for his heart.

"I'm sure he was provoked. Digby wouldn't hurt a fly."

"Roe—"

"He's the one, dammit! I know it!" he yelled. "Now get on the telephone and get him back to work!"

Chub mumbled something reluctantly affirmative before hanging up.

The mayor breathed deeply before setting the cordless phone in its cradle next to his chair. After a minute or so, the throbbing went away. One damn thing after another, he thought. If it wasn't his heart, it was his knees. If it wasn't his knees, it was the chronic bronchitis that had reared up about a year ago.

Not what it's cracked up to be, life in your ninth decade, he thought with a bitter smile. The doctor appointments every other week, the aches and pains that never stopped, the pills that lined his medicine cabinet like soldiers on parade—all were testaments to his waning mortality.

"Aw, screw it."

He eased the chair into a reclining position, cranked up the volume, and drifted off to the high-pitched whines of Stukas dive-bombing Warsaw.

CHAPTER 16

After scanning the crowd to make sure no one was looking, Pete Schaefer raised his pen to his nose and took a little sniff. Sharpies had a strong ammonia smell that never failed to give his olfactory nerves a jolt. It was a little trick he sometimes employed for sleep-inducing events like this one—the groundbreaking ceremony for The Historic Lewis and Clark Land Bridge and Dragon's Ice House Park.

Up on the podium sat old Roe Tolliver and a cast of Pridemore luminaries, including *Headlight* publisher Larry Truesdale. Some of them stifled yawns as a pasty-faced professor rattled on about how, if Lewis and Clark had possessed the foresight to make their historic passage through Pridemore County, they probably would have gotten to the West Coast a day or two earlier. Sadly, they hadn't.

"Many believe Meriwether Lewis killed himself because he thought his dream of finding a water route to the Pacific was a failure," the professor said. "In spite of such a sad ending, he was a very brave man."

"That's what bravery'll get you," whispered Rhett Blauser, the *Headlight*'s sloth-like photographer and nobody's idea of a brave man.

Pete managed a smile. He had been up half the night trying to make the final round of "Grand Larceny II: Intend to Defraud" on his phone, and his head was still swimming with fund misappropriations and tax shelter schemes.

The professor finally surrendered the podium to the mayor, who waved at the crowd of thirty or so onlookers with a thickly veined hand. He was wearing his signature American flag tie and an olive suit that looked too big for his frame. The mayor seemed to have aged a lot in the past year, and, as he walked slowly but determinedly to the podium, Pete thought about old footage he'd seen of sickly Soviet premiers saluting the troops at the May Day Parade. It was as though a whole era was passing before his eyes.

Once at the podium, however, the mayor cast a broad grin of yellowed teeth at the crowd. His voice, after a few initial crackles, flowed smooth and strong.

Roe Tolliver was in his element, and, though the ceremony recognized a project that involved state funding, a team of architects, and hundreds of workers, he was sure to pepper his speech with plenty of "I's" and "me's."

"Today I'm as proud as a turtle sitting on a fence post. You kind of figure that turtle didn't get to such a lofty height all by himself," he said. "Today, we're all turtles."

Pete didn't know what the hell that meant, but he jotted it in his notebook. He also had his tape recorder running in case the mayor wanted to quibble about his quotes in tomorrow's paper.

"My friends, these haven't been the easiest of times for our little town," the mayor said with a frown. "Some of my critics have described this project as impractical, as a boondoggle."

Pete looked over at Bryan London, who sat to the mayor's right and whose face was its usual shade of crimson. London, of course, had opposed the project. And now he paid the price of public humiliation, something to which he'd grown accustomed in twenty years as the mayor's rival.

"You know, the hardest thing to do in times of trouble is hold tight to your dreams," the mayor said.

At least it was a pretty day, Pete thought as he scribbled in his notebook. It was gorgeous, in fact—upper sixties, not a cloud in the sky. It was one of those April days, just after the time change, when Pete liked to get home early and walk the streets around his apartment building. It was a working-class neighborhood where the housing stock wasn't the best, but people took care of what they owned. The yards were neatly trimmed with tulip bulbs and daylilies poking out of garden beds. Kids rode bikes up and down the street or chased each other through the sprinklers. Aromas of freshly cut grass and burning charcoal reminded Pete of backyard football games and blackened hamburger patties on Wonder Bread buns. He was almost relieved to remember such things, even as he ate fast food over the coffee table he'd fashioned by stapling an oversized chessboard to a plastic plant pot.

The speech was winding down. The platform and podium faced the sun, so that everyone onstage wore crimpled brows that suggested either too many rays or severe incontinence. Everyone except the mayor, who stared into the light with such blissful certainty that Pete wouldn't have been shocked if the man began levitating toward the heavens. Guess the old buzzard's happy for things to get started, he thought.

The mayor led the dignitaries to the threshold of the soon-to-be-paved trail that would wind its way under the Lewis and Clark Land Bridge and terminate at Dragon's Ice House. There, he used a chromium shovel to scrape a handful of soil from ground hardened by an unusually dry spring. The others followed suit, one by one, until the ceremony concluded and everyone was asked to stick around for cookies and punch. It was an ideal time, Pete thought, to approach some of the town's bigwigs with a few questions.

"Peter!" The mayor draped his arm over the reporter's shoulders like he was a dear, old friend. "How are you, my boy?"

This came as a surprise, since Pete's last exchange with Tolliver had involved a stern lecture on the difference between "on the record" and "off the record." Now they were buddies again, and the mixed scent of mothballs and Bengay overpowered Pete as the mayor pulled him close.

"You like my speech?"

"Yes, very much," Pete said, slowly wrenching himself from the mayor's grasp. "There's just a couple of things I'm confused about."

"You know, you're standing right where we're going to put a visitor's center with a little museum on Lewis and Clark. Gonna have a thousand square feet of artifacts and exhibits."

"Really? Well, that kind of relates to what I was going to ask."

"All right." The mayor swayed back on his heels, both hands clasped behind his back.

"I've, uh, looked at the plans and artist's renderings and everything," Pete said. "But you still haven't told me what part of the city budget is going to pay for all of this."

The mayor frowned at the little black tape recorder Pete had pulled from his jeans pocket. "You really need that thing?"

"The way I figure it, the city's got to come up with four million for this project," Pete said. "But nobody can tell me where that money's coming from."

He'd finally asked The Question. *How the hell are you going to pay for this?* His skinny chest swelled a tiny bit. For the first time in months, Pete felt like a real reporter doing a real news story.

His subject frowned, then quickly switched to an expression of grandfatherly amusement.

"It's all very simple, Pete. And if you'll come by my office first thing Monday, I'd be happy to explain it to you."

He put out a knotty hand and squeezed Pete's shoulder with surprising force.

"But it's far too pretty a day to be mulling over assets and liabilities," he said. "Let's enjoy it, shall we?"

Before Pete got in another word, the mayor introduced him to the pasty-faced professor, who embarked, as if on cue, on a ten-minute lecture about how construction of the Hannibal Bridge in eighteen-whatever made Kansas City an economic force. By the time he was done, the mayor was yards away, courting a couple of state senators and grinning like he was atop the tallest fence post in the county.

PART III

SUMMER

CHAPTER 17

Digby awoke to the sound of someone coughing uncontrollably. It came from downstairs.

He rubbed his eyes and looked at the skinny black arms on his Mickey Mouse alarm clock, which read a quarter past three in the morning. His mother was on the night shift and wouldn't be home until breakfast time. He heard the hacking cough again and realized there was a stranger in the house.

He froze, too spooked to pull the sheet over his head. The light in the downstairs den was on, and, once the hacking stopped, he heard two men talking.

"If he can't do it, I don't know who can," one voice said.

"Dammit, he's just a kid," said the other. "You don't send a kid in to do a man's job."

"I suppose you know somebody better?"

"I can think of a few."

"Then name 'em," the first voice challenged. "Name a man who can do it better than Digby Willers."

Digby shuddered at the mention of his name. His eyes scanned the dark bedroom for something to use as a weapon. A baseball bat, never used for anything more than hitting rocks over the neighbor's fence, leaned near a pile of dirty clothes in his closet. A bowling-pin lamp stood on the dresser, and a softball-sized paperweight rested atop a stack of comic books on his desk.

"Let's go up and see what he thinks," said the man with the hacking cough, who apparently was Digby's friend in this argument. "Then you'll have your answer."

Two feet creaked up the stairs, accompanied by a cadence of heavy breathing. Digby stared across the room, trying to will himself to leap out of bed, grab the baseball bat, and beat the intruder to a pulp. His body would not respond. He lay paralyzed beneath the sheet, sweat rolling slowly down his neck. He silently prayed that, by lying very still, he somehow would become invisible to whoever was coming up the stairs.

The stranger stood in the doorway, a tall silhouette with a baseball cap perched high on his head. Smoke curled around him, and Digby recognized the cherry of a burning cigar in his hand.

"Hello, son."

The man ran his hand along the wall until he found a light switch. Sudden brightness made Digby blink once or twice before he settled his eyes on the gray, wrinkled face of the mayor of Pridemore.

"Remember me?" the old man said, sitting on the edge of the bed.

Digby nodded, feeling a little more at ease, though he couldn't imagine what brought the mayor to his house in the middle of the night.

"Where's my mom?" he asked softly.

"Your mother's working. She won't be home until seven-thirty."

"Does she...." He rubbed his forehead and tried to the think of the right words. "Does she know you're here?"

"Oh, certainly," the mayor said, smiling. "Certainly she does."

He puffed his cigar and stared thoughtfully at the model planes hanging from the ceiling. Digby had worked at City Hall for more than a year, but he couldn't recall seeing the mayor smoke.

"Do you know why I'm here?" the mayor asked.

Digby vigorously shook his head to indicate that he hadn't the faintest idea.

The mayor chuckled and squeezed Digby's leg. "Well, maybe you'd better put on some clothes and join us downstairs."

Digby pulled on shorts and a shirt from his dirty clothes pile. He followed the mayor to the den, where two other men sat on the big sofa with the faded floral pattern. Digby recognized one of them as his boss from the construction site. He'd seen the other man around town—a handsome guy with wavy hair—but couldn't recall his name.

"You remember Mr. Hughes," the mayor said.

"Hey there, Digby," said his old boss, wearing an odd-fitting smile. "Nice seeing you again."

"And this gentleman," the mayor continued, "is Mr. Truesdale."

The handsome guy gripped Digby's hand and pulled him close. He smells nice, Digby thought.

The mayor sank into a leather lounger, letting out a small fart in the process. He took a puff from his cigar before setting it on the edge of the coffee table.

"I guess you're wondering why these three fools came to visit you tonight?"

Digby nodded.

"Well, I can assure you we wouldn't come here at o-dark-thirty if it wasn't absolutely, positively necessary. You understand that, don't you?"

"Sure," Digby said, though he didn't understand at all.

"Why don't you have a seat?" the mayor said, motioning for his friends to make room on the sofa. Digby slowly lowered himself between the two men, half-expecting a trapdoor to open or three hundred volts of electricity to surge through his body. He was grateful when his bottom sank into a comfortable sofa cushion instead.

The mayor groaned as if it had been a very long day. He was strangely dressed for three in the morning; along with the baseball hat, he wore a dark brown suit with a tie that looked like someone had run an American flag through a paper shredder. Digby noticed that the mayor's pants and shoes were splattered with mud.

"We're friends, aren't we, Digby?" the mayor said. "I mean, we've known each other a long time, haven't we?"

"I guess."

"You know that I would never steer you wrong."

Digby thought for a moment about the many times he'd brought mail to the mayor's office and how the old man almost always had a Baby Ruth or a Kit-Kat bar waiting in his desk drawer. When the mail room job went away, the mayor had put in a good word for him with Mr. Hughes. Yes, Digby decided, Mayor Tolliver was a person he could trust.

"Sure," he said.

"That's good," the mayor said. "Because what I'm going to ask you to do will sound strange, maybe even dangerous. But you're going to have to have faith that ol' Roe Tolliver would never intentionally put you in harm's way."

"Okay."

The mayor leaned forward so that he was balanced on the edge of the lounger. Digby and the two men leaned in, too, like football players huddling up for the next play.

"We've received information from a very reliable source," the mayor said, "that a bomb has been planted somewhere inside the Dragon's Ice House."

He said this so gravely that it sent a chill up Digby's back. It was the kind of news that left you gasping for something to say, like when his mother sat him down and explained that his father no longer loved them and would never, ever come home.

"Now this is probably somebody's idea of a practical joke," the mayor said. "You'd be surprised how many bomb threats we get at City Hall."

The other two men nodded solemnly.

"But we have to check out every one of these threats," he said. "And there's something about the level of detail on this one that makes you sort of wonder if it's for real."

As if on cue, Chub Hughes pulled some paper from his breast pocket. He explained that it was a diagrammed map of Dragon's Ice House and the surrounding area. He pointed a stubby finger at an "X" someone had drawn in Magic Marker, marking a spot deep within the meandering cave.

"I found this in my office early this morning," Hughes said. "With a note explaining about the bomb and that we have forty-eight hours before it goes off. That 'X' is supposed to be where we'll find the bomb."

The mayor rose with a grunt and strode across the room. He stopped near the fireplace mantel, which held an array of framed photos from Digby's childhood years.

"It makes sense, when you think about it," he said. "Not everyone in this town shares my vision to turn Dragon's Ice House into one of central Missouri's premier tourist destinations. Some folks, frankly, are dead-set against it.

"A well-placed bomb would blow the whole place to smithereens. Bye-bye, Dragon's Ice House! Bye-bye, last, best chance to do something great for Pridemore!"

He shot Digby a worried look.

"Who knows?" he whispered. "It might be al Qaeda."

The mayor picked up a photograph. It was a studio shot of two-year-old Digby, ankle-deep in shag carpet and grinning as he held a red rubber ball.

"That's where you come in," the old man said.

Digby suddenly felt ill. Dragon's Ice House was a place he had visited frequently during his stint on M&M Construction

Co.'s road crew. Most days, he'd eaten lunch up there to get away from Travis and the other guys who made fun of him. He realized now that these men had come in the middle of the night to arrest him, and it took all his strength to keep from bursting into tears and begging for his life.

"I don't know nothing about a bomb," he said.

The men looked at each other and chuckled.

"I don't!"

Truesdale smiled and patted Digby's knee.

"We know you don't," he said.

The mayor unleashed a hacking cough and spit into a handkerchief.

"You're not a suspect, Digby. But we know you've spent an awful lot of time in and around those caves. Probably no one in Pridemore knows their way around them as well as you."

Digby wanted to tell the mayor that he, in fact, was terrified of the caves, daring only to peer once or twice into the pitch-black nothingness of the Ice House before scurrying back down the trail. But he said nothing. He didn't want to disappoint the mayor and his friends.

"We need someone who's brave enough and strong enough to crawl through that cave and tell us where the bomb is—if there is a bomb—so we can send some people in there to disarm it."

The mayor suddenly clapped his hands and smiled, as if hunting for bombs in a closely confined network of caverns was his idea of a grand time.

"I'd do it myself, you understand. But I'm getting a little long in the tooth for these kinds of things."

Digby sat there, overwhelmed. Part of him was glad that the mayor thought enough of him to offer this important mission. Another part imagined the snakes, spiders, and other creepy things he'd encounter crawling through the Dragon's

Ice House. He wished his mother were here to tell him what he should do.

The mayor leaned over him now, peering at him with eyes as blue as a cloudless sky.

"What do you say, Digby? Will you do this for us?"

The men looked at him. The handsome one, Truesdale, placed a hand on his shoulder and gently squeezed.

"Will you do this for me?" the mayor asked.

Digby rubbed the sleep from his eyes and thought how nice it would be just to pad his way upstairs and go back to bed. He would burrow under the covers, leaving only a tiny crease through which to breathe. It was his firm belief that, if you shielded your entire body with a bedsheet, you could go undetected by the outside world and the troubles that came with it. Digby could kick himself for not covering his head the instant he heard the mayor creaking up the stairs.

Too late for that now. He thought about what his all-time favorite hero, Dakota Marx, would do in this kind of situation. There was a movie coming out this summer called *Banzai Nights 2* in which Dakota was a police detective who rescued kidnapped children and, judging from the previews, also wore a lot of tight-fitting leather outfits. It was supposed to be even better than the first *Banzai Nights*, in which Dakota heroically landed a passenger plane that had been taken over by a bunch of ninjas.

Digby figured Dakota would jump at a chance to find a hidden bomb and probably would even insist on shooting the thing into outer space so no one would be killed when it exploded. This wasn't the movies, of course, but the least Digby could do was crawl through a cave and find out if there was even a bomb or not. And there probably wasn't, the mayor reminded him.

It was what Dakota would want, and it would make his mother proud. Still, his lip quivered as he looked at the three men and gave them his decision.

CHAPTER 18

About three football fields from the mouth of Dragon's Ice House, in a thicket where a man could safely hide even on a moon-bathed night, Berry B. Duncan sat in his camp chair, thumbing through a paperback of *The Fountainhead* by flashlight. He'd read it more than a dozen times since college, where he had "discovered" Ayn Rand. He kept coming back to it, along with *Atlas Shrugged* and a few other favorites. There was something about the individual's triumph over the proletarian masses that always got his juices flowing. And the heroes of Rand's books were always redheads, just like Berry.

As ballistics expert for Region 7 of the Southern Missouri Paramilitary Freedom Corps, Berry Duncan knew firsthand how one individual's spirit and creativity could knock down walls, in addition to office buildings, radio towers, military barracks, and aging suspension bridges. He received most of his demolition training in the US Army's Long Range Reconnaissance Patrol back in the 1960s. For four years, Berry had roamed the Vietnamese and Cambodian countryside, blowing up enemy convoys, ammunition dumps, gunboats, and whatever else Uncle Sam had in mind. The Lurps, as they called themselves, were real tough mothers, strapping themselves to palm trees and sometimes waiting days for Charlie to show up. They made Berry more than just a trained assassin. The Lurps made him a man.

He received a Purple Heart and an honorable discharge in '69 after a putty bomb he tossed into a Vietcong tunnel exploded prematurely. In the waning years of the Vietnam War, most GIs couldn't wait to finish their tours of duty. Berry cried for three days after his. He called it "the day the music died."

Berry bounced from town to town before settling into the Southern Missouri Paramilitary Freedom Corps in the late 1980s. While not exactly active duty, it was a nice escape from his day job at a chicken plant in Sikesville. And it's where Chub Hughes found him. The Freedom Corps, always in need of cash, sometimes contracted out its members for special projects. Berry jumped at the assignment. The idea of blasting a Missouri cave dating back to the Ice Age was intriguing, a chance to match wits against something that literally took millions of years to build.

The job required months of prep work. Berry'd spent entire days in that damn cave, finding just the right pressure points in the limestone to plant his explosives. He had to figure the precise amount of TNT to blast the cave entrance without harming the structural integrity of the interior caverns or scaring the crap out of the farmers who lived nearby. In the end, he decided on three 500-foot spools of PETN-filled detonating cord and more than 20 pounds of dynamite. He hoped it was enough: there was always a fair amount of guesswork in these sorts of jobs.

He looked at his watch. For four hours, he'd sat in the dewy leaves with his firing plunger and a walkie-talkie, awaiting the signal to blow a cloud of limestone powder toward the sky. His lone companion, save for Ayn, was a runt of a man named Rufus. The guy was a used-car salesman or something. Liked to brag about his National Guard service and strut around in the brand-new hunting camos he'd probably bought from Bass Pro Shop. A real power tool, Berry thought. But he kept that to himself. The client wanted someone tailing Berry to make sure the job was done right, and that was okay by him. Like his barbershop father used to say, the customer always knows best, even when he really doesn't.

Still, Berry couldn't help thinking, as Rufus snored the hours away curled in his Eddie Bauer sleeping bag, how easy it would be to walk up to the car dealer and calmly, quickly slit his throat. He could do it without even waking the guy up.

"Rufus?"

No response.

"Rufus!"

The little man rolled toward Berry, uncorking a snort that sounded like a refrigerator dragged across a linoleum floor.

Berry picked up a pebble and hurled it, beaning Rufus square in the head. He woke with a yelp, and Berry shone the flashlight in his face.

"Now that I have your attention," he said, "do you mind telling me when we can blow this noodle stand and go home?"

Rufus rubbed his face and nodded toward an ancient oak.

"That tree knows as much about this damned charade as I do," he said. "Probably more."

Berry doubted that. The car dealer might have been out of his element, but he carried himself in a chest-thumping way that told the world he was a man in charge. Rufus probably insisted on knowing everything that was going on. Berry had only met two of the characters behind this scheme—Rufus and Chub Hughes—and he didn't care to know anyone else, or why someone would want to blow up Dragon's Ice House in the first place.

It was better not knowing. It kept his mind on the task at hand. Berry had learned long ago that you only knew what you needed to know on jobs like this. Once a month since September, he unlocked his post office box and retrieved an envelope thick with $6,000 cash and a coded letter with the latest instructions. The client had insisted on doing business with as little personal contact as possible, which was fine with Berry as long as the cash arrived on time.

The last envelope was an especially bulky one, containing a walkie-talkie and a one-page note instructing him to camp near Dragon's Ice House with his firing plunger at the ready on Memorial Day weekend. That meant it was go time.

But when, exactly? Berry checked his watch. It was 5:35 a.m., less than an hour from twilight.

He nodded toward the wooded horizon.

"First hint of sunlight through those trees," he said, "and I'm out of here."

Rufus nodded like he was of a similar mind.

"The hell are we doing, anyway?" Berry asked.

Rufus said nothing. Just looked in the distance and smiled. There was something in the man's smirk that Berry didn't like. Calmly, slowly, he pulled a hunting knife from his belt, walked behind Rufus, and wrapped a forearm around his neck. His other hand held the knife against the car dealer's cheek.

"I asked you a question," he said. "What are we doing here?"

Years of reconnaissance experience gave Berry a sense of whether he could break a man's spirit. Rufus, he correctly guessed, was an easy mark.

"The mayor's behind it," he gasped. "It's all his plan."

"That's not what I heard."

"I swear to God it's true."

"I hear this was your idea," Berry growled. "That you're the brains behind this operation."

"Please don't kill me," Rufus said. "I got a wife and kids."

"Who is Howard Roark?"

"Wha—?"

Berry pressed the blade deeper into the man's neck.

"Who does Howard Roark work for?"

"I swear on my kids' graves, I don't know what the fuck you're talking about."

144

Berry released Rufus from his grip so suddenly that the man went headfirst into a lilac bush.

"Howard Roark," Berry said.

Rufus sat up and brushed the leaves from his hunting outfit.

"Huh?"

"He's an architect. Main character in a little book called *The Fountainhead*." Berry tossed the paperback toward Rufus. "Maybe you should read it sometime."

He cackled as if Rufus were the butt of a wonderful joke. A little over the top, Berry knew, but what the hell? He was bored and his tail was sore from four hours in the damn camp chair, and if Rufus thought he was a few oars short of a dinghy, then so what?

"You're fucking certified, man," Rufus said. "You're nutso."

Berry was about to argue to the contrary when his walkie-talkie crackled with a man's voice.

"Golden Eagle to Lost Bear. Golden Eagle to Lost Bear. Come in…"

Berry frowned. Golden Eagle's voice was gravelly and had a twang to it. Berry had expected the deep monotone of Chub Hughes. He glanced at Rufus, who nodded that everything was kosher.

"This is Lost Bear," Berry said. "We thought you'd stood us up."

"Never mind that, Lost Bear. Are you ready for some skinny dipping?"

"We're in our skivvies and ready to play. Just give the word."

There was a pause on the other end of the walkie-talkie.

"You there, Eagle?" Berry asked.

"The coast is clear," the voice said. *"Come on down to the swimming hole."*

Berry grinned. "I read you, Eagle. We'll be there momentarily. Out."

He shut off the walkie-talkie and slipped it into his backpack. Then he picked up the firing plunger and made sure everything was wired correctly. It was a rather innocuous-looking piece of equipment: no bigger than a shoebox and made mostly of plastic. But the spring-loaded gadget could bring down bridges if wired to the proper amount of explosives. By pressing the palm-sized button, Berry would shoot electronic currents along two coils of wire that would detonate the cave in about a second. So long, Dragon's Ice House.

He crouched like a baseball catcher in front of the plunger, listening to the birds beginning to stir in the trees above, looking at the first hint of sun through the branches. In seconds, those birds would take flight. It was a moment every demolitionist savored.

"I sure wish I knew what this was all about," he said.

"You and me both," Rufus said with a not-too-convincing shrug.

Berry pressed the button. A heartbeat later, the ground shuddered with two tremendous blasts. There was just enough daylight to see a wall of dust rise from the cave's entrance. The ground continued to tremor under the stress of rocks settling into the rubble. For a moment, Berry wondered if the earth beneath him might collapse into some prehistoric cavern far below. It was an exhilarating moment.

Then it was over. The birds settled. The dust cleared. And the forest looked as it had before the blast. Berry would have liked nothing more than to walk down to the cave entrance and assess his work. But that would be imprudent. Instead, he packed his equipment into his backpack and an oversized duffle bag, both of which he would later toss into a far-off lake.

Rufus sat with his knees tucked under his camouflage jacket, still taking it in.

"That," he said, "was awesome."

"Not a bad way to make a living, eh?"

"I think I'm deaf in my right ear."

"It'll wear off in a few hours."

"You think so?"

Berry zipped his duffle bag, swung the backpack over his shoulders, and scanned the area to make sure he left nothing behind. He waited for Rufus to stand up, and the two men shook hands.

"Well, I'm off," Berry said. "I advise you to get a move on as well."

He walked in the opposite direction of the cave entrance, through a part of the forest where the underbrush was neck high. His Ford pickup was parked on a dirt road about half a mile away. He would head east on Interstate 70, stop in St. Louis for a quick visit with his Aunt Linda, and maybe grab a burger from Jack in the Box. That would put him back home in Sikesville by nightfall. There, he would quietly wait for his final payment to show up at the post office.

Digby didn't know what hit him. One instant, he was slogging through a muddy cavern, feeling his way around the waxy cones that drooped from the ceiling. The next, he was flying headfirst through the musty air. He didn't know what caused the cataclysmic bang that set his ears ringing or the eruption that made the ground give way beneath him. All he knew was, for a moment, he was airborne through no voluntary act of his own.

Then he landed face-first in the mud. After a few seconds of groping all his extremities to make sure nothing was missing, Digby crawled onto his hands and knees, fished his flashlight out of the muck, and found a dry place to sit and collect himself. His body shivered, though he wore three layers of clothes. Wrapping his arms tightly around his chest, he realized that he was crying.

They were deep, gasping sobs that left him short of breath—he hadn't cried like this since he was little. His ears were buzzing. His nose and mouth were filled with dust. He couldn't see more than two feet in front of him. He was lost in this dark place where probably no one would be able to find him. Not the mayor, not Mr. Hughes. Not even his mother, who always warned him to never, ever leave the house without checking with her first. The thought of defying her was almost as unbearable as the realization that he was utterly, maddeningly alone.

He sat in the glow of his flashlight, his mind latched onto this grim prospect. Every few minutes, he heard rocks colliding in some other part of the cave. He beamed his light against the cavern walls each time, expecting to see a massive boulder rolling his way.

The tremors grew faint and less frequent until they were little more than a rumble from time to time. Other than the settling dust, his portion of Dragon's Ice House seemed insulated from the explosion. For now.

Digby had traveled what seemed like a vast distance within the caverns and crawl spaces that made up the Ice House. The mayor and his friends had loaded him into the back seat of Mr. Hughes's SUV, delivering him a few minutes later to the cave entrance with a flashlight, a parka, a canteen, a backpack filled with power bars and M&Ms, and a bright yellow box with a receiver that the men called a cave radio. "Keep it turned on," the mayor told him, "so we can check in and track you at all times."

Those were the last words of advice before Digby crawled into the Ice House. Just a few feet in, he noticed a drop in temperature (so that's where it gets its name, he thought). The cave walls, wet and slimy, closed in on Digby as he advanced until there were only a few inches of wiggle room to spare. He stepped slowly, the mossy walls sometimes brushing his cheeks and causing a shudder to run down his spine. He could only imagine what kinds of strange creatures lived in this place.

"Pick it up, Digby," Mr. Hughes had yelled from outside the cave. "We don't have much time."

Digby felt like replying that he'd trade places if Mr. Hughes felt he could do better. But he sucked in his gut and carried on, eventually sliding though a narrow passageway and into a small cavern that Missouri spelunkers called the Living Room. It was like no living room he'd ever seen, filled with muck that slopped over the tops of his Dingo boots. And there was a moldy stench that reminded Digby of the unfinished part of his mother's basement, only ten times worse.

He'd heard a flutter and beamed his light in time to see something small flying directly toward his face. Digby covered his eyes and let out a scream that surprised him with its girlish pitch.

"What is it?" a voice called from the radio.

Another one flew past, missing his face by inches.

"These birds are attacking me," he said.

One of the men—Digby thought it was the mayor— chuckled through the frequency.

"Those are bats," he said.

Digby shivered. It was one of his worst fears realized. A bat had gotten into his house once, flying crazily around the bedroom ceiling until his mother trapped it in a wastebasket. Seeing its fangs and beady eyes up close was enough to give Digby nightmares for a full week.

"They won't hurt you," the mayor said. *"Ever heard the phrase, 'Blind as a bat'? It's true. They can't even see you."*

After he collected his senses, the men had told Digby to attempt what one of them called the Snake Crawl. This, Digby learned, was a good description. As he walked deeper into the Living Room, its walls narrowed until he found himself crawling on his belly through a tube of rock that, at some points, seemed barely wider than his torso. Crawling like a worm through mud that seeped into his mouth and eyes, he thought more than once about turning back and going home. But that would require him to crawl in reverse. So he pressed on, shining his flashlight into the blackness.

After what seemed like an eternity, he'd crawled out of the wormhole and into the cavern where he now sat after the blast, covered in mud and sobbing like a little baby. He could be thankful, at least, that he wasn't in the Snake Crawl when the bomb went off, which he imagined would have crushed him under several tons of rocks or, worse, left him breathing in a closed-off space no larger than a casket. He may be cut off from the world in this cavern, but he could breathe. He flashed his light around. The dust had settled enough for him to make out some of the features of his new home. In some places, the ceiling rose as high as twelve feet. He couldn't get a feel for how large the cavern was; his flashlight beamed only a few feet in any direction.

As if being practically blind weren't enough, Digby was also freezing. He pulled the mud-caked sleeves of his parka over his hands and hugged himself as tightly as he could, hoping to generate some warmth.

"*Digby?*"

It took him a few seconds, but he found the radio a few feet away and hoisted it from the slime.

"*Digby!*"

The mayor's voice, loud and clear. Digby's heart did a cartwheel. At least he wasn't entirely alone.

"Yessir?"

He heard what sounded like a sigh of relief from the other end.

"Thank God. Are you all right, Digby?"

"I think so."

"Nothing broken? You aren't in any pain?"

"No, sir."

"Good, good. Now, Digby, I want you to listen very carefully—"

"I'm sorry, Mr. Mayor."

"Sorry for what?"

"About the bomb. I musta crawled right past without seeing it."

Digby felt himself wanting to cry again. The mayor and his men had placed their trust in him, coming to his home in the middle of the night and practically begging for help, and he let them down. He failed, just as he failed to watch the cement spreader a few weeks ago and lost his job on the construction crew. Just as he failed to deliver on every job he ever had. There was a long pause before the mayor spoke.

"I'm the one who should apologize, Digby. It was irresponsible for me to put you in harm's way, and I don't expect you to forgive me."

Digby didn't understand how this could be the mayor's fault, but he decided not to argue the point.

"Well," he said, "all right."

"What's important right now is that you remain safe and conscious, and that we get you out of there just as soon as possible. And we will get you out. Understand?"

"Yessir."

"Here's what I need you to do, Digby," the mayor said. *"I need you to tell me exactly where in the cave you think you are."*

He thought for a moment about the long, cold journey and gave the mayor his best estimate.

"Very good. Do you think you could find your way back out the same the way you came in?"

The bomb had definitely gone off behind him. Which was where, exactly? Digby looked around with his flashlight, not seeing anything familiar. He wouldn't know where to start looking for a way out of here.

"I don't know," he said. "I could try."

A long pause.

"*Tell you what, Digby. I want you to shut off your radio and I want you to set it down.*"

"Okay."

"*Then I want you to stand up and scream just as loud and as hard as you can. Understand?*"

"Yessir."

"*And then after you've yelled and screamed for a couple of minutes, I want you to turn your radio back on and we'll talk some more.*"

"Mr. Mayor?"

"*Yes, Digby?*"

"What do you want me to scream?"

"*You scream anything your heart desires. You can scream a rendition of* The H.M.S. Pinafore, *for all I care.*"

Digby did what the mayor asked, setting the cave radio next to his feet, standing up as straight as he could, and then screaming the first thing that entered his mind.

"Shhhiiit!"

Over and over he screamed expletives until it seemed like a couple of minutes had passed. Screaming felt good after what he'd been through. It took his mind off things for a little bit. He was about to scream one last time for good measure when he heard a faint, muffled voice. The mayor was calling his name through what must have been several feet of rock.

"Digby? Can you hear me?"

He puffed out his chest and bellowed as loud as he could.

"Yes!"

The mayor told him to turn his radio back on, then said he thought that they could pinpoint Digby's location in the cave and get him out in a few hours.

"You're probably going to run low on your batteries pretty soon, so if you need to tell us anything, you just holler like there's no tomorrow, you hear?"

Digby said he'd do that. The mayor said he would have to go back into town to get some help, but that he'd be back shortly.

And just like that, Digby was alone again, though not quite as hopeless as before. The mayor would take care of things, he thought. The mayor had never let him down. He turned off the flashlight and radio, to save the batteries, and sat in the darkness, rubbing his arms to keep warm and singing his favorite Dakota Marx song in a quivering but brave voice.

"Things'll be all right soon," he sang to himself. But he wasn't sure he believed it this time.

CHAPTER 19

The mayor slipped the radio receiver into his coat pocket and made a mental note to dump the device when he got home.

"You did it, Roe," Truesdale said, his perfect teeth gleaming in the twilight.

"Did what?"

"Did *it*. I've gotta hand it to you. I had my doubts. But you pulled it off."

The mayor picked up the plastic cup he'd been carrying and spit a sizable wad into it. His old vices were with him tonight: cigars and chaw. Everything but alcohol, which he'd kept mostly under wraps for the past twenty years.

He looked down to see that Truesdale had extended his hand. The mayor shook it, though this was no time for congratulations.

"How's that old song go?" he said, starting to sing. "We've only just begun?"

"You got that right," said Chub Hughes, leaning against a tree. After the explosion, the three men had walked to the mouth of the Dragon's Ice House, which looked surprisingly unharmed. A few steps inside the crevice, however, revealed that one interior wall had collapsed against the other, effectively blocking the only way into the cave. Given the size of the explosion, Hughes estimated that rescuing Digby could require drilling through at least twenty feet of crumbled rock.

The contractor wore a particularly grim frown as he twisted a tree branch in his hands. "I've got a few concerns."

"Which are?"

"Well, for one thing, what happens when they dig the kid out of that cavern and find his radio?"

The mayor shrugged. "I don't know."

"Aren't they gonna wonder who he was talking to?"

"Perhaps."

"And what happens when Digby tells them how the mayor and two other men broke into his house in the middle of the night with some crazy-ass story about a bomb hidden in Dragon's Ice House?"

"Don't know," the mayor said. "It'll be interesting to see how that plays out, won't it?"

Hughes snapped the tree branch in half and flung the pieces into the woods.

"Glad to know you've thought this through," he said. "I'll be waiting in the car."

They watched Hughes trudge down the path, twigs and mulch crunching under his engineer boots.

"Gee," Truesdale said. "I've never seen Chub like that."

The mayor chuckled as he fished a plug of chaw from his bag of Red Man.

"Oh, he gets that way from time to time. He's scared, that's all. Thinking about all the what-ifs. Of course, it's a little late for second-guessing, isn't it?"

He stuffed the chaw firmly between his cheek and bridgework, enjoying the flavor for a moment before continuing.

"Digby Willers has the intellect of a little boy. He watches Saturday morning cartoons, leaves milk and cookies out for Santa Claus every Christmas Eve, and deeply believes that, if he tries hard enough, he can shoot adhesive strings from his wrists just like Spider-Man."

He spit out a string of tobacco.

"You remember being that age, Larry?"

"A little," he said. "All that mattered to me, at that age, were baseball cards and collecting enough proofs of purchase from Cheerios to get my own *Lost in Space* poster."

"Did anyone take you seriously?"

"No."

"And, if you were to speak one day of a conspiracy involving the mayor, a time bomb, a deep, dark cave, and two of Pridemore's most powerful businessmen, would anyone listen?"

"Probably not."

"That's a pity," the mayor said. "We could probably learn a lot from the imagination of a young boy, or a twenty-three-year-old who thinks like one."

Truesdale smiled wearily. Dawn had given way to daylight, and the mayor saw the circles under his friend's eyes. It had been a long night for both of them.

"His mother is kind of a head case, you know. She could be trouble."

"I'll worry about that. You worry about turning this into a national story."

The publisher nodded.

"I'm serious. Tomorrow I want to see it top-of-the-fold in the biggest bold-type you can print."

Truesdale put an arm around the mayor's shoulders and steered him along the trail that led to Hughes's SUV.

"It's as good as done," he said.

The mayor answered with a grunt. His body was like a rubber band wound up to the point of snapping, his muscles strained from all the running around he and the boys had done since six in the evening. He wanted nothing more than to collapse into bed for a week. But the adventure had just begun. In a few minutes, Chub would call the police dispatcher from a public phone and describe hearing a loud explosion near Dragon's Ice House. The cops would investigate, and the mayor figured *his* phone would start ringing around 8:00 a.m., first from Public Safety, then the county sheriff, then Stodemeyer, Treadwell, Chester Maddox, and all the other butt-smooching, sniveling sycophants who wanted their little piece of the glory.

From that moment, he'd be on call 24/7, answering reporters' questions, consulting emergency personnel, badgering the governor to send in the National Guard. He should be excited. He should be elated. This was what he'd worked toward for more than a year. But all he felt was the throbbing pain in his battered old knees from too much standing and too much moving around.

He glanced up. The sun was now over the trees, revealing a layer of fog that covered the ground like a lumpy down comforter. It was going to be a beautiful spring day. Sunny and seventy-five degrees.

The mayor leaned against a tree and wheezed heavily.

"You okay?" Truesdale asked.

"If we don't get back down to the car right now," he said, "you're going to have to carry me there."

CHAPTER 20

Pete Schaefer watched his cell phone ring through a pair of hazy eyes. He knew it was either his editor, Beatrice Reilly, or his mom. No one else called before eight o'clock on Saturday morning.

He picked up on the fourth ring. It was Beatrice.

"I'm listening to the police scanner," she said. "Something's happened at Dragon's Ice House."

"Yeah?"

"Somebody's trapped in the cave. Pretty sketchy info at this point, but cops are all over the place."

"All right."

"I want you out there," she said. "If it's something big, call me and we'll bump the press run back to get it in the paper."

Pete sat on the edge of his futon and blinked at the sunlight streaming through the window. He had planned to spend the morning trying out some new apps on his phone.

"Wouldn't this be more down Tom's alley?" he asked softly, referring to the *Headlight*'s veteran cops and courts reporter.

"He's fishing in Colorado, in case you forgot," she said. "You're my guy on this one."

Pete said nothing, hoping his silence spoke for itself.

"This could be a cool story, Peter," she said. "That's how you get ahead in this business. Do you really want to write obituaries and the crop index for the rest of your career?"

That would be a most definite "no," Pete thought. He thanked Beat for the assignment and placed the phone gently on the floor so he wouldn't wake the sleeping mass next to him. He tiptoed across the room and slipped on a golf shirt and a pair of wrinkled khakis.

"Where to?" asked the voice from the bed, accompanied by a luxuriant yawn.

"Dragon's Ice House," Pete said. "There's been some kind of accident. I might have to file a story on it."

He stopped short of adding that it was probably time for her to leave, too. They'd been flying pretty close to the sun lately. Her folks thought she was at a sleepover with the cheerleading squad. All it took was one phone call to blow that little ruse.

Pete sighed, knowing they would soon have to have another one of their talks. It was something he kept putting off like a dreaded item on the weekly to-do list. *Get milk... Change the oil... Break up with Angela.*

"I'll wait for you."

"Don't you have something better to do," he said, "than sit around my apartment all day?"

"Maybe I'll clean it. Except for the bathroom. You're on your own there."

"Angela."

"Maybe I'll go get coffee and doughnuts for when you get back."

He shot her a stare that was meant to be stern. Pete hated confrontation, so he hoped a dirty look would express the fact that he wanted her gone when he returned. He was prepared to say something if absolutely necessary. Somebody had to be the adult in this relationship, a responsibility that gnawed at him since they'd gotten back together in February. He never should have taken her back. It wasn't even fun anymore.

Angela apparently got the vibe, because she crawled out of bed and put on her shorts. He tried kissing her, but she turned away. Her eyes were getting puffy.

"Fuck you," she spat when he asked what was wrong.

She slammed the door and stomped angrily down the rickety stairs. He watched her march across the dandelion-strewn lawn and onto the sidewalk that led to her house less than a mile away.

Pete gulped down a half-empty Diet Coke and headed out the door, figuring the day could only get better.

He drove north on Old Highway 54, turning at the glossy new sign that proclaimed *Lewis & Clark Land Bridge—Dragon's Ice House Park, Next Right.* He drove about a mile on the newly paved blacktop before a sheriff's deputy in an orange vest waved him over.

"I need to get in there," he told the officer. "I'm a reporter with the *Pridemore Headlight.*"

"I don't care if you're with the *Daily Planet.* You'll have to park your car and hoof it the rest of the way."

Pete pulled off on the side of the road, behind a red pickup that he recognized as belonging to Rhett Blauser, the *Headlight's* photographer. It was rare for the indolent Blauser to beat him to an assignment, especially on a Saturday.

He walked until the trees lining both sides of the road gave way to a gravel-covered clearing. What would one day be a parking lot and information center for Pridemore's two natural wonders was, at the moment, a carnival of flashing red and blue lights. Pete counted two ambulances, three fire trucks, four sheriff's patrol cars, two Pridemore Public Safety cars, and more than a dozen vehicles belonging to volunteers of the Rural District 2 fire brigade. As with most emergency scenes that drew more personnel than needed, there was a lot of milling around. The firemen clumped about in their heavy gear, inspecting some gauges on the pumping trucks. The sheriff's deputies were busy closing off the entrance to the Lewis and Clark Land Bridge with yellow crime scene tape.

Most of the volunteers glumly sat on the tailgates of their Ford F-250s, waiting to be given something to do.

"What say you, Pete?"

He turned to find Rhett Blauser grinning down at him. About six-foot-four with long graying hair, a crooked mustache, and a T-shirt that barely covered his protruding gut, the photographer was like a shaggy dog you still loved no matter how many times he shit on the carpet.

"Don't know," Pete said. "I just got here."

"Well you haven't missed much. They're not letting us anywhere near the action. And nobody's saying squat."

The photographer looked over Pete's head and winced.

"Watch your back," he said. "Ernie Pyle at six o'clock."

Pete glanced over his shoulder to see Ferris Castleberry walking toward them in short, jerky strides. He carried a clunky black tape recorder that looked to be about half his own weight. Blauser called him Ernie Pyle because Castleberry had been a reporter at 1080 AM (the Home of Country Hitzz!) for as long as anyone could remember. And the excitable little man covered every assignment like it was the marines landing at Iwo Jima.

"What's the story here, boys?"

"They won't let us up there," Blauser said, nodding toward the entrance.

"I heard on the scanner that the cave collapsed and trapped a man inside," Castleberry said. "Sounds strange, don't it? Someone sneaking in that cave in the middle of the night."

"I dunno," the photographer said, a smirk crossing his face. "I paid a few midnight visits to the Ice House back in my youth."

"I'll bet you did, you old dog," Castleberry said. "I'll bet you weren't alone, either."

"Well...there was a bit of conjugal activity."

"Nice," Pete said. "Thanks for the mental image."

Blauser's smile widened. "Happy to oblige."

"Okay, boys," the radioman said. "Something's happening."

He nodded toward the park entrance, where Pridemore Chief of Public Safety Cole Turner had emerged from behind the yellow tape. Castleberry punched a button on his huge recording machine and whispered into the microphone: "Testing, testing, one-two, one-two! The quick brown fox jumped over the lazy hound..."

Chief Cole Turner was a grim, unsmiling man who more than made up for his lack of charm by possessing an ego the size of Mt. McKinley. The head of Pridemore Public Safety owned at least five official uniforms, including a royal blue number with enough ribbons and gold piping to make a Prussian general blush. He'd even been known to break out a swagger stick at ribbon cuttings and other formal events.

Today, Turner was dressed like a Navy Seal: black jacket, black pants tucked into black, shiny boots, and black utility belt holding a gun and other ominous devices, which were also black. As Pete and his colleagues approached him, the chief puffed out his chest like a gamecock spoiling for a fight. Because the Lewis and Clark Land Bridge and Dragon's Ice House had recently been annexed by the city of Pridemore, this was a Public Safety Department matter, and he called the shots.

"Chief, what's going on up there?" Blauser asked.

"What I can tell you right now is that a man ventured into the cave and is now trapped behind some rocks. We are assembling rescue personnel to get him out of the cave."

Pete rolled his eyes. The chief had a tendency to emit police dribble in a monotone voice that could make a triple homicide sound like a parking violation.

"Is the man hurt?" someone asked.

"There appear to be no serious injuries."

"How was he trapped?"

"There appear to have been some collapsed rocks that cut him off from the cave's entrance. Fortunately, we are able to communicate with him, and he appears to be in good condition."

"Can we go up there?" Blauser asked.

"No."

"When do you hope to have him out?"

"Difficult to say. As I said, we're assembling personnel and will have him out as soon as possible. But we have to take precautions."

"What's the man's name?" Pete asked.

"Pardon?"

"What's his name?" Ferris Castleberry asked.

"Uh, we're not giving out the identity at this time until the man's family is notified."

"Is he local?"

"How old is he?"

"What was he doing in that cave?"

"Can't give that information out," Turner said. "You'll have to—"

Whatever the chief said next was consumed by the machine-gun sputtering of a car that had long since parted ways with its muffler. A white Pontiac Fiero circled the parking lot at high speed, spitting a trail of dust and gravel before stopping a few feet from the nearest ambulance.

A big, round woman in blue hospital scrubs hopped from the car and stormed toward Chief Turner, her red-faced scowl instantly parting the throng of reporters. Two sheriff's deputies grabbed her by the armpits as she lunged for the chief, who had wrapped his arms around his head in a classic duck-and-cover.

"Where the fuck is he?" she screamed. "What have you done with my boy?"

Another deputy converged on the woman in time to take an elbow to the nose. She weighed three hundred pounds, Pete figured, but her arms were long and sinewy. They worked the cops over like the guns of a prizefighter, jabbing the rib cage, the lower back, and, when they had the chance, below the belt.

Four cops finally brought her down. She thrashed under their weight, spewing profanities between gasps for air.

"Cocksuckingmotherfuckingsonuvabitches. Get these apes offa me."

"Not before you calm down, miss," said Turner, regaining his cock-of-the-walk posture.

"I'm a RN, for fuck's sake," the woman said, still struggling. "I save lives."

"Ma'am—"

"I deliver babies."

"Okay, ma'am."

"You and your fucking storm troopers—"

"If you do not calm down," the chief said in a shrill voice, "we will take you to the stockade, where you can scream and kick and carry on for as long as you want."

This seemed to break her. She lay there, panting as the deputies held her to the ground. She apologized for the Nazi reference, and the brown-clad officers helped her up.

"Who are you?" Castleberry asked.

"I'm Susan Willers," she said, brushing dirt from her scrubs. She glared at the chief, but much of the fury was gone. She had bags under her eyes and long stringy hair that came out of its bun during the scuffle. She looked like she hadn't had a full night's sleep in weeks.

"My boy's the one who's in that cave."

"What's his name?" Pete asked.

"Digby," she said. "Digby Willers."

The reporters jotted this in their notebooks. Rhett Blauser snapped shots of the woman with his digital camera.

"I wouldn't report that, if I were you," Turner said. "Nothing's official until it comes from my office."

"You guys reporters?" the woman asked. "Boy, do I have a story to tell."

"We like stories," Castleberry said.

"Now, hold it!" the chief cried. "Hold it just one minute!"

He walked over to Susan Willers and placed a hand on her back.

"Mrs. Willers," he said, lowering his voice, "if you've got some information about this case, wouldn't you like to discuss it somewhere more private? You know, we might just know some things that would be useful to you, too."

"Is that a fact?"

"But we're not going to share it with you out here."

This seemed to rev her up again. Her dark eyes smoldered at the chief with a fresh batch of hate.

"Cole Turner," she said, "I've known you since you were a little punk hanging stray cats by their tails and shooting at them with your .22. And if you think for one minute that I am going to go sit in your patrol car and pour my heart out to you and beg you to come save the day on your big white stinking steed, then you're even more of a demented prick than the one I knew back in junior high!"

Pete didn't catch all of that, but he could tell from Turner's expression that he'd just been zinged. The chief quickly recovered, throwing his shoulders back and walking purposefully toward a group of EMTs behind the yellow tape.

Susan Willers brushed the rest of the dirt off her scrubs and gave the reporters a tired smile.

"Well, boys," she said. "Where should I begin?"

CHAPTER 21

The *Headlight* went to press late Saturday morning, about an hour before Pete could file his story. That meant his account of the rescue operation at Dragon's Ice House wouldn't hit newsstands until Monday afternoon since the *Headlight* didn't publish on Sundays.

Realizing her reporter had a fast-breaking story, Beatrice Reilly took the unusual step of posting Pete's article on the *Headlight*'s website (usually the sole domain of crop reports and high school sports scores). She also sent a condensed version to the wire services on Saturday afternoon. The story ran Sunday in most of the state's newspapers, including the *St. Louis Intelligencer*, the *Springfield Call*, and *The Kansas City Journal*. Though thrilled to see his work in the major dailies, Pete was a little discouraged at how the big-city editors cut and rewrote his copy. The truest version, the one he laminated and kept in his files for years to come, graced the front page of the nearby *Possum Trot Tribune* under the headline, "Cave Collapses, Traps Pridemore Man."

PRIDEMORE, Mo.—Emergency crews from three mid-Missouri counties converged Saturday in an effort to rescue a man trapped inside a cave.

Police would not confirm the identity of the man who, as of press-time, was trapped behind several feet of collapsed limestone inside Dragon's Ice House, a network of prehistoric caverns popular with tourists and area cave enthusiasts. Pridemore Public Safety Chief Cole Turner said on Saturday that the man is in good condition and is able to communicate through the obstruction with emergency workers.

"He does not appear to be in any immediate danger," Turner said. "We're calling in personnel who have expertise in this kind of rescue, and we hope to have him out of there in a few hours."

One Pridemore resident at the scene claimed to be the mother of the unidentified man. Susan Willers, 45, said she rushed to Dragon's Ice House after receiving a phone call from police informing her that her son, Digby Willers, was trapped in the cave.

The elder Willers, who is a registered nurse at the Pridemore County Hospital, said her son was missing when she returned home from a night shift at 7 a.m. Saturday. She suspected her son, who is 23 years old and mentally challenged, had been kidnapped.

"He is very trusting, very innocent," she said. "I know he wouldn't go into that cave all by his lonesome."

Turner said he could "neither confirm nor deny" that the man trapped in the cave was Digby Willers. He said police had no reason to believe an abduction had taken place.

Asked what might have caused the cave to collapse, Turner said he didn't know.

"We have top people looking into that," he said.

Dragon's Ice House and the Lewis and Clark Land Bridge were to be the centerpiece of a multimillion-dollar recreational park that Pridemore began constructing in early spring. Officials said work on the project, which includes $8 million in matching state funds, will resume once the rescue operation has concluded and a damage assessment can be made to the cave.

"This is just a temporary setback," said Charley Shall, president of the Greater Pridemore Chamber of Commerce. "Lewis and Clark sure didn't give up because of a setback, and neither will we."

The mayor began his Sunday morning at the Grab-n-Go, ordering a tall cup of decaffeinated coffee (black as always) and picking up every regional newspaper he could get his hands on.

Later, in his study, he laid the newspapers end to end across his big oak desk and opened each one to the page that carried Pete Schaefer's story. The big papers buried the article deep within their metro sections, while the rural rags tended to give it better play. The newspapers within a 100-mile radius of Pridemore reserved front-page space for the story, with bold-faced headlines.

Throw in the briefs that aired Saturday on a couple of Columbia TV stations, and you had a nice tally, the mayor thought, for day 1 of the Great Adventure. It was his idea to put the story out on the news wires to ensure that other newspapers picked it up, an order Larry Truesdale passed along to Beat Reilly. They were fortunate that the last Saturday in May was a bone-dry news day: other than a car wreck fatality in Wellington and a bass-fishing tournament in Rushville, there wasn't a lot going on. Small-town editors across the state were more than happy to play up a strange tale of a man trapped in a cave.

Now the hope was that the big-city TV stations would dispatch their reporters to the scene. That was key: the electronic media's involvement could spread the story like wildfire from affiliate to affiliate. With luck, and a shortage of bizarre crime stories coming out of the cities, Pridemore could be a national news story by the end of the weekend.

Roe Tolliver had good reason for selecting the last weekend in May to roll the proverbial dice. And that was because nothing of great note usually happened around Memorial Day, save for car accidents, the Indianapolis 500, and the obligatory feature stories on grumpy old war veterans.

The mayor wrapped his arms across his chest and giggled. A fat, juicy worm was dangling from his hook, he thought, waiting for a big fish to bite.

Of course, lots had happened since Schaefer filed his story on Saturday afternoon. Susan Willers screamed her damn fool head off until finally breaking down and cooperating with the police, who brought her to the Ice House to hear her son's muffled voice behind the layers of rock. Late in the day, a six-county task force converged to mount a rescue operation, adding to the impressive mass of emergency vehicles gathered around the site but getting very little accomplished in the way of actual rescuing. Fact was, Digby Willers was crouched behind twenty feet of limestone, and nothing short of a small mining operation was going to spring him. It would take time to assemble the right professionals and hardware for the job. The mayor put out a call to the governor to see if the state guard or the Army Corps of Engineers might lend a hand. But Missouri's chief executive was playing a charity golf tournament and couldn't be reached.

That afternoon, after the handful of media left to file their stories, Chief Turner led the mayor and city council president Rufus Stodemeyer down the meandering path beneath the Lewis and Clark Land Bridge, through a thicket of trees, and, finally, to Dragon's Ice House. A sheriff's deputy took them a few feet in to a cavern that ended abruptly in a collapsed mass of large rocks, some the size of a compact car. Three men wearing hard hats examined the mass with their flashlights. One of them was the city engineer for Fairsfield, a little burg about thirty miles away.

"What caused this?" the mayor asked.

"Could be anything," the engineer said. "My expertise is street design, not geology, but I don't believe it's unusual for caves to collapse from natural stress. Maybe even a small tremor. We're not too far from the New Madrid fault."

The mayor nodded solemnly.

"How do we get him out?"

"You'll need a hell of a lot more than what we got today," he said. "And you can't get any heavy machinery up here. You'll have to use rock drills, the hand-held kind. That could take days."

The engineer sighed. Even in the darkness, the mayor thought he saw weariness in the man's eyes.

A long, baleful moan came from somewhere behind the rocks. It lasted nearly a half a minute, rising to a pitch that made the mayor's ears tingle.

"That's him?" he asked.

"He does that from time to time," the engineer said. "We've been talking to him, trying to keep his spirits up, but the poor kid's confused."

"You can communicate with him through all that?" Stodemeyer asked.

"Lots of air pockets between the rocks," one of the other hard-hats said.

Another moan echoed into the cavern, so forlorn that it made the mayor wince. It was almost primal, the sound of an animal losing its will to fight.

"Jiminy Christmas," he said softly.

"You wanna say something to him?" Stodemeyer asked.

The mayor stared at the mass of rocks and shook his head. Roe Tolliver could be as cold and venomous as a southern Missouri diamondback, as many political rivals could attest, but he deplored human suffering. Couldn't stand it. Couldn't abide it even as a nineteen-year-old in the South Pacific, when his unit had captured a few starving Japanese soldiers and tied them to a cluster of palm trees until they could be transported off the island. He was the only GI who shared his rations that night with the Japs, and he felt bad that he couldn't do more.

No one, least of all that rat fink Stodemeyer, would ever believe it, but at that moment the mayor would have traded places with Digby Willers. He wanted to say something like that to the boy, but he didn't dare.

"Just get him out," he told the men.

CHAPTER 22

Digby had long since adapted to the dried mud that covered his body as dawn broke on the second day of his ordeal. The musty smell no longer offended him, and the sound of men's voices and the scrapes of their tools against rock were as grand and heartening to his ears as his favorite church hymn, "Onward, Christian Soldiers."

For the many hours before the rescuers arrived, he had shivered in his Levi jeans and hooded parka. But he soon learned to appreciate the ankle-deep layer of muck that covered the cavern floor. Digby discovered that, by coating himself in the mud and letting it dry, he had a natural shield against the cool humidity that reminded him of a drizzly March day. He slapped on a new layer every couple of hours and soon got used to the sensation of dirt under his fingernails, on his face, and in his hair. Mom would pitch a fit if she could see him, but the mud kept him warm.

Digby also found comfort in his own voice. It felt good to release a long, low moan from time to time. He liked how it bounced off the cavern walls, almost like someone was answering him. When the first men arrived, as the mayor said they would, they asked a flurry of questions: Was he feeling okay? (Depended on what they meant by "okay.") Did he have any food? (He had a few granola bars and a canteen of water.) Was there any other way out of the cave? (None he could tell.)

Answering muffled voices through several feet of rock could be exhausting. Pretty soon, the men stopped asking questions and got to scraping and tapping with their tools. Digby returned to his moaning and, when he tired of that, recited a song off the new Dakota Marx CD. "QueenFest" was Dakota's darkest song to date, an angry answer to all that the artist found lacking about the music business. It wasn't Digby's favorite Dakota Marx song, but the words and melody were easy to recite and kind of fit his mood:

> QueenFest,
> You failed the test.
> I knew you'd never make the grade,
> You're bought and paid.
> QueenFest,
> You've had your rest.
> They want to see you on the stage,
> Now act your age.

He stopped singing each time he heard a particularly jarring clap of metal against rock. He would slowly open his eyes, hoping to see a ray of daylight shooting through the cavern. Each time, seeing only blackness, he took a few minutes to gather himself before singing again:

> QueenFest,
> You failed the test.

CHAPTER 23

More than a hundred miles away, Charlie Lauterbach studied a road map spread across the hood of his 1991 Buick LeSabre. He had stopped in Olathe, Kansas, for gas and a twelve-pack of Pabst Blue Ribbon and suddenly realized he hadn't the faintest idea how to get to Pridemore.

Lauterbach had never even heard of the place until about six hours ago, when he got the phone call from Perry at Gold Star, the talent agency that sometimes booked him for speaking gigs. "I don't know who these people are or how they got my number," Perry told him, "but they've got an emergency and they need your help immediately."

He was a little fuzzy about the rest of the call. Lauterbach had been at Russell's Tavern, where the cell phone reception was weak. Examining the notes he'd scribbled on a cocktail napkin, he surmised that someone was trapped inside a cave and a big rescue operation was underway. He hadn't seen mention of it on the Oklahoma City TV stations, but anything this time of year that didn't involve barn-tossing twisters or the University of Oklahoma spring football game usually went unreported.

So first thing Sunday morning, he'd tossed his crumpled-up Missouri road map and a duffle bag with a change of clothes into the LeSabre and headed north on Interstate 35. He never stopped to puzzle over why someone in Pridemore, Missouri, would take the time to look up a civil engineer who had almost no practical experience working in caves or other geological formations. He knew why they called, and he would help them if he could.

They called because of what had happened more than twenty years ago in Prairie View, Ohio. On September 23, 1989, to be precise. That was the day two-year-old Alison May Funderburk fell down a twenty-foot water well in her family's backyard, setting off a frantic rescue mission that drew volunteers from more than seven states.

Lauterbach was one of them, at the time a thirty-five-year-old captain in the Army Corps of Engineers out of Dayton. He arrived at Prairie View on day 2 of the operation and was quickly briefed on the plan of attack. The little girl was believed to have broken both her arms in the fall. The well that swallowed her whole was a dried-up, cylinder-shaped structure that gradually widened from a ten-inch opening into a three-foot-wide floor of mud and leaves. Since no adult could fit through the opening, the plan was to dig a twenty-foot-deep trench next to the well, punch a hole near its bottom, and pull out Alison May.

The plan failed. Tremors from machinery used to dig the trench caused part of the well's century-old structure to collapse, and the crew suspended the operation. Digging the trench by hand would take too long, so the engineers huddled around the Funderburks' kitchen table to devise a new solution. Lauterbach had one—he suggested lowering a small, gated platform that the little girl could crawl onto and that would keep her secure as the team used a pulley system to lift it out.

The platform, which Lauterbach brilliantly rigged to include a Snicker's candy bar and Alison May's favorite stuffed bunny, Boo-Boo, worked on the first try. The crisis ended after sixty-five gut-ripping hours, and Lauterbach was universally praised as a hero in what became known as the Baby Alison Incident.

His life, as they say, was forever changed, even though the hubbub died down after a few months. Lauterbach had been relatively happy with the moderate income the Corps provided. He and his wife lived comfortably in a split-level home on the edge of Dayton, with a couple of munchkins running around the yard and a cherry-red Firebird in the garage. But two weeks after Baby Alison, they got a call from Parks & Dobson, Inc., the country's fourth-largest engineering firm, asking Lauterbach if he would spearhead their new Community Building Division. Of course he said yes, got his discharge, and moved the family out to Los Angeles.

The job, as it turned out, was a public-relations play. An excuse to launch an advertising campaign about how progressive the folks at Parks & Dobson were—the kind of people an engineer-hero like Charlie Lauterbach would be proud to join—even as the firm bid on government contracts to build a seven-billion-dollar spy plane. Public relations required a lot of travel, a lot of pressing the flesh in cities where the firm had big projects. There was a lot of wining and dining, a lot of sitting-around-the-hotel-bar-till-one-in-the-morning   activity. Lauterbach rarely saw the bottom of his suitcase in those years, but he saw the bottom of a lot of double martinis.

The wife and kids eventually left him, followed by an engineering firm that suddenly had no use for a faded hero. Lauterbach had moved to Oklahoma City, where he ran a company that repaired derricks for the state's chronically depressed oil industry. Every now and then, he got a call from Perry at Gold Star about a chance to speak to a company retreat or a high school class about Baby Alison (his booking fee was $1,000 for corporate events). He usually got a Christmas card from one of the Funderburks; the parents had long since divorced, and Alison May, last he heard, was waiting tables at Denny's after failing to get a scholarship to a design college.

Every couple of years or so, Lauterbach got a phone call from some desperate stranger caught up in another one of God's practical jokes. Most of the calls involved children

175

trapped somewhere—an abandoned mine shaft, a condemned building that collapsed at the worst possible moment—and a rescue operation that was running out of time. Four years ago, the Mexican government flew him down to Monterrey to help save a school bus full of kids trapped under a collapsed highway overpass. By the time Lauterbach's plane touched down, however, a concrete beam had disintegrated and the children were crushed to death.

So it was no surprise that Lauterbach was beating a path to Pridemore as fast as he could. He had no idea if what he had to offer could help these people, but he'd be damned if he was going to sit on his ass thinking about it.

Now, leaning over the battered map across his car hood, Lauterbach traced the red line that branched off Interstate 70 and meandered into a part of the state where most of the town names were printed in the smallest available type. It looked like he had four lanes all the way to Farley, then a quick jaunt west on something called Old 54. Running a hand through the graying hair that circled his bald dome, Lauterbach figured the drive would take three hours, which would put him in Pridemore by mid-afternoon.

He stuffed his map in the glove box and eyed the silvery twelve-pack of Pabst propped in the passenger seat. In his haste to get out of Oklahoma City this morning, he'd forgotten the trusty red Igloo cooler that accompanied him on most trips.

He quickly scanned the Olathe filling station to ensure that no cops were on the prowl before pulling out a can, popping the top, and taking a deep, long sip. The frosty liquid felt awfully nice on his parched tongue. It was going to be a hot day, creeping into the low nineties by lunchtime, and a few cold beers would have to compensate for the Le Sabre's conked-out air conditioner.

He eased the car into drive and pulled slowly onto the four-lane suburban road that would take him back to the interstate. He clicked on NPR in time for the local news report, but there was no mention of anyone trapped in a place called Pridemore. Lauterbach silently prayed that he wasn't already too late.

He had a nice buzz working by the time he pulled into Pridemore that afternoon. A sad little burg, he thought. One of those dying country towns where you slowed down just enough to abide by the speed limit signs, then gunned it back to sixty the instant the shuttered stores, abandoned grain elevators, and sagging clapboard houses were out of view.

Actually, as he scanned the downtown strip for a place to pee and ask directions, Lauterbach thought that perhaps Pridemore was a little better off than some of its peers. Next to the dreary thrift store and antique mall was a cute little malt shop called Truman's that looked to be straight out of Norman Rockwell. The wood-framed churches had a whitewashed sheen to them, and the city hall was a brick-and-mortar giant surrounded by dogwoods and trimmed hedges. And there was a surprisingly large Ford/Lincoln/Mercury dealership that must draw customers from miles around. The patient definitely was on life support, Lauterbach thought, but there was hope for a recovery.

He pulled into the malt shop, took a leak, and ordered a chocolate shake with Oreo cookies (it was a damn hot day, and Lauterbach was grateful for something thick and cool to absorb the six PBRs he'd consumed since Kansas City). The kid behind the counter gave him directions to Dragon's Ice House.

"You with a TV station?" the kid asked.

Lauterbach replied that he was an engineer.

"Just wondering," he said, straightening his paper hat, which Lauterbach supposed was meant to give the shop a 1950s aura. "We've had some TV people in here asking how to get to the Ice House. One of them came all the way from St. Louis."

He peered at Lauterbach through a pair of oversized bifocals. "You ain't dressed like a television guy, though," he finally added.

Lauterbach thanked the kid and hopped back into his Buick, empty beer cans rolling around the back seat as the car rambled down Old 54. The access to Dragon's Ice House was a scene straight from Prairie View: police cars, fire trucks, television trucks with antennae reaching to the sky, reporters practicing their live shots, a crowd of onlookers kept at bay by sheriff's deputies. This was just the beginning, Lauterbach thought. It would build in intensity until the crisis was resolved, for better or worse.

He explained his presence to one of the cops, who took him to a doublewide trailer along the side of the road. Lauterbach felt nauseated from the combination of chocolate shake and cheap beer, and the hot sun over his head didn't help things. He felt vulnerable without his hat—a cloudless day was like Kryptonite for bald guys. He could almost feel the sun burning little patches of skin cancer across his scalp.

"They're all in there," the deputy said, nodding at the door that read "M & M Construction" in blue lettering.

Inside, Lauterbach found thirteen men sitting around a conference table. They were watching a tall man with silver hair jot ideas on a white board. Lauterbach recognized him as Dwight Riddick, a vice president for Hurd\Douglass Engineering Corp. and, in Lauterbach's opinion, one of the biggest charlatans in the business. The guy couldn't find his way around an erector set, yet he had achieved fame for swooping into high-profile calamities from Baltimore to Bombay and devising engineering solutions that invariably saved the day. He was especially skilled at charming the media and taking credit for ideas that weren't necessarily products of his own gray matter.

Lauterbach had seen Riddick on a daytime talk show a few weeks ago, pimping a book called *They Soared with Angels* that was about the effect those rescue operations had on his spiritual life, or some bullshit like that. The fact that Pridemore pried Dwight Riddick away from his book tour could mean only one thing: this gig held the promise of garnering some serious national press.

"Well, now, there's ol' Charlie Lauterbach." The name came out like *Chaawlee Louder-back.* Riddick grew up in Traverse City, Michigan, but he'd cultivated a thick-as-molasses southern accent during his years of working in Hurd\Douglass's Atlanta office.

"Hey, Dwight."

"Charlie is one of the finest civil engineers I've ever known," Riddick said. "Some of you are no doubt familiar with the Baby Alison rescue back in '89. Well, here's the fellow who figured out how to get her out of that little well down in Texas."

"Actually, it was Ohio," Lauterbach said.

"Oh, of course. Eden Prairie, Ohio."

"Prairie View."

"Whatever. You did one hell of a job. We're glad you're on the team."

Some of the men nodded and smiled. Lauterbach recognized a couple as Riddick's toadies from Atlanta. The rest were the usual assortment of government officials and private contractors thrown together at a moment's notice. Most of the men wore golf shirts and khakis, save for the police chief and an elderly gentleman in a seersucker suit with a lemon-colored bowtie. Lauterbach guessed the old man was the mayor or some similarly ranked dimwit. Only a small-town pol would show up at a task force meeting dressed like he was in a local theater production of *The Music Man.*

Riddick directed Lauterbach to a vacant spot at the table, where he found a meeting agenda and a folder filled with mimeographed maps.

"Pardon the informality, Charlie, but we're brainstorming how to bust into this cave," Riddick said. "Feel free to dive in when you feel like it. Now, Eliot had a very interesting idea that I'd like him to expand upon."

Eliot Owens was one of the toadies, a structural engineer with rimless glasses so narrow they barely covered his beady little eyes.

"Basically, you've got twenty feet of limestone bedrock separating us from the subject," Owens said. "We've got a team of men trying to penetrate that rock with hand-held drilling equipment. But the structural integrity of the cave is such that any hole you dig into that stuff almost immediately collapses upon itself. They've been at it twenty-four hours now, and the progress has been measured in inches, not feet."

Lauterbach unleashed a long, low belch that tasted like beer and the pulled-pork sandwich he'd eaten three hours ago in Olathe. Riddick shot him a look.

"Sorry," Lauterbach whispered.

"Now," Owens continued, "if we get a truck-mounted drill rig up there, maybe one of those mobile B-59s, we could break through that limestone in just a few hours."

"Well, that's the trick, isn't it?" said another man with a name tag that identified him with something called Magellan Corp. An East Coast consulting firm, no doubt. "You've got acres and acres of dense forest around the base of the cave, plus a pretty rocky terrain. You'd be hard-pressed to get a golf cart up that trail, much less a twenty-one-foot drill rig."

"He's right," said the police chief, whose name tag read "Turner." "It's no picnic walking up there, either."

Riddick jotted bullet points on the white board as the men talked. When he finished, the silver-haired guru faced the group with the beaming expression of someone on the cusp of the Next Big Idea.

"Nice work, fellas. Let's think outside the box for a moment. What would be the easiest way, supposing it was even possible, to get a three-ton drilling rig over the river and through the woods to grandmother's house we go?"

"Airlift one in," Eliot Owens said.

One of the other engineers heaved a sigh.

"Seriously," Owens said. "You cut out a clearing near the cave entrance and you helicopter it in."

"We could get the National Guard involved," someone else said.

"No need," Owens snapped. "We have contractors do that kind of work for us all the time."

"I like where you're going with this," Riddick said, jotting furiously. "Keep it coming."

"I'd like to say something, if I might."

Everyone turned to the old guy in the seersucker suit. He had a strange smile on his weathered face, and his hands were gently raised, like the Pope might do when blessing the crowd outside his balcony.

"Dragon's Ice House, for those of you who aren't from these parts, is one of the largest, most extensive networks of caves in Central Missourah. It's just a few feet away from a land bridge that Lewis and Clark crossed during their magnificent journey west and which is protected by the state's registry of historic landmarks.

"Both of these treasures are surrounded by some of the oldest and tallest oaks in Pridemore Country. Those trees are part of what gives this area its charm."

Who, Lauterbach wondered, is this clown?

"My point is, on one hand, we have poor little Digby Willers who's stuck in this cave and must be freed as soon as possible. On the other hand, we have some very fragile, very historic natural wonders that we must preserve and protect."

The old man paused a beat, then slammed a fist on the table with such force that coffee cups rattled on the opposite end.

"And I'm a bow-legged son of a biscuit eater if I'll let any of you tear out half the forest so you can land a whirlybird on top of my cave.

"There's got to be a better way," he said. "Now find it."

He stared down his audience for a few frosty seconds. Riddick stepped behind him and massaged his shoulders.

"Don't worry, Mayor," he said. "We won't touch a limb on those oak trees."

"I know you won't."

The room was silent for several moments. The engineers and contractors stared at each other, eyebrows raised over their designer eyewear.

"Is there another way in?"

Everyone looked at Lauterbach, who held up a handful of the mimeographed sheets from his packet.

"These maps," he said, "are shit. I can't tell from these squiggly blue lines where the cave ends and where it begins."

"Those are the best we could find at the county archives, Charlie."

"Well, the reason I ask, Eliot, is because, if I correctly remember my freshman-year geology class, a lot of these caves have more than one entrance. And since the mayor here is so concerned about protecting the environment, it might behoove us to find another way into the cave."

"That's a thought," said a heavyset man with a hang-dog face and a golf shirt that read "M&M Construction." "But there's a lot we don't know about the Ice House. The maps are sketchy because a good portion of the cave's unexplored."

The mayor nodded. "The lines on those maps are educated guesses on where the cave goes, and the man who drew them died seven years ago."

"C'mon," Lauterbach said. "Nobody goes caving anymore? There's not some sort of extreme-sport spelunking club here in Missouri that goes in there and, like, takes rock samples or something?"

Lauterbach wasn't the sort to dominate meetings, but he was feeling the nice, warm glow of a PBR buzz, and besides, somebody had to set these damned people straight.

"There's got to be someone who knows those old caves backwards and forwards. I'll bet there's a guy right here in Pridemore."

The men stared at their notes. Riddick wiped a bullet point from his white board with a squeegee rag.

"Look, do we want to save this kid or not?" Lauterbach said. "Because I could be sitting at home right now, watching reruns of *House*."

The police chief whispered something to the mayor, who grimaced but gave a little nod that apparently was a go-ahead.

"Um," the chief said. "There's a fellow by the name of Chad Hutchins who might be able to help us."

"Does he live here in Pridemore?"

The chief nodded. "I don't know how reliable he'll be. The man has multiple convictions for reckless driving and use of a controlled substance. But he knows those caves as well as anyone around here."

"Well, there you go," Lauterbach said. "Why don't we get this man on the horn, get him down here and see what he knows. Sound like a plan, Dwight?"

Riddick responded with a toothy grin that barely masked the vicious squint of his gray eyes. It was a don't-fuck-with-me smile if Lauterbach had ever seen one.

"That's a great idea, Charlie," he said. "Let's get right on that. In fact, if the chief here can bring in this Hutchins fellow, you and he can have a meeting and report back to us on what you find."

"I'll do whatever you need me to do, Dwight."

Riddick locked in on him with that clenched smile. "I know you will, Charlie."

They broke for a few minutes so a caterer could bring in sandwiches and Cokes, and so Riddick and the mayor could step out and make a statement to the media that had been gathering throughout the day and could now be considered a legitimate throng.

Lauterbach was heading back to the car to get his briefcase and a pack of smokes when he felt a tug on his sleeve. It was the mayor, who was surprisingly tall and commanding up close, not at all like the frail gentleman on the other end of the conference table. He cast down a great smile that consumed his entire face. It was a smile that Dwight Riddick would do well to adopt if he ever wanted to at least look sincere.

"You know, I'm the one who called your agent the other night," the mayor said, wrapping his hand firmly around Lauterbach's.

"You are?"

"I'm a big fan. I know what you did in Ohio."

"Yeah...well."

"And I know life hasn't exactly been a bowl of cherries for you since."

"Well," Lauterbach said. "I get by."

"That's why I called you. Not everyone wanted you, but I overruled them. What you did all those years ago was brilliant, and I know you've got another one in you."

"Thanks."

The mayor gripped Lauterbach's hand so tightly it hurt.

"Don't prove me wrong, son. And leave your boozing ways back in Oklahoma."

He walked off before Lauterbach could muster a retort. A pair of deputies helped the mayor onto the back of a flatbed truck, where he stood and invited the crowd of reporters and television cameras to gather around. He bragged on the great team Dwight Riddick assembled, smiled wanly as he recounted Digby Willers's incredible run of Pinewood Derby wins, and spoke in grave tones about the difficult fight ahead. Then Riddick climbed up next to the mayor and offered a few euphemism-laden statements that gave the impression of candor without saying much of anything at all. The reporters ate it up.

It was still awfully damn hot, and Lauterbach repeatedly wiped perspiration from his forehead as he watched the press briefing. Riddick's upper lip was glistening and his golf shirt clung to the contours of his middle-aged chest. But the mayor was hardly sweating at all in his seersucker suit. In fact, he looked almost blissful standing there, taking it in, beaming down at everyone as if they'd come here just to see him.

It was a little unnerving, considering the circumstances. At one point, while he was talking to the throng, the mayor looked directly at Lauterbach and winked, a motion so swift that no television camera could possibly track it.

CHAPTER 24

After the press conference, Pete Schaefer rushed to the *Headlight* newsroom to file more stories. The *Alliance Press* had hired him as a stringer on the rescue operation until its regional reporter returned from vacation, which meant Pete had to feed them an updated story every three or four hours. It was kind of a pain in the ass, but the prospect of having his byline run in newspapers across the country more than made up for the paltry freelance pay.

He was also working on a package of stories for the *Headlight*, which had decided to publish a four-page special section on the crisis for Monday's edition. It would include a profile on Digby Willers (for which Pete drew liberally from old stories on the kid's Pinewood Derby exploits), a question-and-answer with Susan Willers (conducted in her driveway because she was convinced that her house was bugged), and an article speculating on the cause of the cave's collapse (earth tremors were one professor's guess; a law enforcement expert speculated it was explosives belonging to a terrorist cell). Of course, the section also would have plenty of space for advertising, which was really the point of the whole thing.

Though little more than twenty-four hours old, the pending operation to save Digby Willers was the biggest thing to hit the region, old-timers said, since the summer of 1976. That was when Milton Pemberton, an insurance claims adjuster from nearby Guthridge, went on a highway shooting spree that spanned three counties and took four lives before he wrapped his lips around a shotgun muzzle and pulled the trigger.

Realistically, the Digby rescue was already a bigger story involving many more players. About three hundred people were at the site: police from six counties, firefighters and paramedics from across Missouri, and dozens upon dozens of support people. Experts from some of the top engineering firms in the country had flown in to devise a way to get a truck-mounted drill up to the Ice House. Beginning late Saturday night, when it was apparent that the rescue would be measured in days instead of hours, several doublewide trailers, refreshment tents, and port-a-potties trickled in from across the state to aid the workers. An area soda distributor donated a truck full of pop to the rescue team, and the local churches had gotten together to grill free burgers and hotdogs. There was a makeshift infirmary where injured workers could go for treatment or even a deep-tissue massage. By Sunday morning, the half-finished parking lot outside Lewis and Clark Land Bridge was a small city of trailers, tents, and pickup trucks.

The media rolled in Sunday morning from across the state: every TV station in Kansas City, Springfield, and St. Louis had a camera propped outside Dragon's Ice House. Two of the national cable channels, the left-wing World News Network and the blatantly conservative Patriot Television Corp., sent correspondents to cover the unfolding drama, and there was word that crews from the big networks were on their way. A few of the gadfly groups that always popped up at any sort of media gathering had pitched camp in Pridemore. Members of the radical Church of Revelations were already picketing the site with their familiar rainbow signs blaming everything on the gays.

The spotlight, Pete knew, would intensify as the rescue lumbered on. And "lumber" was the operative word—an engineering source told him off the record that it could take as many as five days to get the proper equipment to the Ice House and dig Willers out.

It was amazing, now that he thought about it, how quickly things changed. Twenty-four hours ago, the most pressing thing on Pete's mind was whether he should drive to Memphis to visit a college friend. Beale Street would have been a blast, but there would be plenty of other weekends to sit shit-faced on a curb outside B.B. King's bar.

This was the reason Pete got in the business, the payoff for almost two miserable years toiling in bum-fuck Missouri. After filing a final story late Saturday night, Pete collapsed on his futon but wriggled under the covers for hours, story angles filling his head like a stream of movie trailers. He couldn't sleep. So he went back to the newsroom and spent the night scrolling through old issues on the microfilm machine, preparing for the next day's story. For once in his life, Pete felt that he was exactly where he needed to be.

Larry Truesdale called the whole staff into the *Headlight* newsroom on Sunday morning. Once everyone gathered, the publisher climbed atop the nearest desk and announced that the newspaper would publish a special section for the first time since bin Laden knocked down the Trade Center (that effort garnered $20,000 in ad revenue, he noted). Digby's rescue, Truesdale said, would last several days (Pete thought later that it was curious of him to say that, since there was no official estimate at the time), and the *Headlight* would work around the clock to cover it. Everyone would put in long hours and work weekends until the story concluded. Truesdale, being the stand-up guy he was, would pop for free pizza and Cokes throughout the crisis.

"I want to cover this thing like the Second Coming is scheduled tomorrow at the Dragon's Ice House, and we're the only ones who've talked to Mary Magdalene," he said, waving a fist in the air. "This is why we're in the newspaper business. If you can't get pumped about this, you should find something else to do."

A few hours after the meeting, Pete sat drumming his fingers against his desk, puzzling over how to edit Susan Willers's diatribes for a family newspaper. The phone interrupted his train of thought.

"Schaefer here."

"Peter?"

It was Angela. Shit. He instinctively cupped a hand over his mouth and ducked behind his computer.

"Please tell me you're not calling me at work right now," he whispered. "Please tell me you're not breaking Rule Number 1 of our friendship."

"I'll call you whenever I want, my love," she said.

"Did you dial in through the front desk?"

"Yes."

"Shit! You want everyone in town to know?"

"Quit being such a Nervous Nelly," she said. "Besides, I've got an important news tip."

"You have five seconds before I hang up."

"Fine. You know about the Digby Willers drama?"

"I'm familiar with it."

"I heard my dad talking about it on the phone last night," Angela said. "Way past midnight, when all good parents should be in bed. I think he was talking with Mayor Tolliver."

"Okay."

"There's something going on, Peter. I think my dad knows something about this whole Digby thing."

Her voice cracked as she spoke. Pete felt a little guilty for snapping at her. The Truesdales, Angela once told him, didn't exactly lead the fun-filled, happy home life they projected to the community. She never said much beyond that, but Pete sensed a dark side to the family. He had never pressed her on it. He'd probably rather not know anyway.

"You okay?" he asked.

"Yeah," she said, though she was now in full-fledged sniffle mode.

"You want to tell me what's going on?"

"Maybe later. Can I come over to your place?"

"God knows when I'll be home," he said. "I'm sort of at the mercy of this crazy story."

"Peter, what I've got to tell you *is* the story."

This sent a shudder down his back. Could a tip from his high school girlfriend break open the Digby Willers saga, or was this a ploy to get into Pete's apartment and talk for four hours about their relationship?

Something told him to trust her. She'd never misled him before, at least not lately. Plus, the cracking voice on the other end of the line was real. Angela didn't break down over little things like a forgotten birthday or a callous remark. Something was definitely up.

"Okay," he said. "Let's shoot for ten o'clock."

CHAPTER 25

Chad Hutchins was pushing thirty-five years old but still bore the trappings of a high school skateboarder: hooded sweatshirt with an artist's rendering of Tupac Shakur on the front, denim shorts hanging low enough to reveal a glimpse of Scooby-Doo boxers, and an elaborate tattoo on the right calf depicting Ronald Reagan with a forked tongue. Hutchins's bleached hair was shaggy and full, but his face had the baggy eyes, smile marks, and crow's feet of middle age. If anything, too much sun, alcohol, and other recreational elements over the years made him look older than his actual age.

Public Safety Chief Cole Turner bore a look of barely controlled fury as he watched Hutchins flip through the mimeographed maps of Dragon's Ice House that Charlie Lauterbach had provided. The three men stood on Hutchins's front porch, so rickety and weatherworn that Lauterbach half expected it to collapse, sending all of them tumbling into a weedy lawn that was littered with children's toys and various parts of a rusting Camaro.

"You're right," Hutchins said, handing the papers back to the engineer. "These pretty much suck."

"We know that," Lauterbach said. "We need you to draw us a better map."

Hutchins settled into a wooden porch swing that was removed from its moorings and rested atop two concrete flower pots.

"Dude," he said. "It's been six years since I shot the 'House. And I'm pretty sure I was on mushrooms at the time. No offense, officer."

The chief glared.

"It's not a particularly interesting cave, anyway."

"What do you mean?"

"I mean you can only cave so far, like maybe nine hundred feet, before things get a little too close for comfort. Compared with caves down in southern Missouri and Arkansas, where you can go for miles if you want, the Ice House is like a kiddy pool for true spelunkers."

"He's not interested in spelunking, Hutchins," Turner said. "In case you missed it, there's a kid trapped in there, and we don't have a lot of time to reach him."

"Which bums me out," Hutchins said. "You know I taught Digby how to rollerblade? Tried to, anyway. Right down that street. He skated into a drainage ditch and broke his ankle. His mom was *pissed*."

"Do you think," Lauterbach said, "there might be another way into the cave?"

"There's always another way. The trick is figuring out where it is, and if it's wide enough for a body to get through. Based on my experience, I'd say no chance. The 'House is one skinny-ass bitch, so you'd have to be some sort of contortionist to make your way through."

"Thanks a lot," the chief said sarcastically. "You're a great help."

"I could be wrong," Hutchins said. "But you're not going to know until you check it out for yourselves."

"Will you go with us?" Lauterbach asked. "I don't know much about caves. Neither does anyone on our team. Having you as a guide would help."

Hutchins pointed toward a metallic anklet clamped below his Reagan tattoo.

"I'm not supposed to leave the premises without permission from my parole officer."

"Dealing to a minor," the chief explained. "Six months in jail and another six on parole. Pretty light sentence for frying the brains of our youth."

"Hello! The kid was six weeks from his eighteenth birthday and the biggest pothead at Community R-2," Hutchins said. "It's not like I was giving dime bags to kids coming off the curly slide."

"You're lucky we're not alone, Hutchins," the chief hissed, hovering inches away from the perpetrator's face, "or you'd get a real, nice pop in the mouth for that remark."

"Guys!" Lauterbach said. "Can we stick to the task at hand?"

The chief planted an index finger against Hutchins's shoulder, but slowly backed away. The aging skateboarder just chuckled and nodded his shaggy head. Lauterbach wasn't one to side with the establishment, but he could kind of see what infuriated Turner about this guy.

"You're chief of police, right?" he said, turning to Turner. "So we could bring Chad up to the Ice House under your custody."

"Technically speaking, that would be okay. But I've got enough things on my plate right now without spending the afternoon babysitting this moron."

"No need worrying about me, chief," Hutchins said. "If I decide to run, I won't get far in those caves."

"Damn straight, you won't."

"Two hours," Lauterbach said, looking directly at the chief. "That's all I need with him."

Turner stared at the men for a moment, then lowered his head and muttered a flurry of indiscernible words to the sagging porch floor. One of them sounded to Lauterbach like "guacamole," but the chief said it so fast and at such a low decibel it was hard to know for certain.

When he finished, Turner ran a hand through his hair a few times, looked at Hutchins, and grimaced.

"Give me the name and number of your parole officer," he said, "and let's get this over with."

CHAPTER 26

"Pete, have you got a minute?"

He didn't have a minute. He didn't have half a minute, with everything that was exploding around him. But Larry Truesdale was leaning out of his office with a concerned look on his usually jovial face, so Pete supposed he'd better make a little time for the boss.

"Just a minute, okay, Pete? I know you're busy."

"Uh-oh," said Edna Bright, looking up from her monitor. "The boss-man calleth!"

Pete ignored the society editor's remark but felt a roiling in his belly as he walked into the paneled office and Truesdale closed the door behind him. The publisher strode to his desk and motioned for Pete to take a seat. Truesdale settled into his own Herman Miller executive chair, took a drag from a half-smoked cigarette, and crammed it into an ashtray shaped like a Mustang convertible.

"This is going to seem strange at first, but bear with me," he said, smiling. "There's a method to my madness, okay?"

Pete nodded. His boss looked like he could use some sleep. His eyes were red and his graying hair, usually perfectly coiffed, clung in strands around his skull like legs of an enormous spider. It had been a long Sunday for everyone at *The Headlight*. Most of them had been there since seven o'clock.

Truesdale's hands shook slightly as he lit another cigarette and took a long drag.

"You've met my daughter, Angela," he said, nodding at a framed picture on his bookcase of a willowy girl walking on the beach. "She's been in the newsroom a few times, wrote a couple of articles for our teen section?"

"Yes," Pete said, shifting in his seat. His throat was dry. He clicked and unclicked the ballpoint pen he always carried with him.

"Well, Angela has been in some trouble at school. Her teachers tell me she's skipped a few classes."

Truesdale's smile was gone, replaced by a grimness Pete didn't recognize in his boss.

"Her mother and I were naturally worried," he went on. "Angela's always done so well in school. I mean, most kids you expect to skip a few classes, come home with a 'C' on the report card now and again. Christ knows I did. But Angela has always been so good."

Larry let out a hollow-sounding laugh and crammed the cigarette into the ashtray.

"I feel bad about this next part. I wish we hadn't done it," he said. "But we were worried. You know how parents get worried? Well, you will someday. Anyway, one afternoon when Angela was out, we went through the things in her room to see if we could figure out what was going on.

"We found this." He lifted a manila envelope from his desk and pulled out a ziplock bag of ground-up leaf particles that Pete guessed was not herbal tea. He dropped it on the desktop as if the bag had suddenly become very hot. "I'm sure you know what this is?"

Pete nodded. He ran his tongue around his mouth, trying to build up enough saliva to swallow. No such luck.

The publisher drew in a heavy breath. "We also found some pictures of you, Pete.

"And we found a letter Angela apparently was writing you." He pulled some light blue stationery from the envelope and handed it to Pete. "They described some of the things you two have been up to during your working hours."

Pete took the pages and looked at them, not so much reading as studying the light blue tint, Angela's favorite color, and thinking this isn't real, this isn't real, this isn't happening to me. He was covering the biggest news story of his life. Just hours ago, Larry Truesdale had been standing on a desk in his pinstriped suit, singing Pete's praises, calling him "the best young reporter we've hired here in a long damn time."

He looked up to find Truesdale leaning over his desk, hands gripping the corners like a lineman about to burst out of a four-point stance. He glared at Pete, his big, fleshy face red as a hot poker.

"Well?" he demanded. "Care to explain?"

Pete stared at the stationery and found his name in the flowing, ornate cursive Angela had mastered after years of practice. She used to spend hours copying her great-grandmother's longhand from old letters and the backs of photos. Angela felt she did her best writing in this arduous style.

"I'm not going to fire you, if that's what you're thinking," the publisher said evenly. "Not just yet. I'd love nothing better than to kick your sorry ass to the curb, but the fact is the newspaper needs you right now. And I'm not going to let personal problems override what *The Headlight* needs. I was going to talk to you after this Digby Willers thing got settled, but, well, I just couldn't contain myself. You understand, don't you, Pete?"

Pete nodded.

"Now, before we wrap this up—and I do hope for your sake that this is the last time you and I will ever be alone in a room together—I want to give you a chance to explain yourself. Even though I'm a sales guy who probably couldn't write a ten-inch crime blotter to save his life, I do believe in getting both sides of a story. So here's your chance, Pete, to explain how this is all some crazy, *Three's Company*-style mix-up, and that you aren't actually sleeping with my daughter every Thursday afternoon at three."

Truesdale pulled another cigarette from his pack of Camel Filters, but he fumbled it onto the carpet and uttered a swear word. He dropped the Camels into a desk drawer, pulled out a pack of nicotine gum, and tossed a piece into his mouth.

"So what you do have to say for yourself?"

Pete replied in a quivering voice he barely recognized.

"I'm sorry—what was that?" Truesdale growled.

Pete repeated himself. "I—I didn't give her the marijuana."

Truesdale slammed a fist down on the massive desk, bouncing the Mustang ashtray to the floor and sending a cloud of ash into the air.

"My daughter," he said, voice cracking, "is eighteen years old!"

He swung around the desk like he was about to attack but stopped short, grabbed the arms of Pete's chair, and looked him square in the face. There were tears in his eyes.

Pete fought the urge to look at his lap, feeling he at least owed the boss some eye contact. Maybe that way he could say something to put the man at ease, to make things better between the two of them.

He muttered something stupid instead.

"What did you say?" the publisher roared.

Pete opened his mouth and said it again. "I'm sorry."

The big man lifted his hands off the chair and turned away. He collapsed into a leather couch in the corner of the office and ran his hands through his hair.

"Get out of my sight," he said softly.

"Larry, I—"

"Go!"

Pete rose slowly from his chair, carefully placing Angela's letter on the desk. He opened the office door and closed it behind him, making as little noise as possible.

"And stay away from my daughter!" the publisher yelled through the glass-paneled wall as Pete retreated to his cubicle to somehow craft a fresh lead sentence for his news story.

CHAPTER 27

A storm rolled in late that afternoon, blackening the sky and
dumping rain on the mass of rescuers, reporters, and curiosity
seekers who gathered in the muddy parking lot of Dragon's Ice
House and the Historic Lewis and Clark Land Bridge. Some
scurried to their trucks or huddled beneath tarps that the local
Jaycees set up to give shelter from what moments ago was a
seething, merciless sun.

Charlie Lauterbach's only relief from the downpour came
from the tree branches overhead and the bright orange poncho
he'd borrowed from the Pridemore Department of Public
Safely. Chief Cole Turner and Chad Hutchins wore similar
garments as the three men tromped through the woods,
searching for a new way into the Ice House. They'd been
wandering through the muck for more than an hour, and
Lauterbach was starting to doubt Hutchins's professed
knowledge of the area.

Hutchins was supposed to lead them along the cave's
general course from the mouth of the Ice House, up and down
steep ridges, and through a heavily wooded valley that the
locals called the Bottoms. But they'd lost their way in the rain
and had to return to the cave's origin to start over again.

Even under the canopy of trees, the rain came down in
sheets that made it impossible for Lauterbach to make out
anything but Hutchins's poncho as he scrambled up the ridge.

"This," the police chief grunted, "is a complete and utter
waste of time."

Crawling up the slope before grabbing a sturdy root that
poked from the muck, Lauterbach wondered if Turner wasn't

right. Maybe jackhammering away at a twenty-foot wall of limestone rock, no matter how long it took to break through, was the best approach. Maybe trusting a convicted dope dealer to find another way to save Digby Willers was as pointless as Lauterbach wiping his glasses in the middle of this typhoon.

"Tell you one thing," Hutchins said as they crested the ridge, "it keeps raining like this, and we can say so long to our little friend."

"What's that supposed to mean?" Turner asked.

"I mean storms like this can fill up a cave real damn fast. I was caving one time in Arizona and this thunderstorm came out of nowhere. The water kept rising and rising. Good thing I got my lifeguard badge, 'cause we had to fucking swim our way out."

"Nothing we can do about the weather, Chad," Lauterbach said. "But are you sure we're going about this the right way?"

"Come again?"

"I mean, how can you be sure we're tracing the cave's path going entirely off your memory? Shouldn't we look at the maps?"

"I told you, the maps are shit."

"Chad," Lauterbach said, taking on what he thought was a fatherly tone. "It's okay to admit you're lost. You said it yourself—you haven't been around these caves for years."

"Fuck you, man! I didn't ask to be dragged out here in the pouring rain looking for some magical passageway that probably doesn't exist. I'm only out here for my man Digby. You want my help? We roll my way.

"And this," he said, pressing an index finger against his scalp. "Is all I got."

The chief swooped over Hutchins like a florescent orange flash, grabbing the skateboarder's poncho hood and slamming him headfirst into a tree. Hutchins bounced off the trunk and collapsed into a pile of wet leaves.

"Jesus!" Lauterbach said. "Ever heard of police brutality?"

"I have," Turner said in low rasp that was a little too TV cop for Lauterbach's taste. "And you could be next, my friend."

"*Dudes!*"

The men looked at Hutchins, who sat upright in the leaves. "Check this out."

He balled his hand into a fist and hit the ground, generating a noise that sounded strangely metallic. He repeated the motion with the same result.

"It's hollow," Lauterbach said.

The men pushed aside leaves and dirt to reveal a metal, six-panel door—the kind found on a typical suburban home—embedded in the ground. Lauterbach wiped the rain from his glasses to make sure he wasn't seeing things.

"I'll be damned," the chief said.

Lauterbach reached down and lifted the door. Below was a hand-dug tunnel barely wide enough for a grown man to lower himself through. The chief pulled out his flashlight and shone it down the hole, which dropped several feet before hitting limestone, then appeared to make a bend so that it was almost horizontal with the ground. Lauterbach lowered his head into the opening and heard trickling water.

"There's your second entrance," Hutchins said.

The engineer stood up and brushed mud and leaves from his Wranglers. The rain was still coming down, and, despite the poncho, his clothes were soaked.

"I'm going in there to see where it leads."

"Hold on, Kemosabe," Turner said. "I'm no cave explorer and neither are you. And I'm not exactly sure Hutchins here knows what the hell he's doing."

"The cave's filling up with water," Lauterbach snapped. "I can hear it. We've got to move fast."

"So tell the task force. They'll know what to do."

Lauterbach stared down the hole, his hands resting on his hips. It didn't make sense. Hundreds of workers had rushed to the scene, along with a panel of more than a dozen experts, in a rescue mission that grew more desperate by the hour. And yet here in the woods, no more than half a mile away from the rescue site, was a man-made tunnel covered by a six-panel door that might lead directly to the retarded kid.

The chief was right. Lauterbach knew nothing about caves. The task force had resources and people to take this thing on. Yet something told him that going through official channels was the worst thing he could do.

"I'm going in."

"Yeah!" said Hutchins.

"I don't think you should," the chief said.

Lauterbach ignored him. He threw off his poncho and asked for the nylon rope that Hutchins had hooked to the belt loop of his cargo shorts. He had started wrapping the rope around his waist when he heard the unmistakable click of a gun being cocked. He turned to find Chief Turner's Glock thrust in his face.

"I don't want to be an asshole about this," the cop said with his best Dirty Harry squint. "So why don't you gentlemen come with me?"

All Digby knew of the storm outside was the steady stream of water running down a ledge that hung over the cavern floor like one of those gravity-defying boulders in a Road Runner-Coyote cartoon. More than two days of sitting in the muck gave him ample time to explore his surroundings, and Digby was amazed at the depth and size of his natural prison. The ceiling looked to be three stories high in some places, with waxy cylinders hanging like the icicles that appeared outside his window after a winter storm. Any spelunker could tell you these were called stalactites, and that the similarly shaped cylinders protruding from the floor were stalagmites. Digby knew nothing of this, so he called all of them the same thing: cave candles.

There was a cluster of cave candles along one wall of the cavern, forty paces from the collapsed archway Digby had passed through just seconds before the explosion. They looked like pipes of a once-grand organ that had collected a thousand years of rust. Just above the organ rose a twenty-foot wall that jutted into a rocky overhang. Water flowed over this ledge for much of the day, leading Digby to believe it might represent a way out. He had snaked his way slowly up the wall, one modest foothold after another, getting to the point where his back was almost parallel with the ground, his big hands clinging to the overhang, ice-cold water splashing his face. He could almost peer above the ledge to what must certainly be an escape route (that was how it worked in the movies, wasn't it?) before losing his toehold, tumbling down the wall, and nearly impaling himself on the pipe organ below.

This was how it went through at least a dozen attempts to climb the ledge, each time more slippery than the last because the water was steadily increasing in volume. On his last try, the bright yellow cave radio slid out of his backpack and shattered on the rocks below. No big loss, Digby thought. The batteries were almost dead, and he had been unable to reach anyone on the radio since the mayor signed off shortly after the blast. Still, the broken piece of equipment was another reminder that Digby was closed off from the rest of the world and might never see daylight again.

So he took a little break, sitting cross-legged in the mud and munching one of his last power bars, his chance of salvation looking about as dim as the bulb in his flashlight. The workers were still drilling into the rock, still making their around-the-clock racket, but the noise didn't sound any closer than it had yesterday or the day before. Pretty soon, he'd run out of power bars and clean water, and he would be reduced to lapping at the water coming over the ledge, the stupid ledge that might be his only way out of here if he could just hoist his big, fat body over it.

He scooped up some mud and flung it against the ledge, making a splat that echoed through the cavern walls. Then he grunted and went back to his power bar, nibbling tiny bites to savor the apple cinnamon taste. He'd thought a lot about food over the last two days: his mother's pot roast simmering in the Crock-Pot, ice cream sandwiches at the city pool on a hot summer day, hot apple crisp with a scoop of homemade vanilla ice cream—

"What do you think you're doing?"

Digby pointed his flashlight toward the ledge, where a young man in gold lamé trousers and an unbuttoned shirt stood, holding a red guitar against his waist.

It was Dakota Marx.

"Hi," Digby said shyly.

"Hi, yourself," Dakota said. "You're just gonna give up, aren't you? You're just gonna sit there and pout."

Digby shrugged, not sure what to say. The rock star walked over and leaned against one of the larger cave candles.

"Look, I know it's hard," he said. "You think I don't know? Read the bio on my website. That'll give you some idea."

Digby nodded. He hadn't read the bio, but he was familiar with the ninety-minute documentary about Dakota Marx that ran at least once a day on the celebrity channels.

"You know my song, 'Keep on Burnin'?" he said, strumming a chord on his Gibson. "*Keep on burnin' through the night, making sure you get it right*? That's a true story, man. That's about me."

Digby smiled as though he had the slightest clue what Dakota was talking about.

"Growing up in Southern California wasn't easy. All the houses looked the same. Almost from the time I could crawl, I knew I was destined for something bigger. And on that fateful day I heard my first Bon Jovi song, I knew that music was my way out of the suburban sameness. So I hit LA, landed a record deal, and cut my first album."

The superstar threw his head back and laughed, revealing a set of thick, white teeth.

"Okay, so it wasn't quite that easy, but you know what I'm saying."

Digby nodded.

"Look, the point is we all have problems. Some of us don't get the right record deal. Some of us get trapped in a dirty cave with no food and water.

"The thing is, you've got to keep trying. You've got to pick yourself up and find a way out of your jam. That's what I'd do. You gotta keep on burnin', man. Even in the tough times, when it doesn't look like there's a ghost of a chance."

"Okay." Digby squinted so he could see Dakota's face a little better. The rock star was somehow haloed in light.

"You're like me, Digby. You're a burner. You're meant for great things. You're going to get through this. You're going to set the world on fire. Just keep on burnin', baby."

"Yessir."

"Say it."

Digby looked down at his mud-caked hands. "I'm gonna keep on burnin'."

"C'mon, man. Give it to me loud."

"Gonna keep on burnin'."

"That's a little better." Dakota sauntered toward the ledge until he could no longer be seen. Digby had hoped he would play one of his songs, maybe something off the *QueenFest* CD. He didn't stress about it too much, though. He'd had several conversations with Dakota Marx over the past two days. He always seemed to show up when Digby felt his lowest.

He pointed his flashlight toward the ledge, where the water was now spilling over in a thin sheet. He flicked off the light, closed his eyes, and breathed deeply in and out. He thought some more about his mother's pot roast, the aroma of beef so tender it almost melted in your mouth.

He would tackle the ledge again soon, but not just yet.

CHAPTER 28

The rain turned to steady drizzle by dusk. The clouds gave way to a purplish sunset, which cast a dreamy filter on everything from the stately oak trees around the courthouse to the stoplight on Main. It was a time that Pete's movie geek friends called Magic Hour, the early evening light that made for optimal filmmaking. Any other day, Pete might have stopped to admire it. Tonight he wanted only to get to his apartment, collapse on the couch with a bag of chips, and watch TV until he drifted to sleep. He was physically and mentally whipped, too tired to dwell on the disturbing encounter with Truesdale, too spent to pull up his résumé on the computer and start a job search.

He arrived at his duplex to find Angela standing in the drizzle, long strings of hair clinging to her T-shirt and face. Her shoulders sagged from the weight of her oversized book bag and her eyes were puffy, like she'd been crying for a long time.

He let her inside. "How long you been out here?"

"An hour. Maybe more."

She pressed her head against his chest and clung to his sweatshirt. Pete took her hand and led her up the stairs to his apartment. Once inside, he sat her on the futon and rubbed her shoulders, occasionally kissing the back of her neck until she finished sobbing.

"Talked to your dad today," he said. "I think he wants to kill me."

"My dad," she said, sniffling, "is the biggest coward in the world."

"He can be a pretty scary coward."

"He promised me he wouldn't say anything until this Digby business was over. I thought I'd have time to warn you."

"When did he find out?"

"Last night." She looked down at her hands and Pete noticed that one of them was badly bruised. "My brother had to hold him back."

"Jesus."

"I begged him not to fire you, at least not until you finished this story. I know it's your ticket out of here."

Pete frowned. "I'd like it to be. Part of me thinks maybe I should load up the truck and get out of town now before your dad comes after me with a shotgun."

"You can't do that."

"Why the hell not?"

"Because you can't," she said. "Because I have a story for you."

He smiled. "I've already got a story."

Angela sighed deeply and reached into her book bag. She pulled out a lighter and a pack of Marlboro Reds, handing one to Pete and lighting one for herself. Taking a long drag from the cigarette, she seemed many years beyond the goofy cheerleader Pete thought he knew.

"This story's bigger," she said.

They sat on the futon, burning through one Marlboro after another as Angela recounted the late-night conversation she overheard between her father and Mayor Tolliver. She had picked up her bedroom phone, intending to warn Pete that his job might be in jeopardy, but instead heard the two men talking.

"They were talking about Digby Willers," she said. "But not in the way you'd expect."

"How's that?"

"Well, for one thing, Dad was totally wigged out. He kept asking the mayor what happens if the FBI gets involved, and the mayor told him to calm down, that everything was going as planned and that my dad shouldn't be worried. And I wondered, 'What do they have to worry about?'"

Pete nodded.

"And then they talked about hush money and explosives and ways to keep Digby Willers's mom quiet. And I suddenly realized this was no accident."

"What wasn't an accident?"

"The whole thing!" she said, sticking her cigarette butt in an empty Coke can. "I don't know how they did it, but somehow my dad, the mayor, and some other guys figured out a way to trap Digby in that cave and leave him there. They planned the whole thing."

Pete extinguished his cigarette, stood up, and glanced around. Mrs. Wesley, a prune-faced widow and one of the biggest gossips in town, lived just down the stairs, and Pete always took great care sneaking Angela in and out of the apartment at times when he knew the old lady wasn't working her job as a dispatcher for the county hospital. He imagined Mrs. Wesley with her ear cupped against the plaster walls right now, taking in this conversation about two of Pridemore's most powerful men.

"You mean to tell me," he said in a low voice, "the mayor and the newspaper publisher conspired to lure a mentally retarded man into a cave and then triggered some sort of avalanche that would trap him behind twenty feet of limestone rock?"

"Well," she said. "I think they had help from some other people."

"Why would they do that, Angela? The mayor is spending millions of dollars to turn that place into a tourist stop. Why would he throw that away so he could trap someone in a cave?

"And, even if Mayor Tolliver happens to have gone completely off his rocker, which I certainly can see happening, why would your father go along with it?"

"I don't know."

He crouched next to Angela and draped his arm around her. She was still soaked to the bone.

"I'm not saying the conversation didn't happen," he said. "I just wonder if you heard it right."

"Thought you'd say something like that." She reached into her bag again and pulled out a leather-bound notebook. "I brought evidence."

The notebook was Larry Truesdale's. With a sinking feeling that he was about to get into even deeper trouble with his boss, Pete thumbed through the pages, which appeared to make up a personal billing ledger. He stopped at a page that listed a couple of payments to someone named Berry Duncan. What caught Pete's eye were the words "Missouri Militia" on the memo lines.

"Uh-huh," Angela said. "There's more."

Several more. Pete counted nine entries to Berry Duncan— each for $6,000—over a nine-month period. Each had the "Missouri Militia" tag.

"Your dad have any pals in the survivalist community?"

She rolled her eyes. "What do you think?"

Pete frowned. "I'm having a hard time seeing how this points to anything."

"My guess," Angela said, "is this Duncan guy helped with the conspiracy. Some of the other payments look fishy, too. There's $20,000 written out to M&M Construction."

"So?"

"So my dad doesn't keep that kind of cash lying around. And why would he make personal payments to a company that only works on public contracts?"

"Strange," Pete allowed. "But it's not enough. For one thing, if he's doing something shady, why would he keep a record of it?"

"A good question," Angela agreed.

"I mean, what could be dumber than recording something you're trying to keep on the down-low, then further incriminating yourself in the memo line?"

"It's dumb beyond belief. Yet somehow believable, if you know my dad."

She laughed, but not in a humorous way. "When you're used to getting what you want all the time, like my dad is, you tend to ignore the precautions most normal men would take. I mean, why would Nixon tape all those conversations, you know? Why did Clinton hook up with an intern? How could they not know it would bring them down in the end?"

Pete flipped through a few more pages. Angela ran her fingers through his hair in a way that always gave him goose bumps.

"Know what a smart reporter would do?" she said. "A smart reporter would make copies of that ledger, then figure out a way to go through the books at City Hall to see if the dollar amounts match up. My dad's too chickenshit to do something like this alone. The money has to be from somewhere else."

Pete stared at the notebook, his heart sagging with a sense that something seriously twisted was going on and he now was in the middle of it. And he didn't want to be. He wanted to be on the road to Florida.

"I've got to make copies of these."

"Okay," she said. "But I need this back on Dad's desk before he misses it."

Something in those words pissed him off, like Angela had done her duty and could now return to normal life. So much like a girl, dumping this massive weight on him and then running off. He suspected, not for the first time, that she would ultimately let him down, like all the girls in his life. And what was with the dimebag Truesdale had shown him? Why was a high school honors student with her whole future ahead of her smoking weed? He would have to talk to Angela about that, but now wasn't the time.

He grabbed her by the elbows in case she had any thoughts of escape.

"Look," he said. "We're both in this now. Okay?"

She nodded slowly before wrenching herself from his grip. "I know."

Pete's heart was thumping. It was like the scene in *All The President's Men* where Ben Bradlee tells Woodward and Bernstein to get their butts back in gear because only *The Washington Post*, the Nixon presidency, and the Constitution of the United States were hanging in the balance.

"All right," Pete said. "Let's get to work."

Beatrice Reilly opened her front door wielding a fire poker in one hand and a cordless phone in the other. She lowered both when she saw her cub reporter standing on the stoop, soaked clothes clinging to his frame.

"Cheese and rice, Peter!" she said. "Couldn't you call first?"

"No time. Can I come in?"

She led him into a narrow kitchen wallpapered with old *New Yorker* magazine covers. At one end of the room was a breakfast bar decorated with a vase of freshly cut daisies. She tossed Pete a kitchen towel to cover one of the bar stools before he sat down.

The editor sat on the other stool and squinted at him, her chin propped in one hand. Her robe was tied loosely over cotton pajamas that were patterned with cartoon monkeys.

"So what brings you to my door at eleven o'clock at night?"

"Can I talk to you in confidence?"

"You mean off the record?"

Pete looked around the room. The stove and countertop were immaculate, and there was the faint smell of Lemon Joy. He thought of his grandmother, who seemed to spend a large part of her solitary life scrubbing a spotless kitchen.

"I mean better than off the record," he said. "You can't tell anyone, not even the publisher."

"If this has anything to do with you and Angela Truesdale, I'm not interested."

"It does, in a roundabout way," Pete said. "But it's a story. Maybe *the* story."

Beat Reilly rested her elbows on the edge of the breakfast bar and ran her hands through her hair. She squinted over Pete's shoulder, as if spying a microscopic scrap of food she'd missed while cleaning the oven door.

"When I was a reporter, back in the Dark Ages, I went upstairs once a week for tea at my landlady's apartment. Miss Birdsong used to fill me in on all the juicy gossip floating around town. You know, who was sleeping with whom, who was a drunk, who was going broke. She was a county clerk and so she knew a lot. Anytime she had something for me that I was not to repeat, she would point to this plastic bouquet she kept on the dining room table and she'd say, 'This is between you, me, and the flowers, Beatrice.'"

Beat nodded at the daisies on the breakfast bar. "So I guess I can do the same for you, Peter."

He told her what he knew, recounting what Angela had heard and pulling out copies of the ledger he had photocopied at the *Headlight* office.

"You really think Mr. Truesdale's involved in this?"

"From what I understand, he's one of the instigators."

Beat was no great fan of the *Headlight*'s publisher, which emboldened Pete to feel that he could trust her with this news. But now he wondered if he'd made a mistake. The editor stared at the photocopies, eyed Pete suspiciously, and then looked down and read some more.

"Whole thing seems pretty far-fetched, don't you think?"

"How do you explain it, then? How do you explain the notation for the Missouri Militia?"

"I can't. How do *you* explain it?"

She folded the pieces of paper and handed them back to him.

"Pete, you're a nice kid, and you write clean, snappy prose," she said. "But I don't trust you. You've been seeing the publisher's daughter right under our noses, even during working hours, for goodness' sake. It won't be long before the whole town knows if they don't already. And now you want to do a story, based on some vague information on a personal ledger, about how Mr. Truesdale, the mayor, and some of the most powerful men in Pridemore are part of some conspiracy to kidnap Digby Willers?

"I don't buy it," she said, "and I'm certainly not going to stake my job on it."

He looked down at his lap, as he usually did when confronted by a superior.

"The friend in me, Peter, would tell you to drop this information, follow the Digby Willers story to its end, and tidy up your story clips and portfolio. You've got a few days left here at best, so make them count."

"What would the editor in you say?"

Beat groaned softly and tightened the robe over her shoulders.

"Follow the trail. See where it leads. If you've got sources at City Hall, use them. But do it on your own time. Maybe you can sell it to another newspaper. This isn't something the *Headlight* would be interested in, for obvious reasons."

Pete thanked his editor for the advice and walked out into the downpour. He had an idea of where he could start.

CHAPTER 29

The year was only half over, and it had already been a spectacularly bad one for Leland Summer. Not only was he embroiled in divorce proceedings with his third wife, who under New York law was entitled to claim half of the $5.1 million he collected each year from Freedom Television Network Inc., but *The Last Word with Leland Summer*, the evening news show he'd hosted through seven presidential administrations, had found a home in last place among the Big Four networks. It was the bottom feeder in the key demographics of men and women ages twenty-six to forty-five, according to the Nielsen numbers. Focus groups of men ages eighteen to twenty-six used words like "depressing" and "lame" to show how they felt about *The Last Word*, and females in the same age bracket described the anchor's trademark pencil-thin mustache as "creepy."

Leland Summer took cold comfort in the fact that he still ranked first among women ages sixty-five to eighty-five, meaning his core audience was, quite literally, dying off by the hour.

The bad ratings and the money-grabbing wife got the best of him on the May 15 telecast, when he went on a five-minute tirade about everything from how plaintiff lawyers were ruining the country to the excellent Indian dinner he'd enjoyed with Donald Trump the previous night.

The response was crushing. A *New York Times* editorial, titled "Summer of His Discontent," demanded that FTN fire the venerable newsman. The American Bar Association filed a defamation suit against the network over the anchor's remarks.

And Trump told reporters he hadn't broken bread with Leland Summer in at least six years.

It was a dark time in Leland-Land, which is what staffers called the three floors in FTN Tower that housed the network's news division. So, in an effort at damage control, the company's PR flack encouraged Summer to take a feature writer from *Images* magazine on a rare, behind-the-scenes look at *The Last Word*.

"Do I have to?" the anchor asked in that slight Mississippi drawl so many Americans had come to know. "I fucking hate reporters."

"I know you do," said the flack, a particularly juicy dish named Pamela. "But *Images* has a readership of two million and is as easy a mark as we're gonna get. They've agreed to run all their questions by us in advance and not ask anything about the divorce."

"Oh, why the hell not?" he said with a sigh. "It's draped across the *Post*'s front page every other day."

He looked across his desk at the PR lady and imagined how she'd look stretched naked across the bed in his West Village brownstone. A little flat-chested, but, boy, that leather miniskirt didn't leave much to imagine. Plenty of junk in that trunk, Summer surmised.

"I'll do it," he finally said. "God knows I don't need another reporter getting in my girdle, but I'll do it for you, Pam. Because I like you."

The best-paid network anchorman then leaned across his desk, tucked in his chin, and made a little-boy frown.

"Does Pammy like me?"

The following Monday morning, Summer had his limousine pick up the *Images* reporter, a wisp of a man named Grey Glass whom Summer believed he could probably crush with the sheer force of his charisma. The drive from the *Images* office at the mid-30s to FTN tower at 57th and Avenue of the Americas took about twenty-five minutes, enough time for Summer to finish his cigar and offer his new friend a tumbler of brandy.

Once on the thirty-fifth floor, he led the writer into the Bullpen, a glassed-in office in the middle of the newsroom where about a dozen producers sat along a semicircle table, clicking through images on their computers or barking orders into phone headsets. This, Summer explained, was where the team "huddled" to decide what stories would make each evening's *Last Word with Leland Summer*. They held two meetings each day, one at 9:00 a.m. and one at 4:00 p.m., to put the show together. Summer, quite naturally, was "quarterback" of this team.

"And every quarterback needs some talented guys to get the ball to. Or the team suffers. Ain't that right, Cooper?"

He placed both hands on the shoulders of a startled-looking female producer and squeezed gently.

"Just like my playin' days at Ole Miss," he said. "The girls are just as pretty—and almost as young!"

The men in the room laughed mildly at this remark. Grey Glass jotted furiously in his notepad.

"That's off the record, of course," Summer added.

The reporter nodded. "So how do you guys decide what goes on the air?"

"Great question. Basically, these guys are in contact with people in the field all day long. They work with the affiliates and other news sources all across the country, and they start piecing together our program as the day goes on. We powwow in the morning, decide on twenty stories we want to pursue. At four o'clock, we gather by the river again and cut that down to six or eight."

Summer approached a bespectacled man huddled over his computer and clamped a hand around the back of his neck.

"See, Broward here is tracking some of the top stories, and he ranks them by importance throughout the day."

"Broward retired," the man said, not looking up from his monitor. "And I don't keep the master list. That's the associate producer's job."

"Who are you?" Summer asked.

"I'm Cookson. I'm a line producer."

The news anchor clasped his hands together and let out a laugh. "So many new faces around here. They keep me young."

"I've been here six years," Cookson said.

"Of course you have," Summer said. "And we're pleased to have you with us."

He leaned toward Cookson's computer, which beamed streaming video of a TV newscaster wearing a blue raincoat and shouting into a microphone. "What's that from?"

"St. Louis."

"Crank up the sound a bit."

Summer and the *Images* writer peered over the producer's shoulder as the footage told of a mentally impaired man who had been trapped in a collapsed cave for more than two days.

"They can actually hear him wailing through the rock?" Summer asked after the story finished. He wore the solemn frown he liked to use when covering state funerals or hurricanes.

"Appears so," Cookson said.

"My God, that's horrible."

The writer scribbled in his pad. "What town was that?"

"Pridemore, Missouri," Summer said. "Isn't that the watermelon capital of the Midwest or something, Cookson?"

"I have no idea."

Summer stroked his mustache with a thumb and forefinger. "I'd like to go there."

"You would?" Cookson and the writer said in unison.

"It's a story with legs," the anchor said. "Poor dumb kid stuck in a cave for days on end with no rescue in sight. A crisis in America's Heartland. It's the kind of story we do well around here, the kind that hooks viewers in the heart and grabs 'em by the balls."

Summer placed his hands on his hips, assuming the pose of Guy in Charge. Somewhere along the way from his corner office to the Bullpen, he'd shed his Armani jacket and rolled his shirtsleeves up to his elbows, looking like a man ready for a long day of sifting through the nation's news. Too bad the *Images* wonk hadn't brought along a photographer.

"Grant!" he said.

A large, balding man rose from his console at the other end of the Bullpen and walked over to Summer with a legal pad in hand.

"Grant, this is Grey Glass from *Images* magazine." Summer turned to Grey. "Grant McCauley is associate producer for *Last Word*."

"Pleased to meet you," Grant said without taking his eyes off his boss. "What do you need, Leland?"

"We're going to Pridemore, Missouri."

"Are we?"

"I want to broadcast *Last Word* in front of the county courthouse or whatever striking visual they have out there."

Grant jotted something on his pad. "You realize we've got you going to Beijing for the economic summit Wednesday."

"Fuck the summit!" Summer said. "Nobody cares about a bunch of foreign ministers posing for a photo op. I'm talking about a *real* story, Grant. Boy trapped in cave. Townspeople frantic. You seen the footage?"

"I have."

"It's the sort of story we're known for. It's fresh."

221

"It's not bad," Grant said. "Not sure it merits the presence of a major news anchor, though. The promotions department is really going to shit over this one."

"Christ, Grant. Let's lead the charge for once."

With that, the country's fourth-place news anchor clapped his hands for everyone's attention and began barking out orders.

"Pridemore is where we'll be doing the Tuesday night cast," he said. "That means we have to hustle, people. I need to be on the ground in St. Louis tonight."

Summer glanced down at Grey Glass and gave him a wink.

"I hope you're getting all this," he said.

CHAPTER 30

At about the same time Leland Summer plotted his return to journalistic relevance, Roe Tolliver sat in the front pew for Monday morning Mass at the Lady of Our Heavenly Father Church. The little chapel overflowed with worshippers, some the mayor knew for a fact weren't even Catholic.

News cameras were allowed inside to record the service, as willful prayer seemed about the only thing the good people of Pridemore could do for Digby Willers now. Heavy rain had pounded the area from Sunday afternoon into Monday morning, turning the trail that led to Dragon's Ice House into a mudslide and swamping efforts to bring in the heavy-duty drilling equipment. They canceled a planned candlelight vigil in front of City Hall, killing what the mayor felt would have been a wonderful image for the TV stations and morning papers. More perplexing was the five-day forecast: another storm system coming down the Northern Plains and growing concern that any more rain could flood the caves, drowning Digby before the workers reached him.

The mayor softly moaned as Father Ron Matheny called the congregation to pray. The pain of bending his knees to reach the red velvet cushion below almost brought tears to his eyes. No big mystery why he hadn't been to Mass in more than a decade.

Once in position, however, he clasped his hands over the railing, and a kind of peace settled over him. It was a ritual rooted in him from childhood, though he never was particularly good at praying. His mind would wander, rolling through the previous day's baseball scores or a particularly daunting court case, or he would steal a glance at whatever young lady sat nearby. Sometimes he stared up at the crucifix, wondering what Jesus must think of Catholics decorating their churches with depictions of him nailed to two planks of wood. It always seemed to him a strange way to honor someone, portraying them in their greatest moment of suffering. The Crucifixion was supposed to be a great victory, he knew, but he wondered if Christ felt that way at the time.

He wasn't sure he believed in the Almighty. Never really pondered it much. He'd leave that to the clergy and academics who had time for such lofty ideas. He did pray on occasion, on the off chance that someone up there might be listening. He had prayed a lot after his son died, then stopped after a few months when things weren't getting any better, when it didn't seem that he was getting much of a return on his emotional investment.

Monday morning was one of those times when the mayor really prayed. He silently asked the Lord to watch over Digby's soul and comfort him in his time of suffering. He asked God to stop the rains. He asked him to help the workers pierce through the layers of limestone as quickly as possible.

Finally, taking a gulp and shutting his eyelids as tightly as he could, he asked God for forgiveness.

No need to go into details, he thought. *You know what I did. And I know that this will come back on me some way or another. But if there's a way to spare a man's soul after such an act, I pray you will. And please don't let this boy suffer for it. Amen.*

The mayor was certain this mea culpa would raise his spirits. But he left the church feeling numb, like a lawyer who followed the book in defending his client but whose heart really wasn't in it.

CHAPTER 31

Chad Hutchins let out a primal scream, rattling the jail bars as fiercely as his skinny arms could muster.

"This is bullshit!" he cried. "Total bullshit!"

Charlie Lauterbach nodded in agreement from his perch on the top bunk. For twelve hours, he'd sat on the bed, not quite finding the courage to rest his head on the yellow-stained lump that passed for a pillow. During that time, he and his cellmate had learned precious little about why they were incarcerated. No word on when they could use a phone, when they could see a lawyer, or what charges were being brought. The Pridemore chief, Cole Turner, never read Lauterbach and Hutchins their rights. He just drove them into town and handed them over to the guards at the County Stockade.

"You can't hold us here forever, you know," Lauterbach told the young guard who served them biscuits and cold coffee for breakfast. "You've got to arrest us or let us go."

"Not my business," the deputy said, his face as stiff as the rim on his beige Smokey Bear hat.

"Well, could we speak with your sheriff, or whoever's in charge here?"

"Sheriff's up at Dragon's Ice House, likely to be there all day. Big goings-on up there."

Lauterbach threw up his hands. "That's what I want to talk to him about!"

The deputy turned on his heel and didn't look back until he slammed shut the wrought iron door that connected the jail to the sheriff's office. He stared at the prisoners for a few moments through the glass slit in the door before turning away.

That was three hours ago. Not a peep from anyone since. The other cells along their row were empty, save for some derelict two doors down who snored most of the night.

It was making Lauterbach crazy—the snoring, the cold coffee, the inability to get an answer out of anyone. The fact that he was trapped in a cell with a man whose coping mechanism was singing "You Had a Bad Day" from *American Idol* over and over again didn't help things. He could really go for a nice, cold beer right about now. A nice, cold beer and a juicy steak. But mostly a beer, if he had to choose. That would make things almost tolerable, he felt.

At about eight o'clock Monday morning, Hutchins employed his own strategy for getting the sheriff's attention. He screamed. He grunted. He yelled every profanity he could imagine. He climbed up and down the bars like a monkey, even peeling off his Air Jordans and banging them against the bars.

He went at it for an hour with no success.

"I need my insulin, you bastards!" he cried. "Type II diabetes is nothing to fuck with!"

"You've got diabetes?"

"No," Hutchins whispered with a grin. "But it'll get their attention."

The skateboarder had ripped the mattress from his bed and was contemplating how to set it afire when the iron door opened with a tremendous clang. In walked a stout little man wearing a khaki uniform and sporting a trim red mustache. He strode with his shoulders back and his chest out in military fashion. Unlike Chief Turner, who often assumed the same posture, this man looked like he had actually seen the inside of a barracks. This, thought Lauterbach, must be the fellow in charge.

Seeing that his ploy had worked, Hutchins shimmied up the bars in his bare feet and let out a war whoop. The officer unsheathed his billy club and slapped it against the bars, smacking one of Hutchins's hands and sending the skateboarder flying across the cell.

"Chadwick Hutchins," he said, "do you want to go to the naughty seat?"

He nodded down the walkway to a massive chair bolted to the floor. The thick leather binding straps hanging from the naughty seat's arms and legs testified to its effectiveness as a disciplinary tool.

"You see, Chadwick has been on this row before," the cop said, still admiring the chair. "And it wasn't always what you would call a pleasurable visit for any of us."

With his cellmate writhing on the floor in pain, Lauterbach wasted no time explaining his case.

"Sheriff Miller," he said, reciting the name on the man's chest, "we've sat in your jail for half a day without the faintest idea why we're here. If I'm being charged with something, I'd like to know what it is, and I'd like to be able to call my lawyer."

The sheriff smiled thinly and nodded at the proper intervals as Lauterbach spoke.

"Well, I can tell you exactly what's happened," he said when the engineer finished. "Mr. Hutchins here has violated his parole—again. He's not supposed to walk more than fifty yards from his property at any time. That's why we got him that nice electronic anklet.

"As for you, Mr. Lauterbach. You're charged with aiding and abating Mr. Hutchins's escape, in addition to resisting arrest from an officer of the law. It's all in Chief Turner's report."

Lauterbach drew in a heavy breath. He knew he was in no position to argue. The best thing was to let his lawyer, Artie

Shorr, sort things out. But when could he get Artie on the phone? And what about the poor kid in the cave and the trap door? All these thoughts had been welling up inside him for the past twelve hours. He couldn't run the risk of going another twelve hours without talking to someone who could possibly make a difference.

"With all respect, Sheriff, those charges are bullshit," he said.

"Pardon me?"

Lauterbach climbed down from his bunk and walked toward the bars that separated him from Sheriff Miller.

"There's something else going on here," he said. "Someone is trying to silence me. I don't know why."

He sighed, feeling that this was all a pointless exercise. Miller more than likely was in cahoots with Pridemore's police chief and its loony mayor. But at this point, Lauterbach thought, what did he have to lose?

"I've come across a possible way to rescue Digby Willers."

The sheriff listened as Lauterbach recounted the excursion through the woods with Hutchins and Turner. Hutchins listened, too, occasionally shaking his head and muttering about how this was all a fucking waste of time.

"Well," the sheriff said when Lauterbach finished, "that *is* quite a story."

"Look, I know it's far-fetched, and I don't expect you to believe me. But I hope you'll have one of your men check it out, for the sake of the kid."

Sheriff Miller folded his arms and leaned against the bars that separated him from Lauterbach. His forearms were big, tan, and strangely bereft of hair.

"Sir, I can assure you that we are tracking down each and every lead we can to rescue that boy. I'll take what you've told me under advisement."

"I appreciate that, Sheriff."

"And we'll get you processed and hooked up with a phone just as soon as we can. As you can see," he said, nodding toward the row of empty jail cells, "we're pretty busy here."

The sheriff turned on his heel, just like the deputy who'd delivered the modest breakfast hours ago, and strode down the narrow hall, slapping his club against the bars along the way.

Lauterbach and Hutchins looked at each other.

"Dude," the skateboarder said, "you're never getting out of here."

With every bit of strength his arms and legs could muster, Digby hoisted his body over the slippery ledge that had bullied him for more than a day. Time and again, he had inched his way up that stupid wall, reaching the rocky overhang and clinging by his fingertips just like in the movies, only to be sent rolling back into the muck. Each time, thinking of that silly old ant who thought he'd move a rubber tree plant, Digby took a breath, scraped the mud from his eyes, and tried again.

Finally, success! He rolled onto his back and let out a whoop, then another one. He forgot for an instant about his aching body, about the pain in his stomach that sometimes made him bend over and retch, though there was nothing but air to throw up. Right now, he thought about his old P.E. teacher, the one who ragged Digby for failing to complete a single pull-up. *Up your nose wid a rubber hose, Coach Whitney*, he would have said had the old fart been around to taunt.

After resting for a few minutes, he pulled the flashlight from his bag and waved its dimming beam around. The ground was hard and wet. The ceiling was smooth but barely high enough for Digby to walk upright, and it dropped sharply just a few feet beyond the ledge. He shivered at the thought of crawling for days on his hands and knees, only to arrive at a dark, dead end. That word "dead" kept coming back to him. He was cold and wet. Out of food. The flashlight batteries were almost dead (*dead!*), and he had no idea what lay in front of him.

The smart thing would be to wait for the rescue. "Just stay where you're at and I'll find you," his mother told him in the event he ever got lost. He sometimes did—in the woods, at department stores, and, most frightening, at an out-of-town crafts fair. Always, he stayed put, like his mother instructed, often wailing for her in a high pitch. And, always, she came to him.

But something told Digby that if he waited around this time, he would die just as surely as he would by striking out on his own. Maybe he wasn't thinking straight, but it seemed the rescuers should have reached him by now, with all the drilling and hammering they'd been doing. Now and again, they'd stop their work and call out to him, reminding him to just sit tight and conserve his water and batteries. It had been slow going, because of the rain and all, but help was on the way, they said.

"Okay," Digby answered. But he didn't believe anymore.

A few days ago, or maybe it had been hours (he never had a good sense of time even when there were clocks around), a familiar voice had echoed into the cave. It was his mother. "Stay where you are," she said, "and I'll come get you."

There was something in that voice he'd never heard before. There was fear, which was understandable, but also a dullness. Like she didn't quite buy into what she was saying. Digby wasn't the smartest person in the world, but he knew his mother was a woman who always spoke her mind.

This was different. "Stay where you are," her words said, like so many times before. But her voice said something different to Digby. Her voice said, "Run."

He wished he could. He wished he was made of boulders like that guy from the Fantastic Four, and he could just burst through all the rock and limestone and get out of there. But it was slow, he had learned, crawling and climbing and getting mud in your mouth. Falling down and getting back up again.

Digby pulled the empty canteen out of his bag and placed it on its side, capturing just a little of the thin stream that ran across the floor. He would press on, like his mother wanted. But first he needed a little nourishment.

"They found it."

Chub Hughes recognized the raspy voice over the phone line as belonging to County Prosecutor Tom Treadwell.

"Found what?"

"The door."

"Wha—?"

"I've got two men locked up in the stockade who say they found that door you built into the ground a few hundred yards from Dragon's Ice House."

Chub scratched his head and tried to surmise what in the hell Treadwell was talking about. It was 7:15 a.m., and Chub had yet to fix himself the pot of coffee that helped him get his shit together most every morning. He padded into the kitchen, grabbed the canister of coffee grounds, and listened to the prosecutor prattle on about some door in the forest.

"Hold on," Chub said, suddenly recalling an early blueprint for the Ice House project that called for construction of a man-made escape hatch from the network of caves. "We never built that."

"Well, somebody damn sure built it," Treadwell said. "This guy Lauterbach is describing the exact same door the mayor told us he wanted just in case things got out of hand."

"Shit." Chub poured five scoops of grounds into his coffee filter. Now it was coming back to him. The mayor had pestered him for weeks about building some kind of device to ensure the Willers kid could be retrieved if things in the Ice House got really nasty. Chub hastily added something to the plans last winter to appease his old friend, but he'd never intended to build it. Apparently, someone at M & M Construction had followed through on the project, anyway. Chub would be sure to have that guy's ass in a wringer once all this was over.

"How long have these fellows been locked up?"

"About twelve hours. And we can't hold 'em much longer."

"You're gonna have to."

"Chub, we haven't even charged these guys with anything. We can't just detain somebody without any charges."

"Well, charge them with trespassing or something. You're the top cop around here."

"But Chub—"

"Don't get uppity with me, Tom. This thing will all blow over in a couple of days. They'll have rescued the Willers boy, and that will be that. Then you can let your prisoners go. But if you let them out now, if you even let them talk to their lawyers or their girlfriends now, we could have some real trouble on our hands."

There was a pause on the other line. Chub poured water into his coffee pot and noticed that his hands were shaking.

"Alright," the prosecutor said. "We'll figure something out."

CHAPTER 32

Leland Summer realized he had made a mistake the minute his team touched ground in Pridemore. Hell, he knew as soon as they got fifteen minutes outside of St. Louis. There is no way, the news anchor thought as he stared out at the rolling expanse of corn and soybean fields, that I am going to get laid on this trip.

Not unless he significantly lowered his standards, which Summer wasn't yet ready to do. He should have taken Grant's advice and covered the economic summit in Beijing. It was the politically safe thing to do, the food would have been excellent, and Summer would have gotten to sample some of China's most beautiful concubines. He had a weakness for Asian women going back to his days reporting for the *Stars and Stripes* in Saigon. There was something about their lithe but amazingly durable bodies that made him feel like a muscle-bound Hercules in comparison. And so polite! They'd bang you all night long and then fix you hot tea in the morning. Try finding a Manhattan socialite with that kind of dedication!

Asian women had gotten Summer in trouble more than once in his spotty marital career. But there would be no trouble in Pridemore. He was newly single, and there probably wasn't a woman with a full set of teeth within a sixty-mile radius. And it was raining like a motherfucker. Nope, he thought sadly, there would be no ravenous debauchery tonight.

Summer stood outside the FTN news van holding a golf umbrella. They had scoped out the Lewis and Clark State Park, which had taken so much rainfall over the past forty-eight hours that it was starting to look like the Amazon River Basin, and decided Pridemore's Courthouse would make a better backdrop for *The Last Word with Leland Summer*. But barely. It was one of those brick monstrosities from the 1950s that had all the charm of an East German dormitory. They were going to have a hell of a time making this place look like Main Street, USA.

"Isn't there anything visually interesting in this fucking town?" Summer said to no one in particular. His crew was busy hoisting a tarp over the makeshift *Last Word* set, and his makeup people had gone to get coffee at a drugstore down the street. It was less than an hour from airtime.

"Where the *fuuuuuck* is my makeup!" Summer screamed, but his words were swallowed in the thick sheets of rain.

Screw it, he thought. They think they can do the show without ol' Leland Summer? Let 'em try. Maybe it was time for another impromptu strike like the one he'd pulled seven years ago when the network threatened to cancel his weekend news magazine, *In Depth with Leland Summer*. He'd walked off the set a half-hour before airtime, forcing a panic-stricken producer to fill in. The episode spawned several newspaper editorials and late-night comedy routines about Summer's out-of-control ego, and that led to a two-month leave of absence spent playing golf in Bermuda. And after all that, FTN welcomed him back with a five-year extension and a one-million-dollar signing bonus.

Yes, a day would come when Summer would be back on top of the ratings and could send them reeling with another well-timed tantrum. But not now. Not in Pridemore, Missouri. So he closed his umbrella, brushed the rain off his Italian suit, and stepped back into his motor coach.

It was one of the nicer ones, he had to admit. The converted bus was outfitted with leather seats, a queen-sized waterbed, a forty-inch plasma TV flanked by two smaller screens (so he could watch FTN's three rival networks simultaneously), and a wet bar stocked with three cases of Dr. Pepper, Summer's favorite.

He popped one open and was flipping through the morning's New York papers when he heard a rapid-fire knock on the door. It was Monty, a network publicist and the guy responsible for keeping the public at a healthy distance on road trips like this.

"What is it?"

"A visitor. The local newspaper publisher."

"Christ, now?"

"He just needs five minutes."

Summer muttered something to himself. FTN was constantly catering to clowns like this in hopes of getting some positive local press. Yet another reason to stay in New York and leave the real work to the correspondents.

"Fine. Let 'em in."

A middle-aged man in a blue suit bounded up the stairs and flashed Summer a gleaming grin. He was an okay-looking fellow, with silver hair coiffed in what must have been a very expensive haircut even here in the hinterland. But Summer was more interested in the man's companion, a dark-haired, puffy-lipped girl in a sweatshirt that read "Pridemore Bulldogs" in block letters.

"Larry Truesdale," the man said, squeezing Summer's hand and pumping vigorously.

"Always nice to meet a fellow member of the Fourth Estate," Summer said, returning the smile.

"This is my daughter, Angela," Truesdale said, pushing the girl forward. "She grew up watching *Last Word* every night on our old twenty-four-inch Sony."

"A pleasure," the anchor said, giving her a lightning-quick once over. Even in her sweats, he could tell the girl had a tight bod, one that would look good draped across his queen-sized waterbed on a hot Missouri night.

"And how old are you, dear?"

"Eighteen."

Shit, he thought. You never can tell these days. He could have sworn she was at least early twenties.

"Well, your daddy must be proud to have such a poised young lady for a daughter," he said, giving Larry Truesdale one of those isn't-it-amazing-how-fast-they-grow-up winks. "Can I sign anything for you folks?"

"Thanks, but no," the girl said. "I don't believe in autographs."

"Really?"

"It's nothing personal," she said with a little smile. "It just seems sad, getting validation from another person's signature."

"Well," Summer said, stroking his thin mustache with thumb and forefinger. "That's a very mature outlook."

"I mean, just meeting and talking with you is cool enough."

Whatever floats your boat, honey, Summer thought.

The girl excused herself so her dad could do his interview with the great anchorman. The two men sat on the couch, and Summer gulped the rest of his Dr. Pepper.

"She's something, isn't she?" the publisher said as he fumbled with a tape recorder. "Straight-A student and captain of the cheerleading squad. We couldn't be prouder."

"I'll bet."

"I only have a couple of questions."

"Take all the time you need," Summer said, glancing at his watch.

The newspaperman stammered through the usual queries about FTN, Summer's illustrious career, and why the network chose Digby Willers as a national story. And Summer rattled off the stock answers about how *Last Word* always goes where the news is, how generous the hard-working people of central Missouri had been to the FTN team, and how a small town like

Pridemore was much more emblematic of the American spirit than New York or Los Angeles. It was boilerplate stuff that Summer could blather for days while he thought about other things. Like bending this guy's snotty daughter over the couch and giving her the nice, firm spanking she richly deserved. That would, of course, lead to some things Summer was only beginning to explore by the time Truesdale wrapped up the interview.

"Tell me something," he said after the publisher had tucked the tape recorder into his jacket. "Do you know where a guy can get a good screw in this town?"

"Pardon me?"

"Look, I just got a divorce. And it gets lonely on the road. I was just wondering if you knew someone who could arrange, you know, a visit."

Truesdale nodded like he got this kind of request all the time. But his eyes looked like they were about to roll out of his head.

"I dunno," Summer said. "Maybe an exotic massage parlor or something. Y'all have any of those?"

The publisher's head bobbed up and down as he backed slowly toward the exit.

"I think I know a place," he said, "that can help you."

"Aw, forget it," Summer said. "I can take care of myself. Here, have a Dr. Pepper."

"No, I know a place," the publisher said, backing down the motor coach steps, almost bowing as he did so. "It would be an honor."

Dakota Marx had just conquered the seventh stage of *Criminal Intent II* when his iPhone blew up. He paused his game and checked the phone. Rubin, his punk-ass agent, was calling for the first time in more than a week.

"What up?" Dakota said in a slow drawl that belied his Santa Monica upbringing.

"Turn your television to channel nine now."

"Man, I'm gamin'. I'm taking down the Lopez Cartel."

"Good for you. Now turn on the TV."

With a groan of someone enduring the latest in a life of personal hardships, the pop star did as told. He switched to Channel 9 and got the evening news.

"Who's the old guy?"

"That's Leland Summer," Rubin said.

"He still on? Man, my grandma used to have a thing for him."

"Just watch and listen."

Dakota did. It was hard at first to understand what this had to do with the price of rice in China. There was a lot of footage of trees and rescue workers and this cave in Kansas or Missouri where this dude was buried alive. Then ol' Leland played what he said was audio of the guy singing—they could hear him singing through, like, twenty feet of solid rock. The song got Dakota Marx's attention.

"That's one of mine!"

It was, in fact, a rendition of "Tryin' to Remember," the third single off *QueenFest* that was currently stalled at number 38 on the Billboard charts. Sales of Dakota's latest album had been disappointing since he'd canceled his US tour (for "personal reasons," as the press release put it) last summer.

"This kid has been trapped in a cave for four days, and he's a huge Dakota fan," Rubin said. "He sings your songs as a way to keep his spirits up. They don't know if he's going to make it out alive."

"Man," Dakota said. "That's cold."

"Do you know what this kind of exposure means for us?"

The singer thought for a moment.

"It means we're back?"

"Shit, yeah, we're back! But we've got to act fast. I need you on a plane to Missouri tonight."

"Why the hurry?"

"Well, the kid's stuck in the ground with no food and water, Dakota. You've got to get over there before something happens."

"What am I s'posed to do?"

"Sing him one of your hits. Lead a candlelight vigil. Hug his mom. Don't worry, I'll work it all out."

Dakota groaned. It had been almost a year since he took the stage. It was in Dayton in the middle of July. Playing through a thunderstorm at one of them goddamned amphitheaters. Seven feet from where he stood, his lead guitarist was struck by lightning, and, although the guy recovered, Dakota was thoroughly spooked. It could have been him. Nearly a year later, he still couldn't even think about singing in front of an audience.

"I dunno, man."

"Look, you've got to get over this stage fright thing. It's killing your career."

Dude's right, Dakota thought. Sooner or later, he would have to man up and face his fears. He'd think about this kid-in-a-cave thing, maybe talk it over with Carmen by the pool. It had been an unusually cool spring in Los Angeles. Today was the first in forever when you could get in a swim without freezing your 'nads off.

"Peace," Dakota said, and he hung up before the agent got another word in. There were a lot of distractions when you were a pop star, and it was hard to tune them out. But it had taken Dakota twenty-four hours of nonstop gaming to get to Stage Eight of *Criminal Intent II*, and he'd be damned if he was going to quit now. He was just a few more kills away from controlling 80 percent of the world's cocaine trade.

"Who you talking to?"

"Shit!" Dakota said, throwing his controller to the hardwood floor. "Can't I get no peace?"

"Sorry, Boo," Carmen said. He was a broad-shouldered man with a deep tan and barbed-wire tattoos on each arm. "Just taking an interest in your life, that's all. Want some grapes?"

Dakota dipped his hand into the bowl placed next to his armchair. Carmen put his hands on the singer's bare shoulders and rubbed gently.

"So what's bothering you?"

"Rubin's busting my balls about doing a show in the Flyover. A benefit for some retarded kid stuck in a cave."

"Sounds interesting," Carmen said.

"I dunno."

"You haven't performed in a while. This might be good for you."

Dakota reached for one of the big man's forearms and squeezed it. "You'll go with? I can't do this alone."

Carmen let out a long, low chuckle that sounded like the thumping of a bass drum.

"Sure, Boo. I'll go with."

Wearing a burgundy kimono that was given to him by the late emperor of Japan, Leland Summer sipped from a tumbler of brandy while catching up on e-mail. He lingered on the ones congratulating him for the Pridemore coup ("Bold, brash, decisive—the best journalism we've done in ages," wrote FTN's vice president of programming). There was even a note from his archrival, HTV's Russell Stone, who was holed up in Beijing with the rest of the national press: "Congrats on taking the road less traveled… Yours is the only story people will talk about around the coffee pot tomorrow morning."

Summer smiled and rattled off a quick reply. "Mucho thanks! Rest assured, the food's much better in Beijing.... Bring me back some moo shu pork if you can!"

He closed his laptop and took a sip from his brandy, letting it rest on his tongue for a moment before swallowing it. He listened to the rain pitter-patter on the motor coach's roof. It had been a good day, the best in many a fortnight. And, based on the official reports, the rescue team hadn't made much progress since the storms began. The Digby Willers story might have legs well into next week. One could only hope.

Summer contemplated replaying the DVR of the evening newscast one more time before bed when he heard a knock on the door. It was ten o'clock. The PR flack knew not to bother him unless it was extremely important. He briefly wondered if it was someone of the female persuasion—he had told security to let any attractive young honeys through, in case the newspaperman made good on his promise to deliver some action. Summer felt he deserved to release a little tension after the day he'd had.

He opened the door to a young girl holding an umbrella. It was the smart-mouthed brunette who'd dropped by with the publisher a few hours ago. My God, Summer thought. He appreciated the man's efforts, but enlisting one's own daughter for a one-night stand was kind of appalling. Guess there were no other takers, Summer thought as he ushered the girl in.

"Angela, right?"

"Yes."

He motioned for her to sit on the couch and offered a glass of brandy.

"Sorry," she said. "I'm underage."

The news anchor chuckled and peered at her over his reading glasses, the ones he wore on TV when there was particularly grave news to report.

"But not too young to visit a man nearly four times your age in the middle of the night?"

Summer sat in the armchair across from her and adjusted his kimono so it wouldn't show his stuff. She really was a peach—long hair and brown eyes you could just swim around in for days. Too bad she was so young. A pity, really.

"Look, you probably think I'm a good guy, from seeing me on TV and all. But you don't know me.

"You don't know what's in here," he said, running a hand across his hairy chest. "You're lucky that I have some standards where women are concerned. And while being with someone your age isn't technically illegal in the state of Missouri, it's probably frowned upon, isn't it?"

The girl stared at him. "What are you talking about?"

He walked to the mini-fridge, pulled out a Dr. Pepper, and poured it into a glass. "Don't get me wrong. You've got it going on. Lord knows I've done a few gals close to your age at one time or another. But things are different now. I gotta be careful."

He handed her the soda.

"Come back in five years and maybe we'll talk."

The girl shuddered like someone had dropped ice down her shirt. "You think I'm here to have sex with you?"

"Well?"

"You're, like, eighty years old!"

"Sixty-eight," the anchor said with a frown. "Doctor says I have the prostate of a fifty-five-year-old."

Angela pressed both hands against her temples and groaned.

"I came to talk about Digby Willers."

Summer flipped through his mental Rolodex: Willers.... Willers.... Where had he heard that name before? Oh, yes! The kid in the cave.

"What about him?"

"There's more to the story than you know."

"Is that a fact?" Summer leaned back in his chair, downed his last sip of brandy, and brought the glass down on the side table with an angry clink. "And what's a silly girl like you gonna tell me about my story?"

The girl's face turned crimson as she dug her fingernails into the couch's smooth leather.

"You know what? Forget it. I've lived in this town my whole life. I know the people. I know the culture. I know the mayor is an egomaniacal troll who'll stop at nothing to get what he wants. And I'm pretty sure this whole rescue operation is just a means of achieving that end.

"But don't mind me. I'm just another life support system for a vagina, just aching to spread my legs for the great Leland Summer."

Kid's got some sass, Summer thought. And she wasn't done, sucking in her chest as if girding for a final assault.

"Well, fuck that shit, and fuck you, and fuck your stupid show!"

She stood up, knocking over her Dr. Pepper in the process. Angela had almost reached the door when Summer grabbed her by the arm.

"Wait," he said, peering at her through those famous spectacles. "Tell me more."

CHAPTER 33

Roe Tolliver didn't get home in time for *The Last Word with Leland Summer* because of a late-night cram session with the engineers on the "next steps" in the rescue operation. The bottom line was that they were screwed: it had rained off and on for more than two days, the trail leading to Dragon's Ice House was too steep and muddy for the big drilling machines to navigate, and the caves were taking on more rainwater by the hour. Pounding through the rock by hand—slow, delicate work under the best conditions—was crippled by the downpours. And there was more rain in the forecast for the next three days. No one had a particularly good take on what the hell to do next.

So when the mayor got home around eleven o'clock, he was relieved to learn that Margaret had taped *The Last Word* and had leftover meatloaf waiting for him to microwave. He got through the intro of Leland Summer sitting on a stool at Truman's Malt Shop (mental note: make sure the newscasters work City Hall into their live shots) before the phone rang.

"How are tricks, Roe?" a familiar, raspy voice said. "You watch the evening news?"

The mayor cleared his throat and shifted his lounger to an upright position. It was about damn time the son of a bitch called him back.

"Hello, Governor," he said. "How are you tonight?"

"I'm concerned, Roe. Very concerned. I'm coming to Pridemore tomorrow to see what I can do."

I'll bet you are, you glory-grabbing whore, the mayor thought. He had phoned Governor George Wesley's office at least a dozen times over the past two days and couldn't even get a staffer to call him back. Now the story gets on national TV, and guess who suddenly wants in the game?

"Governor, we would be honored to have you."

"So how is the boy?"

Well, he's been dead for almost fifty years, Roe thought before realizing the governor wasn't asking about *his* boy. Nobody talked about Jack anymore. The governor wanted to know about the Willers boy.

"It's not looking good," the mayor said. "The first couple days, we heard him singing through the bedrock, but we haven't had much of that lately. The weather hasn't helped."

The governor grunted like a man who was either deep in thought or about to doze off.

"Anything you need, Roe, you just ask," he said. "National Guardsmen, the state police, the DOT...whatever you need."

"That's very kind of you."

"Normally we wouldn't get involved in this kind of operation. But this is obviously a special case."

It is indeed, the mayor thought. A governor can lose thousands of votes in an election year if he doesn't show the proper amount of concern. But no matter what the governor did, nobody could save Digby Willers if it rained like this for another day. Well, almost nobody.

"My people will call tomorrow morning to set things up," the governor said. "You take care, Roe."

"See you tomorrow," the mayor said before gently placing the phone receiver in its cradle. With a soft groan, he pushed himself out of the lounger and shuffled to the kitchen window. Watching the drops meander down the glass panes, he tried remembering the last time it had rained so hard over a twenty-four-hour period.

The mayor was, by nature of his profession, a man given to gross exaggeration. But he didn't think he would be too off base in likening what had happened over the past few days to something out of the Old Testament.

CHAPTER 34

Until about a week ago, the worst thing that ever happened in Pete Schaefer's life was the day his parents sat him down to tell him that they were getting a divorce, and that Pete and his mom would be moving to Omaha. That was ten years ago, but not so distant that Pete forgot sitting ramrod straight on the sofa, his fingers digging into the suede cushions as he took in the awful news.

That was a bad day. But lately Pete sensed that he was headed for an even more precipitous fall, one that could result in his body being unearthed off some country road, like those poor Civil Rights workers in 1960s Mississippi. He mulled over this scenario Tuesday night while sitting in his Ford, trying to decide if he should follow up on the information Angela gave him or if he should head down the highway to friendlier climes. Something, perhaps a latent desire to see his life completely destroyed, kept him in Pridemore that night. Or maybe the reporter in him just wanted to see this story all the way through. Whatever the reason, Pete's belongings were packed and waiting by the door of his apartment in case he had a change of heart.

On Wednesday morning—another drizzly day, but with a few spurts of sunshine—Pete went to work, hanging outside the Dragon's Ice House with the ever-growing media circus. All four networks and most of the cable news channels now had correspondents on the ground, and the National Guard had pulled into town overnight. He filed his story from the *Headlight* newsroom at around 4:00 p.m., then walked over to

City Hall to look at some old police files. That's what he said he was doing, anyway.

Pete's real goal was to sneak into the mayor's office and dig through his files, hoping to find incriminating evidence that jibed with what Angela found. If there truly was a conspiracy behind the Digby Willers mess, he was sure Roe Tolliver was neck-deep in it. Maybe the old fox got sloppy and left a paper trail.

Breaking into the mayor's chamber was as simple as walking into the third floor bathroom during working hours and crouching in a stall, both feet on the seat to avoid detection, until the building closed and everyone went home. There was only a skeleton crew on hand—the police and most of the city staff were out at the rescue site. Save for the dispatcher down in the basement, the place was empty by six o'clock, when Pete emerged from his stall, tiptoed down the hall, and gently turned the brass doorknob to the mayor's office.

Pete had been in there before, for an off-the-record interview about the city budget that quickly turned confrontational and ended with the mayor ranting about yellow journalism. Save for the big oak desk and a couple of pictures on the wall of the mayor with old Missouri governors, the room was pretty Spartan. In fact, the desk was cleared of everything save for a silver letter opener and a yellowed, three-by-five photo of a sandy-haired boy. Pete wondered if it was a picture of the mayor as a child—the old man never mentioned having kids of his own. Something about the photo gave him the chills, or maybe it was the fact that someone could burst in on him at any moment.

Come on, Schaefer, he told himself, do what you came here to do. It only took a few minutes to find the filing cabinet key, hidden beneath a box of city stationery in the desk's middle drawer. For the next hour, Pete pored over sheaths of spreadsheets, billing statements, meeting agendas, and personal notes before coming across a file folder intriguingly labeled "Off the Books." In it, he found four letter-sized envelopes, each one about an inch thick with one-hundred-dollar bills. Also interesting was the blue letterhead on the envelopes that read "M&M Construction Co."

"Shit," Pete said. He guessed he was holding more than $10,000 in kickbacks from the area's largest contractor, the company charged with making a tourist attraction out of the Lewis & Clark Land Bridge and Dragon's Ice House.

There was more, including a file marked "Personal Transactions," which Pete opened with the zeal of a cheetah running down a wounded gazelle. After some more digging, he found himself staring at four personal checks made out to Larry Truesdale. Each was for $6,000, the same amount the newspaper publisher paid out to the mysterious Berry Duncan.

Breathing deeply, Pete took his phone out of its holster and snapped pictures of the checks and the envelopes of money, all nestled together on top of the mayor's desk.

He looked at his watch. It was 7:45 p.m. Another half-hour and it would be dark enough for him to sneak out of the building unnoticed. His heart pounding, Pete reminded himself to relax and calmly reassemble the files that were now strewn across the tiled floor. Slowly, patiently, he packed the file folders into their drawers in what was really a blind guess at their proper order. With any luck, it won't matter, he told himself. Good ol' Roe would be hauled off on corruption charges by the end of the week.

He finished his work by 8:15, then hunched in the mayor's armchair until just a sliver of daylight hung over the downtown buildings. Dark enough to slip out of City Hall unseen, light enough to see where the hell he was going.

Built in the 1950s, City Hall was one of the most prominent structures in town. Only the grain elevator and the First Baptist

Church steeple were taller. A three-story edifice of flagstone and yellow brick, the building had massive, floor-to-ceiling windows that were lined outside with thick stone ledges. It was Pete's thinking that he could dangle himself from the ledge outside the mayor's window, then drop into the chin-high hedge that wrapped around the building.

Had Pete done more research, he would have known to take the stairs to the ground level of City Hall and try leaving via the fire exit, which was never locked from the inside. He would also have known that those hedges around City Hall, while big and springy enough to break a twenty-foot fall, were actually a particularly mean strain of sticker bush, with thorns thick enough to puncture a tennis shoe.

Pete realized this while crashing butt-first into the well-trimmed branches, his bare arms and legs scrapped and slashed by dozens of needles. For an instant, he lay on his back atop the bush, extremities flailing in the air, before the branches collapsed and Pete found himself imprisoned in the plant's substructure, stinging pain puncturing every part of his body.

"The hell you doin', boy?"

Through the broken branches, Pete saw a large man approaching, wearing the light blue shirt of either a body shop mechanic or a Pridemore Public Safety officer. Pete wasn't going to hang around to find out which.

With a pained grunt he rolled out of the sticker bush and onto the soggy grass, falling into a four-point sprinter's stance.

"Hey, hold it!"

He broke the man's grip. The big guy was a sky-blue blur as Pete ran across the lawn, puddles exploding around his sneakers as he ran.

Groping through his pockets for the car keys—don't tell me I left them on the mayor's desk, he thought—Pete ran into the street, not seeing the oncoming van until he was flying into its windshield like some kind of hapless sparrow. It was a white van, he noticed in the millisecond before he hit the pavement, driven by a thick, mustachioed man with a look of comic horror on his face.

Then the pavement. Then pain. Then barely making out the people who were huddled over him.

"You okay?" one of them asked.

"He better be dead," someone else said.

Pete knew he would be out soon. He was fading fast. Images of personal checks and cash-stuffed envelopes flew through his head.

"Phone," he said, tasting blood in his mouth. "Where's my phone?"

"Wow, you look like shit."

Angela had come to visit Pete in the hospital. She was right, of course. He had a broken clavicle, three broken ribs, a bruised kidney, and a concussion. In the hand mirror beside his bed, Pete's face looked like a peach that was quickly going bad. His right eye socket was dark and puffy, and his lower lip had swelled to twice its normal size. His body was a landscape of cuts and bruises from the encounter with the sticker bush, the white van, and the Main Street asphalt.

The doctor told Pete he was lucky. The truck that hit him was a news van, speeding through downtown at about forty-five miles an hour. Apparently, the driver, a cameraman for a TV affiliate in Springfield, was in a rush to get some footage of Dragon's Ice House before the ten o'clock newscast. The police let him off with a warning; the local authorities were under orders not to ticket any members of the visiting media.

"Too bad we're not in the Middle East," Angela said. "They'd run that idiot down and tear him limb by limb."

"Not a big deal," Pete said, moving his giant lip as little as possible. "Shoulda watched where I was going."

"Yeah, where *were* you going, anyway?"

She leaned over him, her breath smelling like cigarettes and Big Red gum.

"You know, they're going to arrest you," she said. "They would have done it earlier, but they thought you might be dead."

Pete chuckled weakly at this small victory.

"I guess what I'm saying is," she whispered, "if you have anything to tell me about what you saw in that office, you'd better tell me now."

"I'll do you one better." He nodded toward the chair next to his bed, where his bloodstained clothes were bundled in a trash bag. "Look in my pants."

Angela picked through the laundry, pulling out several balled-up tissues until she found the silvery phone. It was banged up from the collision, and Pete hoped it still worked. A bystander had fetched it from under the news van just before Pete blacked out.

She picked up the phone and pressed a button. After a moment, the phone chirped its happy greeting song. Eureka.

"What do I do with this?"

He thought for a moment about whom he could trust with this information. No one, really. But his editor was a safer bet than most.

"Give it to Beat Reilly. She'll know what to do."

Angela arched an eyebrow. "The *Headlight*? You sure about that?"

"It'll be okay."

She gave Pete a pursed-lip look that seemed to say, *it's your fucking funeral.* He tried contorting his mouth into a reassuring smile.

"Thanks," he said.

"For what?"

"I don't know. For being my girl."

He meant it in a Girl Friday sort of way, like in the old

black-and-white movies about newspapermen. But Angela seemed to take it differently, briefly beaming before settling into a street-smart smirk. "Yeah, you better thank me."

She leaned in and gave him a kiss on the forehead.

"I'll come see you tomorrow," she said. Then Angela was gone, the hospital hallway bathing her figure in fluorescence.

Good, Pete thought. His mom would be here soon, and Pete lacked the energy to explain how he came to know an eighteen-year-old wearing Daisy Duke shorts and an Anchor Club T-shirt.

With a grunt, he pressed the button for the nurse's station. He could use another bag of morphine.

A heavyset woman with forearms rippling from under her scrubs answered the call. Something about her was familiar.

"Pete Schaefer, as I live and breathe," she said. "Boy, do we have a lot to talk about."

Shit, he thought. He was so tired of this story, tired of this town. It would almost be a relief when the deputies came to arrest him. As Susan Willers hooked a new bag to his catheter, Pete thought about Angela Truesdale and how fetching she'd been in the red, spaghetti-string halter top that first day he talked to her, when they wound up kissing on the courthouse steps. He wondered if they would ever rise above that frayed-nerve-ending, hormones-run-amok level. Was this someone he could start a new life with down in Florida? He'd like to think so. After she finished high school, of course.

The big nurse prattled on about her miseries, how she had to work the evening shift while her son's life hung in the balance. Pete pressed the release button, letting the equivalent of a six-pack into his bloodstream. He closed his eyes and pictured a secluded beach, Angela in a sexy but sensible swimsuit, and the manuscript of his future bestseller resting under a Mexican beer.

It was a good place to be.

CHAPTER 35

Like ants to a watermelon rind, the electronic media converged on the sweet juices of the Digby Willers story until their numbers seemed larger than the city of Pridemore itself. By Wednesday night—day five of the drama—the streets were lined with television crews from Britain, Japan, Taiwan, France, Italy, even tiny Lithuania.

Leland Summer's newscast from Pridemore solidified the Willers story as a cultural happening, but the cable news networks had been covering the saga for days, breaking away frequently from the war in the Middle East or the latest missing suburban teen to give updates on the rescue attempt, usually under hand-wringing captions like "Crisis in the Heartland." Gradually, the big networks took greater interest, and then overseas reporters started trickling into town Wednesday morning. Aside from the rescue operation, which was quite literally stuck in the mud, there was the titillating rumor that the fast-fading but still relevant pop star Dakota Marx would play an impromptu show in Pridemore as part of a candlelight vigil. In terms of compelling television, you couldn't do much better in the summer months than frantic rescuers, raging thunderstorms, and a pop music pretty boy thrown together in the same small town.

So great was the crush of TV crews and news trucks that the authorities began requiring press passes to gain access to the muddy lot outside the Lewis and Clark Land Bridge. Those not fortunate enough to obtain a pass were usually relegated to roaming the streets of Pridemore, talking about the story with anyone they could find. Once it seemed that everyone in town had given at least five interviews, the reporters began interviewing each other. The story, in effect, became about how the media was handling the story.

"How would you rate the coverage of Digby Willers so far?" Taft Goldman, one of the dozen or so cable news talk show hosts in town, asked a media critic Tuesday night. "In a time of war and scandal in Washington, does the plight of one Midwesterner merit this much attention?"

The answer, apparently, was yes. The president, vacationing at Camp David, released a statement saying he had watched the televised rescue with "great concern" and that "our hearts and prayers go out to that young man and his family." Halfway across the world, a Saudi prince, deeply touched by the unfolding drama, was planning to fly to Pridemore in his private jet to make a "humble gift" to the Willers family and the city. Pundits were already speculating on whether or not the prince had ties to global terrorism.

Maybe it was the public's growing fascination with "real people" news: runaway brides, missing children, trapped coal miners and the like. Maybe it was the fact that it had been a relatively dull Memorial Day weekend. Whatever the case, the Willers story had legs—Nicole Kidman legs—as far as the media was concerned. It was hard to believe, but tiny Pridemore, Missouri, was muscling for airtime with the likes of Jerusalem, Baghdad, and Kabul, trouble spots drummed into the nation's consciousness. For a week, at least, Pridemore was one of them.

Dakota Marx hated the Boonies. Maybe it was because he was half-Latino, but there was something about rural America that creeped him out. All those lily-white faces—he sometimes wondered how many of them would just as soon see him hanging from a tree. He had taken a canoe trip in Montana a few years back and totally flipped out, convinced the Ku Klux

255

Klan was after him. Except, instead of wearing white sheets and burning crosses, these guys carried glow sticks and danced around their campfires to endless Jimmy Buffet tunes. "Hit 'em, man!" he screamed as a friend drove him out of the crowded campground. "Hit 'em all! Can't you see they're trying to kill us?"

Note to Dakota, he thought, do not smoke a bowl when you're out in the sticks and already more than a little paranoid.

If he had any sense of irony at all (and he didn't), Dakota might have found it amusing that the most pivotal performance of his career would come in a town that was about as far from an interstate highway as the pop singer had ever been. But all he could think about was how much he hated being here. He started hyperventilating the instant his jet touched down at the tiny airfield. The stage fright was bad enough—it had been nearly a year since that fateful show in Dayton, his last live performance. But to take to the stage again here in Pridemore, Missouri (or was it Kansas?), was almost too much for him to handle.

All those flabby white people watching him, sheriff's deputies and National Guardsmen eying him suspiciously, the strange buzzing noise coming from the woods (Carmen said they were probably crickets). For Dakota, it was a perfect storm of bad vibrations.

They led him down a path that ran along a creek and tunneled underneath what was described as a land bridge. The air was cool and thick, and the mossy, slimy wall of the land bridge closed in on the trail so that you had to duck a couple of times to avoid hitting your head. Someone mentioned something about settlers and explorers, but Dakota was too busy stepping around the mud puddles to pay much attention. He had just bought a new pair of Tanino Crisci loafers, and he'd be damned if he would ruin them in this God-awful place.

Clutching his acoustic guitar like a favorite teddy bear, the pop singer arrived at the massive hole in the ground called Dragon's Ice House just before sundown. The place looked like the aftermath of a fierce jungle war. Trees were knocked down and pushed aside, forming a clearing just wide enough to accommodate two truck-mounted drills, several Bobcats, and other heavy-duty equipment Dakota couldn't identify. The ground was a boggy mess, churned up again and again by machinery moving in the rain. The mud was up to Dakota's ankles; he had to ball up his feet just to keep his loafers on as he plodded toward the cave.

Several dozen workers wearing hard hats and overalls awaited him, most of them perched on their muddy machinery. Two aluminum bleachers flanked Dragon's Ice House, one filled with neatly dressed dignitaries and the other with television camera crews. A pair of blonds in business suits handed out candles and were briefing everyone on the proper way to display them. Some of the hard-hats seemed perturbed by the ritual. The politicians looked like they were eating this up.

"Why aren't they trying the save the kid?" Dakota asked Carmen, the bodyguard and personal assistant who had promised not to leave the singer's side.

"I don't know, Boo," Carmen said. "Just keep walking."

The old guy in the seersucker suit, the one who'd met them at the airstrip and introduced himself as the mayor, led Dakota to a small platform and microphone directly in front of the cave's entrance.

"We don't know if he'll be able to hear you," the old man whispered. "The workers haven't had contact with him for almost a day."

The singer nodded. The idea was that, in singing a playlist of Digby's favorite songs, Dakota could offer some calm and reassurance to the kid in his darkest hour. That was the real-deal Holyfield, the reason he was here. Another perk, his agent Rubin explained on the plane, was getting to perform his hits on at least two major networks with no commercial interruption.

But to Dakota, it was mostly about the kid. A kid who, by the looks of it, didn't stand much chance of surviving. That was cold, even to a celebrity like Dakota Marx who loved the bitches, loved the bling, loved his '64 Bentley and his mansion in the Hillz. The singer had a soft spot for children, especially the ones he visited in the burn units and cancer wards, the ones barely strong enough to lift their heads. It was cold what they were going through, and, for Dakota, it meant the world to give those kids just a little bit of joy.

But here's the mayor saying this kid might not even hear the music. What the fuck? Why was he here? To entertain these politicians and keep the hard-hats away from their work? What was the point if the kid couldn't hear the music?

Carmen must have known what he was thinking, because the big man placed both hands on the singer's shoulders and gently squeezed. God love him, Dakota thought, he always knows what to do. Through life's long road, he'd never experienced a connection like the one he and Carmen shared. It was like they had a direct line to each other's senses. Dakota had been with other men, but never considered himself bisexual. It was just part of The Life. When the dessert tray comes your way, he figured, you need to have a bite of everything.

But now he wasn't so sure of his sexuality. Alone with Carmen, he never thought of anyone else. That was unique for Dakota, who almost always thought of himself.

"Be cool," Carmen whispered to him. "You can do this."

"Yeah," he said. The mayor was at the microphone, rambling on about this and that. The old dude could talk, like those television preachers on Sunday morning. So sure of himself. Then the governor of Missouri (or was it Kansas?) got up and gave a little speech, looking smooth and polished in his dark blue suit. Dakota wished he had that confidence, to just get up there and talk to people.

The governor finished and stared at the pop singer with an expectant smile. So did everyone else. All those eyes. Those milky faces. Dakota approached the mic, strummed a couple of chords and looked into his audience. Carmen was below him now, watching with everyone else. Hold it together, boy, he told himself.

"Um," he said. "This is one of Digby's favorite songs."

He looked down, strummed a chord, tried not to think too much. His hands would know what to do.

"Yeah, this is a song of hope."

He launched into "All Right Soon." It was like diving into cold water. After the initial shock, you wondered why you made such a big deal about it.

> *Girl, you want to know what's in my heart.*
> *But I don't want to know,*
> *Just where you get off tellin' me,*
> *which way my love should flow...*

It was a slow, almost folksy ballad without the synthesizer and drum machine. It had never been one of his favorites, though the song made him an awful lot of money. But he liked this version.

One by one, the workers held up their candles, swaying them to and fro. Looking out at the throng, the smallest audience he'd played for in years, Dakota felt a lump in his throat.

> *Girl, you know you are my sunshine,*
> *And you know you shoot the moon.*

And I've got a funny feelin',
Things'll be all right soon.
All right soon. All right soooooon…

The rain started falling during the second chorus. By the song's end, it was a downpour, snuffing out the candles and causing the big shots to duck under their sports coats. Undaunted, Dakota burst into "QueenFest" and then a blistering version of "Tears on Tower 2," his ode to 9/11. An enormous thunderclap took him briefly to the lightning storm in Dayton, when a bandmate was electrocuted through his whammy pedal. But this time, Dakota kept playing.

The next morning, the talking heads would rate the performance with epochal moments like Elvis's comeback special or the Beatles playing Shea Stadium. But history was the last thing on Dakota's mind. All he knew was, for the first time in more than a year, he was feeling it. They dragged him off the stage after about an hour, when most of the crowd had scattered. He had a big smile on his face. The fear was gone.

CHAPTER 36

The concert would have raised Digby's spirits had he heard it. But the power chords that penetrated the fallen limestone and bounced through the contorted passageways faded long before they reached the narrow space Digby occupied, struggling just to breathe.

The past several hours had been a nightmare of twists and turns, of dead ends and death-defying escapes. Digby's journey took him through crawl spaces barely wide enough for him to wiggle through and caverns large enough for a game of full-court basketball. He waded in freezing water and crawled through bad-smelling muck that he slowly realized was, in fact, a huge pile of bat shit.

He'd long ago lost contact with the disembodied voices calling his name, asking if he was all right, telling him to hang in there. He hadn't eaten in at least two days and was left with a dying flashlight (which he used in only the most desperate situations) and a canteen filled with dirty water. Digby had lost all sense of direction, not knowing whether he was moving closer to the surface or deeper into the earth. He wandered blindly, hoping for a thin ray of sunlight around the next corner. If it was even daytime, which he couldn't know for sure.

Like a lot of the passages he'd gone through, this one started as a large crevice and gradually got smaller and smaller until he had to flatten his body against rock just to inch his way through. These narrow spaces, he had learned, either opened into a cavern after a few feet or ended altogether. But this one went on and on, until Digby found himself on his back, water flowing all around him, his face pressed against a crack in the limestone for air.

Total blackness. The flashlight and canteen had washed away. This, he thought, must be what it's like to be buried alive.

He tried reversing himself. But his arms, pinned to his sides, wouldn't allow it. The only way was forward, and then just barely. He used his fingers and toes to push ahead, one painful inch at a time.

He began to lose feeling in his arms and legs, and a burning sensation rose through his chest. The air pocket was gone, and Digby held his breath to keep from taking in water. He felt light-headed, as if he was about to drift off to sleep. His hands and feet pushed frantically, trying to reach another gap in the limestone where there might be a little air. He bit his tongue hard, hoping the pain would keep him focused.

He thought of a game he and his cousins used to play to see who could stay the longest at the bottom of the pool. After a minute or so, he'd start feeling dizzy and his chest and throat would hurt, and he would swim to the surface, gasping for air. But this was no game. And it seemed like it had been much longer than a minute. He was going to die down here in the blackness, in the rock. No one would find him.

The horror of that thought was enough to make Digby try one more thrust, digging the toes of his boots against the rock and pushing hard as he could. He inhaled, expecting water to flood his throat and lungs. Instead, he got air.

He pushed forward and breathed again. The passage widened a little, giving him another inch or so of precious wiggle room. He thrust forward again as though his body were one muscle, like a worm's. He gained a little ground, enough that he could bend his head back and peer into the nothingness ahead. He felt the hint of a breeze in his eyes.

Digby took a few wonderful breaths. He lay on his back, drained and still a long way from home, but filled with the sense that, maybe, the worst was over and he might survive after all. He breathed and listened to water trickling around him. And something else droning in the background. He turned his head so he could get a better listen. It was a noise familiar to every kid in that part of the world, a constant buzz from June until August, when the ugly little buggers fell out of the trees and died.

What were they called? Cicadas! And Digby was pretty sure cicadas didn't live in caves.

CHAPTER 37

The coffee was weak, certainly not up to the usual fine standards of Carl's Machine Shed. But what did you expect at 10:30 on a Wednesday night? Carl was reluctant to open his restaurant for an emergency meeting of the mayor and his cronies. In fact, he was rather surly about it. Said something about missing his favorite *CSI* show, and the mayor silently wondered what kind of man could think about television during a time like this.

"Tivo it," he told him. "Don't you have a Tivo, or whatever it's called?"

It said something about the mayor's powers of persuasion that he not only got the Machine Shed open but also talked Carl into putting some coffee on the stove and frying up some of those delicious sandwiches for which he was famous. People had a hard time saying no to the mayor, who was still proud of his public record despite what had happened the past five days.

"Can I trust you boys to lock up when you're done?" Carl asked when he finished the sandwiches.

"Where you going?" Larry Truesdale asked.

"I'm going to bed."

"Carl, you're a prince and a scholar," the mayor said, handing him two twenty-dollar bills. "How can we make this up to you?"

"Well, you can give me back my liquor license, for one thing."

The men laughed and the mayor said he'd see what he could do. Carl nodded grimly, as if to say he'd heard that one before. He killed the kitchen lights and walked out the front door, a bell merrily announcing his departure.

The restaurant was quiet, save for the men slurping their coffees. The mayor thought how it was just a year ago at this very table when he'd announced his plot to create a new legacy for Pridemore. Chub Hughes, Larry Truesdale, Rufus Stodemeyer, and Tom Treadwell had all gotten a bit grayer since then, particularly Chub, who'd done more than anyone (besides the mayor himself) to put the plan into action. Looking at the four power brokers, hastily called together after the Dakota Marx show, the mayor recalled how they didn't like what he had to tell them a year ago, and they probably weren't going to like what he had to say tonight. Such was the burden on the visionary mind. But the fool on the hill, as they say, sees the sun going down...

"We shouldn't meet like this," Stodemeyer said. "What if Carl goes to the press?"

"What on earth would he tell them?" asked Treadwell, the county prosecutor.

"He could say plenty," Stodemeyer shot back. "Carl knows more than you think."

"Oh, bullcrap," Chub said.

"I'm just saying," the car dealer continued, running a hand through his close-cropped hair, "we might talk about a way to silence Carl. I know people who specialize in these things. That's all I'm saying."

"You're a jackass," Chub said. "Here we are eating the guy's sandwiches, and you want to put a bullet in his head."

"I didn't say that!" Stodemeyer said, wagging a finger. "I did not say that!"

Chub sighed deeply and reached for the Sweet'N Low. "Well, you're right about one thing," he admitted. "We shouldn't meet like this, not with all the media around."

The mayor nodded. It was a risk. But then the whole thing was risky, wasn't it? That, he now realized, was part of the appeal—revving up the city in a way that was a little bit naughty. And instantly gratifying. Bond issues, curbs and gutters, economic development—those are fine and good if you have twenty years to spare. Pridemore didn't. Besides, they'd gone that painstaking route before, and look where it had gotten them. Not on the six o'clock news every night. Not on every network and in every newspaper in the country.

"Before we begin," said Truesdale, looking dapper in a collared shirt and sports jacket, "I'd like to say something."

The publisher stood up, holding a sandwich in one hand and a coffee mug in the other. "I'd just like to say that, when the mayor approached us a year ago with this cockamamie plan of his, I wasn't the only guy in this room who thought he was nuts."

The men nodded and chuckled at the memory.

"That's why I now give credit where it is due. The publicity this town has earned over the past week is more than even I could have imagined. And we're already reaping the benefits. The phones are ringing off the hook at the Chamber of Commerce. There's been talk of the state putting Pridemore on the list of sites for an ethanol plant. And over at the *Headlight*, we've almost made our annual budget. I told my sales staff that, if we string this story out a couple more days, they can all go out and play golf for the rest of the year.

"So here's to you, mayor," he said, raising his mug. "I thought you were crazy as a loon a year ago. Turns out you were crazy like a fox. You had the vision and you made it happen."

"Here! Here!" Treadwell added, lifting a pork loin sandwich that was nearly the size of his head. The men clapped and smiled approvingly at the mayor, who looked down at his weathered hands, not feeling the glow of adulation he normally craved like ice cream on a summer day.

"Enough of the happy horseshit," Stodemeyer said. "Why are we here?"

The mayor laughed in a joyless way. He rose to his feet and gasped at the pain shooting down his legs. The past week's running around had been murder on his knees. He would probably need surgery again, something he wished to put off as long as he could in the hopes that death would take him first.

"Gentlemen," he said, "I spoke with the engineers early this evening, and things don't look good. All this rain has hurt the rescue effort—there's just too much mud and runoff to do much of anything up there. One guy said it's like drilling through quicksand.

"And meanwhile, Dragon's Ice House is filling up with water. The workers lost contact with Digby more than a day ago. They think he's moved to another area of the cave. Which means there's a chance he could stumble into a flooded cavern or crawl space and drown."

The mayor leaned over the table and tried to make eye contact with each of his friends. "The best-case scenario is Friday, maybe Saturday, before the workers get into the cave. Wait that long, and we'll probably be recovering a corpse instead of saving a life."

He paused, waiting for some kind of response. All he got was a soft burp from Rufus Stodemeyer, who had finished his sandwich and was moving on to the coleslaw.

"So I've called you together because we must act now to save the Willers boy's life. We have to implement Plan B."

Larry Truesdale looked surprised. "There's a Plan B?"

The mayor shot him a look, irritated that he had to explain everything a hundred times to what was supposed to be Pridemore's best and brightest. "Remember our contingency plan in case something goes wrong? The escape hatch that Chub installed so we could save the boy if we needed to? I'm saying now is the time to use it. Tonight."

The men looked at each other. Tom Treadwell excused himself to go to the restroom.

"Sit back down in your seat!" The mayor waved a gnarled finger at the county prosecutor, who did as he was told. "No one's leaving until all of us agree on the contingency plan. We don't have much time."

"So what if we exercise this Plan B and Digby Willers just appears out of nowhere?" Stodemeyer asked. "How the hell are you going to explain that?"

The mayor sucked in his chest. This part would be the hard sell. Like Reagan explaining why he pulled out of Lebanon or Clinton explaining why he pulled out of Lewinsky.

"If pressed, I will tell people the truth. I will admit this was a publicity stunt that went horribly awry. As mayor, I'll accept full responsibility. I won't implicate any of you."

"Well, isn't that nice?" Stodemeyer said. "He's not going to implicate us!"

"I'm an old man," the mayor said, looking heavenward. "At best, I have a couple of years left. I don't need to cut a deal with the feds. And I'm not afraid of going to prison. In fact, I'm told the quality of health care is fairly good."

"Well, I've got a good thirty years left," Stodemeyer said. "And I *am* afraid of going to prison."

The mayor stared down the car dealer as coolly as his blue eyes could muster. "Well, you should have thought about that before you joined our little club."

He glared at his collaborators, daring them to defy him. Seeing no takers, he figured it was time to wrap things up. "We gave it our best shot, men. But there's no other choice. Chub and I will take some deputies out to the escape hatch, and we'll bring the Willers boy home."

"I'm afraid we can't do that, Mr. Mayor."

"Come again?"

Chub Hughes didn't look up. He was busy stirring cream into his mug until the coffee was khaki-colored. "The thing of it is, there is no escape hatch."

The mayor felt an electricity surge through his body that he thought he no longer possessed. It was testosterone or adrenalin or one of those other chemicals that kicked in when a man got really mad—or scared. "What do you mean?" he said as calmly as he could.

"I mean we never built it."

"It was too risky, Roe," Truesdale said, leaning in front of Chub as if to shield him. "With all the workers and media running around, somebody was bound to stumble across it, and then what would we do?"

This isn't happening, the mayor thought, his shirt collar suddenly feeling two sizes too small. As a public servant, he'd seen more than his share of infighting, incompetence, and downright skullduggery. But it had been a long damn time since his subordinates had blithely ignored a direct command.

"So you just didn't build it," he said, both arms hugging his torso. "I earmarked two thousand dollars to put in that goddamned door. What'd you do with the money?"

Chub was unfazed. "We put it toward some cost overruns on the public restrooms."

The mayor didn't consciously decide to climb over two men and latch both hands around Chub's throat. He just did it. And while the rest of his body was fairly emaciated, his hands were still thick and strong, and seemed only to tighten their grip as Chub scratched bloody rivulets into the mayor's shirtsleeves.

It took the rest of the crew to pull the mayor back and pin him in his chair. Once everyone stopped panting and wiping food off their clothes, the mayor tried a new approach. Door or no door, they had to get the boy out of there.

"What's the name of that boozy engineer who's looking for another way in?" he demanded.

"You mean Lauterbach?" Truesdale asked.

The men glanced at each other.

"Skipped town two days ago," Treadwell finally said. "Went on some sort of drinking binge."

Stodemeyer pantomimed guzzling a beer with a fist raised over his mouth, and the others cracked up.

"Jesus," the mayor said. "Don't any of you care that there's a human life at stake?"

Truesdale shrugged. "How much time does he have left, anyway? Kids with Down Syndrome don't usually live past their twenties."

"He doesn't have Down Syndrome," the mayor said.

"Well, whatever. Look at it this way: if Digby Willers dies in the cave, it's an even bigger story. We could have a state funeral right here in Pridemore. There's a small chance the president might show up. The kid had one hell of a life. We'll build a statue of him in the courthouse square. There might even be a museum."

"Well," said the mayor. "What's to stop me from going to the press and blowing the lid off the whole story?"

"We can't let you do that," said Chub, dabbing the cuts on his neck with a paper towel. "Wouldn't be good for the city."

"Hell. It wouldn't be good for us," Stodemeyer added.

The mayor looked at his friends and saw the glint in their eyes at the prospect of more glory for Pridemore. He wasn't too old and deluded to know who put that glint there.

"Promise you won't say a word, Roe," Truesdale said, smiling that fierce smile of his. "We'd hate it if you didn't make it home to Margaret tonight."

270

It was past midnight when the mayor got home and collapsed in his lounger. He was too tired to climb the stairs to his bedroom and too anxious to sleep. He took a couple of Tums, which did nothing to calm the roiling acids in his belly.

It was defeat. His guts knew it even if his brain didn't. Complete and utter defeat. Liking an aging lion, he'd flinched in the face of danger, lost the confidence of the pride. He'd promised that snake Truesdale and the others that he wouldn't say a word to anyone about the plot for Pridemore. It was even suggested that the mayor spend a few days at home while everything blew over. Get his strength back. Someone else could cover for him. It was amazing that a man his age hadn't buckled under the pressure of the past week already, they said, false piety oozing from their smiles. He knew what they were saying—get out of the way or we'll put you under house arrest. Or worse.

The mayor would abide. He had no fight left. There was nothing he could do to save the Willers boy, so why not stay at home and watch *The Price is Right*? He had no stomach for all this drama anymore.

He groaned. At least in nature, the pack had the decency to eat your entrails or leave you to perish alone on a frozen plain when it was your time to go. Here in civilization, they plopped you in a comfortable chair and left you to warble endlessly, like an old show in perpetual syndication.

He put the TV on mute, flipped through the channels, and hummed a song from his favorite Rodgers and Hammerstein musical.

This was a real nice clambake,
We're mighty glad we came.
The vittles we et,
were good (you bet!)
The company was the same…

It was, indeed, a nice clambake. A profitable law practice, more than fifty years of public service, a long marriage to a loving wife, a terrific record in the courtroom. Even the tragedies, when seen from a distance, added some beautiful hues to the portrait. "Into every life some rain must fall," and all that crap.

It had been a rich life. Which was why he didn't mind if God struck him dead right now in his living room. In fact, he welcomed it. But God (that old sadist) worked on no one's schedule. If you wanted something done in this world, you had to do it yourself.

The mayor pulled an old Kleenex from his trousers and coughed into it. He wondered if he could retrieve his pistol from the bedroom closet without waking Margaret. Even if he could, he had no idea where to look for bullets. Margaret had hidden his ammo a few months ago for fear he would turn the gun on himself (smart girl, that one!), and he suspected she'd thrown the bullets out with the Wednesday morning trash.

He heard a rap on the kitchen door. Who could be knocking at 12:30 at night? One of Chub Hughes's goons, here to finish him off?

"Please, Lord, no," he whispered, picturing his death at the hands of some tattooed methamphetamine addict. "Let me do it my way."

More rapping on the door. The last thing the mayor needed was for this maniac to wake Margaret, luring her into the bloodbath that was sure to come. Whimpering softly, he hoisted himself from the lounger and shuffled to the kitchen. Through the curtains he saw the unmistakable form of a woman, hands on hips. Assassins come in all types, he supposed.

He opened the door to find Beatrice Reilly. His relief was quickly replaced by a surge of excitement, then panic. Why, after fifty years, was the old lover darkening his door? Whatever the reason, she didn't look pleased.

"Beat! Bless my stars! What brings you here?"

"Don't get excited, Roe," she said. "Can I come in?"

He led her to the kitchen table and asked if she would like some coffee (he hadn't a clue how to work the damn machine, but it seemed right to ask). She declined.

"It's awfully late, Beat."

She nodded. "I waited until I saw your car pull in. I didn't want to leave a note."

His eyebrows rose. It had been a long time since the days when the two of them drank beers in the Mustang. What the devil was this about?

"You know, Margaret's upstairs sleeping. Couldn't this wait until morning?"

"Can Digby Willers wait until morning?"

She reached in her raincoat and pulled out a sheath of papers. They appeared to be copies of some billing statements.

"I know what's going on, Roe. The militia. M&M Construction. Larry Truesdale as the go-between. I know all of it."

The mayor studied the documents, pretending to read what they said. He had the sinking feeling of a kid who'd been caught cheating on a test.

Beat shook her head. "I knew you were a lying, scheming megalomaniac, but I never thought you were capable of something like this."

The mayor shrugged his shoulders. Inside, he was seething. He couldn't believe that idiot Truesdale recorded his payments to the Missouri Militia. And who had the gall to rummage through his files, anyway?

"These are your copies, by the way," she said. "Mine are in the *Headlight* newsroom."

"Beatrice," he said. "You're not writing about this, are you?"

She looked away, but her face softened a bit. And the mayor thought he had an ounce of a chance. He was her mentor, after all. Her guide. He'd taught her city politics when she was a rosy-cheeked reporter fresh out of school. Surely she owed him a favor or two.

"I'm giving you twenty-four hours to save Digby Willers, Roe. I don't know how you'll do it, but I'm sure you have your devices. You always have a back-up plan."

Until tonight anyway, he thought. "And what if I don't?"

"Then Pete Schaefer's story goes to press first thing Friday."

She rose from the table and handed the photocopies to the mayor. "By the way, I realize there may be some difficulties printing this story since our own publisher appears to be in on the plot. So just in case I find myself out of a job tomorrow morning, I've arranged to hand the documents over to the Leland Summer show on FTN."

He grabbed her elbow as she headed out the door. Something about her sense of purpose turned him on. She was not the bright-eyed cub reporter of long ago, nor the frumpy old editor who sometimes kept her hair up with a number 2 pencil. She was a lioness, roaring into the den and putting him in the humble place he deserved. *I'm a coward, Beat. A faker,* he wanted to say. But then she probably knew that all along.

"I can't save him, Beat. I've been stripped of my powers."

She spun toward him, eyes filled with fury. "Get to work, Roe. You've got a day."

She left him holding the door, humidity enveloping him like he was standing in front of a furnace. If this were the movies, he'd have gone after her, swung her around, and planted a deep, forceful kiss. She'd have slapped him, of course. But they would have had that moment, at least.

But this was life. And he was a tired, old fool, holding the kitchen door and letting the moths get in.

CHAPTER 38

Once safely across the Pridemore County line, Charlie Lauterbach pulled into the gravel lot at Saul's Good Time Barbecue and Fillin' Station. He smiled cryptically at the "Liquor, Guns and Ammo," sign over the storefront window. How Red State of them, serving booze and firearms at the same place! Maybe they even had a drive-thru.

Lauterbach knew he should have kept driving until he reached the interstate. But after what he'd been through, he felt entitled to get his drink on as soon as possible. After four days of being held in the County Stockade under no charges, with no due process, the civil engineer was released at eight o'clock Thursday morning with the stern warning from a sheriff's deputy never to return to these parts again if he knew what was good for him.

"No worries about that, bub," he said under his breath as he climbed into his Buick (Lauterbach had no idea who'd transported his car to the stockade, and he wasn't about to ask).

He had finally reached his lawyer, Artie Shorr, on Tuesday. Artie raised all sorts of hell to any Pridemore official he could reach by phone, threatening to call every TV station in the Midwest and get the US Attorney involved. But Lauterbach suspected the lawyer's histrionics had little to do with his release. The local cops had never planned to arrest him. They just wanted him locked down for a few days until the Digby Willers fracas blew over. He considered calling the media as soon as he reached Kansas City.

"Don't do that, Charlie," Artie told him in their last phone conversation. "You want these yo-yos to extradite you back to Pridemore on some phony-baloney charges?"

No, he did not. The damage was done, anyway. The Willers kid had surely perished by now. And Lauterbach didn't have the energy to lead a protest against official corruption in Pridemore County. Who would take him seriously? His name had no clout in Missouri, and his reputation in the rest of the world wasn't what you would call stellar. And he looked and smelled like a vagrant, wearing the same Led Zeppelin T-shirt and jean shorts he had thrown on Sunday morning.

Pulling a case of Pabst Blue Ribbon from the freezer in the back of Saul's, he imagined how that first beer would feel rolling down his throat. He couldn't remember the last time he'd gone as long as four days without a cold one against his lips.

Lauterbach paid for his beer and was headed out the double doors when a familiar, strident voice called out. He looked toward the gun counter, where some old guy was giving the clerk a hard time.

"How the hell can you call yourself a gun shop and not have bullets for a 9mm pistol?" he exclaimed, waving his arms in exaggerated fashion. "It's only one of the most common target guns in the western damn hemisphere!"

The old man looked like a tourist in his Bermuda shorts and a wide-brimmed straw hat, but Lauterbach recognized him as the blowhard in the seersucker suit he'd met on his first afternoon in Pridemore. Without really thinking, he drifted toward the gun counter and waited for the man to pause his diatribe.

"Howdy, Mr. Mayor," he said. "Good to see you again."

The mayor eyed Lauterbach up and down before a glimmer of recognition crossed his face. "What do you want?"

Lauterbach mulled this question for a moment, measuring his response. He was across the county line, safely out of the mayor's jurisdiction. Still, it was unwise to start an altercation only ten minutes removed from a stint in jail.

"I just want to know," he said, "why I was incarcerated for four days in your town for no reason whatsoever."

"I don't know what you're talking about. All I know is you've been seen all over town, drunk off your ass."

"That's crap, and you know it," Lauterbach said, losing all sense of decorum. "You had me and Hutchins locked up because we found the door."

The mayor arched an eyebrow. "What door?"

"Oh, c'mon. The door that was built into the ground. The one that led to Dragon's Ice House."

The mayor grabbed Lauterbach's arm with surprising firmness, tugging him toward the exit. "Let's talk outside."

They walked across the gravel lot to a white Chrysler that Lauterbach assumed to be the mayor's.

"What I don't understand is why somebody went to the trouble of building this door to Dragon's Ice House but doesn't want anyone to use it," he said. "You guys could have gotten Digby Willers any time you wanted. And then I started thinking—I had a lot of time to think during my four days in your jail—why would somebody *not* want this kid rescued? Who stood to benefit if this—"

"Shut up, if you please," the mayor said. "There are things going on here that you don't know anything about."

"Well, no duh."

At this point, pressed up against the side of the car, Lauterbach thought he would have to push this elderly man to the ground if he wished to escape. Normally, the idea of attacking a senior citizen was appalling. But Lauterbach very much valued his life—worthless though it was to most

278

people—and suspected for the first time that it might be in danger.

"Take me there." The mayor leaned in close, his breath smelling like bad onions. "Show me the door."

"There's no way I'm going anywhere with you."

"I'm on your side! I want to save the boy."

"Guys like you don't want to save anything but your own hides."

The mayor stepped back, breathing heavily. His short-sleeved shirt was stained with sweat, and his hat fell to the ground, revealing a pasty dome topped by an unnaturally brown hairpiece. He bent over, hands on his knees, and hacked violently until a thin line of mucus streamed from his mouth.

"You're right—mostly," he said after catching his breath. "I am one self-serving son of a bitch. And I can't begin to explain to you how I got Digby Willers in this mess to begin with. But I want the boy to live. More than anything, I want that."

"It's probably too late."

"Probably. But I've got to try."

The old guy was still doubled over, wheezing heavily now. Lauterbach wondered how someone who had been such a force of nature a minute ago could look so diminished the next. He suspected there was a bit of acting involved. He wouldn't put it past the old dog. Still, the mayor had his number. Lauterbach's life, beyond the drinking binges, chronic depression, and lonely TV dinners, was about saving people. As long as there was a breath of a chance of saving the Willers kid, he knew he couldn't leave Pridemore.

Lauterbach put an arm over the mayor's stooped shoulders and squeezed gently.

"Give me the keys, old man," he said. "I'll drive."

***

It was boiling hot by the time they reached the end of a country road and parked near the charred remains of an old barn that looked to have recently burned (probably the result of a lightning fire, Lauterbach thought). The sun, missing most of the week, was making up for lost time by beating down on them mercilessly. After four days of on-and-off rain, there wasn't a cloud in the sky.

This gave Lauterbach some hope as he and the mayor trudged into the forest. Maybe the rain had stopped in time. Maybe the water hadn't accumulated enough to flood the cave, and Digby was down there, waiting them out.

The two men walked for what seemed like a mile, up and down the narrow gullies that made up a heavily wooded valley called the Bottoms. A couple of times, the mayor stopped to catch his breath, sip a bottled water, and wave the straw hat in his face to cool down. In addition to offering shade, the dense canopy of elms, oaks, and maples cut off any chance of a breeze, adding to the morning's sauna-like conditions.

"I'm too old for these kinds of games," the mayor said, groaning as he pushed himself up from a stump.

"Just keep walking."

Neither of them had a map, so Lauterbach relied on his sketchy memory of landmarks. It wasn't until they reached the foot of a ridge so steep they had to crawl their way up that the engineer felt they were getting close. Cresting the ridge, and stopping for a minute for the mayor to take a sip from his Aquafina, Lauterbach noticed something white clinging to a briar bush a few yards away. Drawing near, he saw that it was a pair of men's underwear. Lauterbach took a stick and carefully lifted the undergarment from the bush. They were size XXL.

"Kids," the mayor mumbled with a sigh. "They'll fornicate anywhere nowadays."

"Digby was a big kid, wasn't he?"

"At least 280 pounds. Would've made a great lineman for the football team."

Lauterbach walked further, coming across a ripped flannel shirt and a pair of mud-covered jeans. A few yards away, hanging from a low tree branch, was a hooded sweatshirt with "Missouri Athletic Dept." emblazoned on the front.

"That's his sweatshirt!" the mayor said.

The two men were now jogging through the trees, past the discarded undershirt, socks and hiking boots, and over another ridge until they reached a conspicuous-looking pile of dead leaves. In the pile, they found the metal six-panel door that covered a dark, narrow hole of indeterminable depth. Judging from the muddy fingerprints on the interior side of the door, someone had forced their way out of the ground. The kid had big hands and must have been strong as a bear to push that door open, Lauterbach thought.

"My God," the mayor said, peering into the hole. "He escaped."

"Apparently so."

Lauterbach looked at the bits of blue sky peeking through the trees and offered a silent prayer of thanks. He wasn't religious in any traditional kind of way, but he'd seen enough rescues to know that, sometimes, intervention by the Almighty was the only explanation.

"You think somebody got to him?"

"I don't know," Lauterbach said. "Looks like he made it out on his own."

"But what about the clothes? You suppose he's running around these woods naked?"

Lauterbach laughed at the image. "Beats the crap out of me. Nothing this past week has made any kind of sense."

"You think he's safe?"

Lauterbach shrugged. "I think he's alive."

"I think so, too."

· The mayor closed his eyes, sucked in his chest, and exhaled very slowly. He took off his hat, wiped the sweat from his forehead, and looked down at the engineer with a little smile.

"Well, my boy," he said, "I guess we have some explaining to do."

CHAPTER 39

Digby Willers, his mother, and two housecats were heading east on the interstate at about eighty miles an hour. Susan Willers had crammed as many belongings as she could muster into her Fiero. It wasn't much more than a few changes of clothes and a silverware set passed down three generations, but, as she explained to Digby, they were both lucky to escape Pridemore with their lives.

He had arrived at his mother's kitchen door shortly before dawn, naked and muddy and shivering from the cold. After pushing his way out of the cave, the first thing Digby did was peel off the filthy, slimy clothes he had worn for the past five days. It seemed like a good idea at the time. But as he wandered for hours in the woods, finally coming across Old Highway 54 and walking, stark naked, back into town, he couldn't help wishing he'd at least kept on his boots and a layer of underwear. The soles of his feet were covered in burrs and blisters, his arms and legs were scratched from underbrush, and there were chigger and mosquito bites on some of his more tender parts.

All this was forgotten when he saw his mother's face switch from shock to disbelief and, finally, to complete and utter joy. There was screaming and crying and dancing and praises to the Lord in the Willers kitchen, until mother and son both collapsed on the harvest-gold linoleum, exhausted but happy in each other's arms.

His mother whipped up some sausage links, along with biscuits and gravy (easily the best breakfast he had ever tasted), and recounted how she had been bullied, oppressed, ignored, and vilified by the Pridemore powers-that-be over the past week. Even the hospital showed no sympathy, forcing her to put in late shifts while she grieved her lost son. It angered Digby to hear how much his mom had suffered while he was gone.

"I'll tell you one thing," she said. "We've got to get out of this town the instant you finish your breakfast."

She lowered her voice, her eyes shifting around the room. "They'll kill us if we don't."

She didn't know exactly how or why, but there was a conspiracy behind all of this, she told Digby. The other night, they'd wheeled in the *Headlight* reporter who had been covering the whole story and had gotten into a "car accident" (she emphasized the quote marks with her fingers). The kid was pretty loopy on meds most of the night, but she managed to extract some information. The mayor and some of the big shots in town had orchestrated a way to trap Digby in the cave, and the reporter had documents to prove it. What the mayor had hoped to achieve through all of this was still unclear.

"I have my own theories on that," she said, serving Digby another helping of hash browns. "Those guys are all Masons, you know."

Digby wasn't sure what that meant, other than he was beginning to realize the mayor and his friends were bad people, judging by the way they treated his mom while he was stuck in the cave. That made him mad. In between bites of breakfast, he swore to his mom that he would get even for what they had done. She smiled and ran a hand through his hair.

"Honey," she said. "You can't fight the system."

Three hours later, they were speeding east on I-70 to visit an aunt Digby hadn't seen since he was a very little boy. They would never set foot in Pridemore again, his mother swore, and they had to take great care to avoid something she called the Liberal Media, which couldn't be trusted because it had something called an Agenda that could only do them further harm.

All of which mattered little to Digby at this particular moment. He would miss Pridemore, he guessed. He would miss the Pinewood Derby races, old Mr. Sanderson's hardware store, the way he could walk down the centerline of Main Street in the middle of the day without anyone caring. He would even miss, in a strange way, the mayor and the candy bars he kept in his desk. Other than his mom, the mayor was the only adult in town who didn't talk to Digby like he was five years old.

Right now, though, he was just content to have food in his belly, two cats purring in his lap, and the green countryside rolling past his window. His mind drifted in and out, happily hearing the familiar tones of his mother's voice but not understanding what she said.

"...which just goes to show that you can't trust anyone in this world, Digby. Not the government, not your employer, not your friends, certainly not that fucking deadbeat father of yours who hasn't so much as sent a greeting card in the last twenty years. My God, I've had bananas that lasted longer than he did after you were born. That's your dad for you—one rotten banana! ...You don't think they put a sensor on the car, do you? You know, a little device that would tell them our whereabouts at all times? I wouldn't put it past those sons of bitches. Maybe we'll look things over when we stop, but I at least want to get to St. Louis first.... Maybe we can pick up some White Castle burgers in the city, baby. How does that sound? Are you hungry? Baby?"

Digby didn't answer. He was fast asleep.

CHAPTER 40

With trembling hands, he placed the record on the turntable and set the needle on the first movement. He settled back in the battered armchair and took in the opening strains of Richard Rodgers's *Victory at Sea*. The mayor remembered watching the documentary series about the Pacific Theater on television in the early 1950s and being impressed by how well the music meshed with footage of beach invasions, jungle battles, and aircraft carrier fleets. It had been decades since he'd even thought about that TV show, but he happened across the soundtrack while archiving some old 33 LPs for the library at Allendale Federal Prison. Now, alone in the reading room, he had a few minutes to soak in a decent symphonic score.

It had been less than three months since he'd checked into Allendale, which *Forbes* recently ranked among the country's cushier white-collar prisons. The mayor wasn't certain about that. Sure, they had a swimming pool, personal trainers, and air-conditioned dorm rooms. But it was still prison. They'd shoot you if you tried to climb the walls just like they would at San Quentin, Leavenworth, or any of those other hellholes. Just because the mayor had broadband Internet access in his cell and clean bed sheets every day didn't mean he was living the good life.

Still, he wasn't unhappy. There was plenty of time for reading and writing, the food was only subpar, and most of his fellow inmates were from the professional class, which made for interesting conversation when he wished to partake. Mostly, he craved solitude. In a short time, the mayor had earned himself considerable freedom within the five-building complex. His job as chief archivist for the Allendale Library, a role he created, was mostly unsupervised. For a large part of the day, it was him alone with a 2,200-volume collection of secondhand library books, as well as newspapers, records, and tapes.

He missed Margaret. Missed her leg rubbing against his in their bed, the way she could calm him by touching his hand, the sound of her singing in the kitchen. He didn't miss the petty arguments, the out-of-control credit card spending, or the surprise visits from her relatives. But he hoped to live long enough to get out of prison and return home to Margaret.

He wouldn't bet on it, though. He had just turned eighty-nine and, after the year he'd been through, felt at least ten years older than that.

It was almost a year ago to the day when he alerted the media of a special announcement about the Digby Willers incident, not sure exactly what he was going to say. He still didn't know as he stepped up to the podium in front of more than one hundred journalists from around the world. Here was the most important statement of his public life, and, for perhaps the first time in his life, he was completely, totally unprepared.

So he let the words go as they came to him. Just let them flow straight from his brain to his mouth. That exacting internal editor, the one that monitored even the most trivial utterances at the most benign dinner parties, had taken a permanent vacation. From now on, he'd say whatever he damn well thought.

"Today I'm happy to announce that Digby Willers's life is no longer in danger," he began. "He has escaped Dragon's Ice House, apparently on his own volition."

There was a millisecond pause as the throng absorbed this turn of events. Then came the predictable clamor of everyone asking questions at once.

"Where is he now?" a TV reporter from Chicago managed to scream over the din.

The mayor raised his arms for silence, which took several seconds to achieve.

"Honestly," he said, "I haven't the foggiest idea. He may be in the woods somewhere. He may be at his mama's house. All I can tell you is, from what I've seen, he appears to have escaped alive and well."

More rumbling from the press.

A talking head piped in: "Are you going to organize a search party?"

The mayor glanced over his shoulder at Pridemore Public Safety chief Cole Turner, who looked like he had just lost control of his bowels. "I don't know. Do you think we should? I mean, hasn't this boy been under enough of a microscope as it is? What do you think, Cole? Should we put together some sort of search party?"

The chief offered a shrug. "Sure thing. Right away."

"Well, there you go," the mayor said. "Any more questions?"

There were many, most of them lost in the frantic shouting match that always prevailed when big news was at hand. The wolf-pack frenzy made one understand why reporters usually ranked below lawyers and politicians, and slightly above criminals, in the American public's esteem.

The mayor waited for things to die down, then pointed toward a corner of the platform, where Leland Summer perched, clutching a thin notepad remarkably bereft of any actual note-taking.

"Mayor Tolliver," the anchor said in a low drawl, "can you explain to us exactly how Digby Willers managed to escape and how you came to this discovery?"

The mayor propped an elbow on the podium and let out a sigh.

"You guys really want to know?"

The throng roared in the affirmative.

"Okay, get your pencils sharpened. 'Cause this one's a long story."

He told them everything, starting from when he cooked up the idea, proceeding through the sham development of the Lewis and Clark Park, and concluding at the moment, two hours prior, when he and Charlie Lauterbach discovered Digby Willers's underdrawers. Along the way, he named co-conspirators, contractors, state legislators, and rank-and-file government officials who, unwitting or otherwise, played a part in the scheme.

It was a forty-minute oratory so startlingly candid that *The New York Times* published it in its entity two days later under the headline, "Small Town Soliloquy: A Mayor Comes Clean."

It was pretty much the same spiel he gave jury members six months later in the criminal trials of Chub Hughes, Larry Truesdale, Tom Treadwell, and Rufus Stodemeyer. The mayor himself had pled guilty months earlier to conspiracy and kidnapping charges. His lawyers worked out a five-year sentence in return for implicating his collaborators, who all received much stiffer terms. Watching his old friends sit stoically as the judge handed down ten-year sentences gave him no pleasure. He made a point of keeping them in his morning prayers (after years apart, the mayor and God had worked out a reconciliation). Still, he agreed with the judge. They were powerful men in their prime, capable of making their own decisions. They never should have fallen for the delusional dreams of a doddering old man.

Pridemore would carry on without them. Bryan London, the outcast of the city council, finally won the mayor's office and, by most accounts, was doing a pretty good job steering through the aftermath of Digby Willers. Pridemore managed to capitalize somewhat on its worldwide fame, though not as much as Mayor Tolliver had hoped. The state legislature, incensed to learn it had spent millions of dollars on a tourist attraction Pridemore never intended to complete, initially demanded its money back. The legal dispute over who should pay up went on for months and kept Pridemore in the news. Eventually, the city and state leaders agreed to open a small museum at the site commemorating the rescue effort and use the ticket proceeds to pay off the bonds.

The museum drew a respectable trickle of curiosity-seekers, school groups, and senior-citizen coach trips—enough to justify the opening of a new Burger Bomb franchise near the park entrance. One of the networks planned to air a "Digby Willers: One Year Later" primetime special in a few days, and there was hope that the coverage might spark some more sightseers over the summer.

For the most part, however, little had changed. There were still vacant storefronts on Main Street. The population continued to decline, and the city remained in the red. You could argue that the whole spectacle actually hurt more than it helped. M&M Construction filed Chapter 7 after its owner went to jail. Rufus Stodemeyer's wife left town and took the family car dealership with her.

It would have been better for Pridemore, the mayor contended, had Digby Willers actually been rescued. They would have handed out keys to the city and staged a downtown parade. There would have been speeches and dignitaries and a commissioned statue in front of the courthouse. They would have done it up right. The mayor would have seen to that.

But it was not to be. The Digby Willers story lacked the tidy conclusion Americans expect of their mythology. There were no heroes. Charlie Lauterbach, who saved Baby Alison two decades ago and came close to pulling off a similar feat, faded back into obscurity. He was in Texas now, a small-time consultant on airport security, out of the hero business for good.

Of course, it didn't help that no one had seen the central character of the whole drama for nearly a year. Eyewitnesses spotted Digby and his mother gassing up a battered Pontiac in St. Louis around the time the mayor was pouring his heart out on national TV. Since then, there were reports of the pair eating at a restaurant in Georgia. Another story had them joining a religious cult in Appalachia. Still another speculated that they ran off to Mexico, where they were kidnapped by highway bandits. None of these tales were substantiated, and the media and law enforcement eventually moved on to more pressing matters. In an age of Homeland Security, spy satellites, GPS systems, and wireless phones, Susan and Digby Willers managed to pull a D.B. Cooper. They had simply disappeared.

Someday they would come forward, the mayor imagined. Just like Mark Felt coming out of nowhere to tell the world he was the man they called Deep Throat, the man who brought down a sitting president. No one could stay out of the spotlight for long, not when they had a story to tell. Not when there was money to be made.

Until then, the mayor would do his part to keep the narrative alive. He had been writing a memoir about the event, but his mind was a little shaky on key dates and pertinent facts. In March, he'd contacted Pete Schaefer, his old nemesis from the *Evening Headlight*, about collaborating on a possible book. Schaefer had long since left Pridemore for a newspaper job in Orlando. But he jumped at the chance to work with the mayor. The two exchanged e-mails several times a week with bits and pieces on the affair. Schaefer's punctuation and spelling left something to be desired, but the kid had saved his press clippings from the *Headlight*, an invaluable resource for checking names, places, and dates.

With luck, they'd find a publisher and get the book on the shelves in time for next year's summer reading. The mayor was working on a query letter to send to the big agencies. It began, "Few people will forget where they were and what they were doing when word spread that a mentally challenged man was buried alive somewhere in America's Heartland...."

Heavy-handed, perhaps. But you had to come out swinging to get these cynical, New York-types interested in a story. Otherwise, they might not make it to the next paragraph.

Something was wrong with *Victory at Sea*. The phonograph needle was stuck, playing three staccato piano chords over and over. He wondered how long it had been doing this before finally rousing him from his thoughts. The audio equipment was third-rate at best, and you had to expect a glitch every now and then.

He thought about fixing it, contemplated the energy it would take to lift his weary bones from the armchair, shuffle across the room, move the record needle with his scratchy old fingers, then shuffle back and adjust the chair to a comfortable position.

It didn't seem worth it, all of a sudden. The music wasn't intolerable. In fact, there was something comforting about an old score that went on in perpetuity, never stopping or starting. Never changing. Going around and around like a moon in orbit, basically telling time to go screw itself.

He closed his eyes, basking in the fractured music. Within seconds, he was asleep.

Digby watched the high-end condominiums rise from the dunes like a giant Florida scrub bush. Every afternoon, he rode his bike along Spyglass Road and parked at the end of the walkway to watch the show: trucks moving in and out, earth movers churning sand, brown-skinned construction crews climbing around the stucco walls and terra-cotta roofing.

It was amazing how fast they worked, how the project went from a cement foundation to a ring of intricate villas in a matter of weeks. Everything moved at a quicker pace in Florida. Everything except the traffic, which crawled along Sea Breeze Boulevard like a lazy worm, especially during the winter months when what they called the Snowbirds came to town.

He liked Florida for the most part. He and his mother shared a small apartment in a part of town where people didn't speak much English. She took a job waiting tables at a nearby restaurant, leaving Digby to himself most of the day. He worried sometimes about his mom. She'd lost weight and had a tired look in her eyes most of the time. She talked about taking a nursing job—there were lots of jobs for nurses in Florida and the money would be better. But she would have to re-register and was afraid that would "arouse suspicion" (a common phrase in the Willers home). So she stuck with the restaurant job, working most nights past the dinner hour, then coming home to feed Digby, collapsing on the couch, and dozing off to the news.

Digby got a bike for his birthday, definitely the coolest thing that had happened since leaving Pridemore. He loved riding on the beach, sometimes steering into the surf and getting his jeans wet. He loved the sound of broken seashells crackling under his tires. It was freedom like he'd never known, spending most days tooling around town, being able to get anywhere in ten minutes or less.

The old beach walkway next to the condo construction site was his favorite spot. He liked how the sunset splashed against the villas in the evenings, giving them a pinkish tint. Some nights, after the workers left, he snuck into the construction site and walked through the units, bounding across the unfinished floors, taking in the smell of sawdust, staring out at the moon-drenched ocean from the balconies. It would be a nice little place for him and his mom to live, but even Digby was smart enough to know they could never afford something on the beach.

Very soon, on a night much darker than this, he'd sneak in with some of those two-gallon buckets like the kind his neighbors kept in their garage. He would douse the hardwood floors and the oak stairways and the kitchen cabinets in gasoline, and he would light a match. Then he'd watch from the walkway as, one by one, the units lit the night like a row of tiki torches. The fire trucks would stream in with their red and blue lights. A crowd would gather to watch the firefighters battle the blaze. It would be like television, only better, because it would be real.

It would be his most ambitious project yet, a long way from the abandoned barns he used to torch back in Missouri. It was a little scary when Digby thought about the chances of getting caught. But that was also part of the thrill. His work might even make the eleven o'clock news. That would be awesome.

Digby pointed his bike toward home and started peddling, smiling to himself and thinking how an old friend once told him never to do anything half-assed. To go all the way, or not go at all.

EPILOGUE

Pete missed Angela. The two had gone their separate ways shortly after Digby Willers disappeared. Once he was released from the hospital, Pete filed a final wrap-up story about the incident, got most of his security deposit back from his landlord, and skipped town. He didn't say good-bye to anyone in the *Headlight* newsroom or tell anyone where he was going. It was better that way. Most of Pete's coworkers disliked him. They weren't exactly going to throw him a cake-and-punch farewell party.

Of course, he went to Florida. Got a low-rent place near Church Street in Orlando and began freelancing. Five months later, the *Times-News* hired him on as a health care reporter, a pretty important beat in the land of the blue-hairs. He upgraded his living arrangements, bought a new car, and tried to get away to Cocoa Beach as often as he could.

Angela took a different path. Despite letting her grades slip her senior year, she got a full-ride scholarship to Duke, where she planned to study pre-law. She claimed to have made peace with her father, though Pete suspected she wasn't giving him the full story. She'd only been home to Pridemore for a couple of short visits since starting college.

Much to her parents' displeasure, Angela spent spring break of her freshman year in Orlando with Pete. They hit the theme parks, checked out Cape Canaveral, and walked on the beach. It was a nice visit, Pete thought, but a lot of time had passed. The white-hot tension between them was gone, maybe because there was no longer any risk of getting caught. With a year of college under her belt, Angela was a more formidable intellect than ever. She wanted to dissect Kant and Nietzsche and Rousseau. She wanted to talk about the upcoming presidential election. Pete mostly just wanted to have sex.

So he had no idea where things were gong with that. Probably nowhere. It had been three months since Angela's visit, and they'd only talked on the phone a couple times since.

Also on hold was a book project with Mayor Tolliver. The two had gotten into a feud about how much the city spent to develop the park around Dragon's Ice House, and the mayor was no longer responding to Pete's e-mails. Too bad. Pete had a draft he was ready to send to publishers, with or without the mayor's blessing.

The crotchety old bastard, Pete thought as he scrolled the *Times-News'* intranet database of breaking stories across Florida. He was vying for an editor position on the city desk, so he sometimes helped piece together the metro section with wire stories. He clicked on an article about a 450-pound alligator captured in downtown Fort Myers and jotted a note to follow up on that one. Readers down here loved a good gator story.

The next story, out of the Panhandle, made Pete blink several times, then utter a swear word, more out of surprise than disgust. He got up, walked to the break room, poured a cup of coffee, came back, and read the story again.

> Destin, Fla. (AP)—More than 30 parents vented their anger at a Monday night public hearing over disputed results in a local Cub Scout derby event.
>
> The winner of the June 12 Seminole District Pinewood Derby, a 24-year-old man who is mentally challenged, should have been disqualified from the contest because of his age, parents argued at Monday's hearing before the District Scouting Board. The subject of the dispute, Destin resident Dakota Williams, did not attend the meeting and was unavailable for comment.

"It's an outrage," said Bobby Jo Grayson, parent of a 10-year-old Scout who competed in the final round against Williams. "What kind of chance do these boys have against a grown man, even if it's racing little wooden cars?"

With the poise of a seasoned reporter familiar with landing the big scoop, Pete grabbed his notepad and tape recorder and strode out into the Florida sun. It was a six-hour drive from Orlando to Destin, so he'd have to get started if he wanted to write something for tomorrow.